MELISS.

a String of Silver Beads

A String of Silver Beads

First Paperback Print Edition: 2018 in United Kingdom

Published by Letterpress Publishing

The moral right of the author has been asserted.

Cover and Formatting by Streetlight Graphics

Map of the Almoravid empire by Maria Gandolfo

Illustration of Tuareg jewellery by Ruxandra Serbanoiu

Kindle: 978-1-910940-14-3
Paperback: 978-1-910940-15-0

Your Free Book

The city of Kairouan in Tunisia, 1020. Hela has powers too strong
for a child – both to feel the pain of those around her and to heal
them. But when she is given a mysterious cup by a slave woman,
its powers overtake her life, forcing her into a vow she cannot hope
to keep. So begins a quartet of historical novels set in Morocco
as the Almoravid Dynasty sweeps across Northern Africa and
Spain, creating a Muslim Empire that endured for generations.

Download your free copy at
www.melissaaddey.com

Dedicated to Abderrahim El Makkouri,
the storyteller in Marrakech.

A glimpse of an older world.

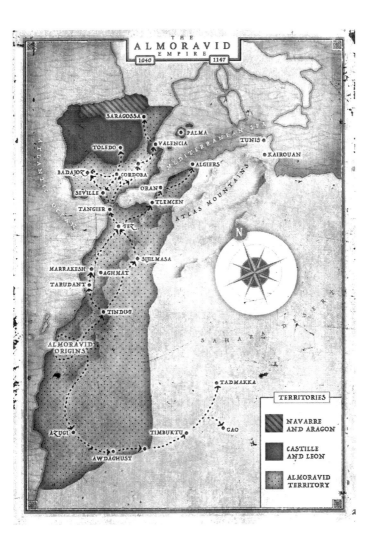

THE
ALMORAVID
EMPIRE
1040   1147

SARAGOSSA

PALMA

VALENCIA

TOLEDO

TUNIS

MEDITERRANEAN SEA

KAIROUAN

ALGIERS

BADAJOZ

CORDOBA

ORAN

ATLANTIC OCEAN

SEVILLE

TLEMCEN

TANGIER

ATLAS MOUNTAINS

FEZ

N

SIJILMASA

MARRAKESH

AGHMAT

TARUDANT

SAHARA DESERT

TINDUF

SAHARA

ALMORAVID
ORIGINS

TADMAKKA

AZUGI

TIMBUKTU

GAO

AWDAGHUST

TERRITORIES

NAVARRE
AND ARAGON

CASTILLE
AND LEON

ALMORAVID
TERRITORY

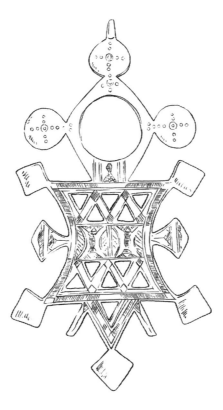

The people of North Africa loosely called Berbers (preferred contemporary name, Amazigh) belong to many tribes and have various names for themselves, including Tuareg. They are known for their blue indigo-dyed robes and beautiful silver jewellery. Women wear the majority of this jewellery and it is highly symbolic, indicating family and tribal ties, marriage status and many other aspects of the wearer's life.

Amongst these peoples it is traditionally the men, not women, who veil their faces.

Marrakech, Morocco, c.1074

A WOMAN'S JEWELS ARE HER LIFE. *I can look at any one of my kinswomen and know her life by the jewels she wears, by their metals, stones, colours, symbols, patterns. I can see her loves and heartbreaks, her children and her family ties. I see all of her while others might see only trinkets bought in the hot jostling souks.*

I sit alone on the tiled floor and look over all my jewellery laid out before me.

I am a woman of the Tuareg people. We are not bound to any one leader to tell us how to live our lives. We are free to wander the desert with our flocks, to move along the trade routes with spices, fruits, nuts, gold and skins. We are free to stay in our villages and care for our crops and beasts. We are many: different, changeable, but all free.

I must choose my path now.

My hands shake. My eyes blur. Across this floor is laid my life, in silver, gold, amber, carnelian, every colour and every symbol that has marked the tale of my days. I begin. I wear only a simple robe. There is no time for fussing over colours and textures to please the eye. I lift each item of jewellery from the floor, in the order in which it came to me. Slowly, I put on each piece, my hands struggling with the clasps.

Watch, now, as I lift up each jewel, for it will tell you my story.

Maghreb (North Africa), c.1067

Tchirot – A Man's Amulet

MY CAMEL THIYYA CAN FEEL the growing excitement around us. Foregoing her usual stance of elegant boredom she shifts back and forth on the spot, even ignoring a tasty clump of foxtail grass nearby. My knees grip the carved wood of my light racing saddle, the red leather trim slick with my sweat. My face is veiled but my bare feet, resting on Thiyya's long neck, give my nerves away, my toes curling into her short white fur.

"Kella! Not again!" The hissed exclamation below startles me and Thiyya's head jerks up, but I steady her. Looking down at my eldest brother's appalled face, I can't help but laugh.

"Sister – "

His voice is too loud. I lean down towards him. "Shh! You'll give me away."

"Tell me why I should not!"

I tighten the veil to make sure my face is well hidden but he can still hear my laughter when I answer. "Because the rest of our brothers have already wagered on my success." I look across at my youngest brother who is smirking at my eldest brother's outrage. "A dagger as the prize, wasn't it?

Very fine. I saw it earlier on that young lout's belt. It will look most grand on you, I'm sure. When I win."

My eldest brother sighs and absent-mindedly pats Thiyya when she nuzzles him.

"Don't sigh like that. Haven't I won you many fine things with my riding skills over these past few years? Where's the harm in that?"

"Would you care to ask our father the same question?"

I shrug. My voice comes out sulky. "I don't see why only men can race."

He walks alongside the camel as we make our way towards the other riders. He gives me his new lecture, the one he has learnt from our father. He never used to be so priggish but having recently been wed he feels he is a grown man and must give guidance to us, his younger siblings. Especially me. "Because, sister. Just because. It is not seemly. Women ride camels for great occasions. A wedding perhaps. And when they do, they have a woman's saddle. They do not ride here, there and everywhere for all to gawp at. And they do not *race* camels."

"But I am the best rider. Five brothers and not one of you can beat me in a race! You have to admit that."

"I didn't question your riding ability. I questioned its propriety."

"Oh, who cares for propriety? I'm dressed like a boy all the time. I ride camels all the time. I might as well enjoy winning the races. Now move away, before the other riders wonder what you're doing escorting me to the starting line. They'll think I'm not much of a man if I have to be accompanied everywhere!"

"And you are such a great man, I suppose?"

I giggle. "Oh, yes. I make a fine young man!"

He raises his hands in despair and turns away.

I call after him, my voice wavering a little now that I'm to be left alone. "Won't you wish me luck?"

He turns back. "I thought you were such a great rider you'd have no need of luck!"

I nudge Thiyya closer so that I can reach out and touch his shoulder. "Everyone needs luck."

My eldest brother is a good-hearted man and cannot stay cross with me for long. He reaches up and puts one broad hand over my smaller one. "May Allah keep the wind from rising and may your camel's feet fly. May you win a great race, my *brother*."

I grin. "Thank you. You may go now."

My brother waves over his shoulder as he walks back to join the gathering crowds.

A big market draws people from a wide area and impromptu festivals spring up. The people come for the food, the trading, the songs and stories and of course for the races, which inevitably take place when the younger men want to show off their camels and their prowess in riding.

For the last few years, ever since I've been tall enough to pass for a young man in my all-encompassing indigo blue robes, I've been entering the camel races at these events and winning more and more often. Now, at seventeen, I am an excellent rider. My camel is a beautiful white beast with blue eyes, a great rarity and a prized gift from my over-generous father. I trained her myself, starting when she was only a baby. I would stand beside her issuing commands, while she peered at me in astonishment through long-lashed blue eyes, wondering who this child-master was. It took a few years, for a camel's training cannot be rushed, but now I have a magnificent beast as my mount, who half-believes she is my sister. I named her Thiyya, 'beautiful', and no-one can argue with my choice of name. I am forever being offered two, three, or even, on a memorable occasion, five camels if I will trade Thiyya for plainer and less speedy animals, but I always refuse. My brothers occasionally race her but she does not try as hard for them as she does for me.

From my high perch I scan the crowds, anxious to avoid my father. My shoulders relax when I fail to spot him. He must be conducting business somewhere. There are traders who buy and sell only one kind of merchandise, such as salt or slaves, skins or jewellery. Their lives are dull to my eyes, always travelling back and forth from the same places, then trading on to the smaller traders such as us. Our family's camels carry delicate perfumes and small packets of herbs or spices, precious metals and stones; some already transformed into glorious pieces rich with patterns and colours, some left unworked for local jewellers who are glad of new materials. There are skins and furs, as well as fine cloths and rugs that are laid flat and then rolled up tightly to keep them smooth and safe from fading in the sun's powerful rays. As we journey we add fresher items to our stock – oranges, dates, nuts – less costly but always desirable. We visit the great trading posts and then go out amongst the little towns, the tiny villages, even to the nomad camps of the desert. We move from dunes to cities and see all manner of people. We are welcomed by all, for we bring news and excitement as well as goods from the greatest city to the most isolated desert tent.

The heat increases and the crowd grows thicker, bodies pressed tightly together. The other camels sidle back and forth, some straining at their bridles, the odd one or two suddenly leaping forward into a run before the race has begun, their owners having to force them back to the start. I wipe the sweat from under my eyes and shift my position to achieve a better balance. There will be no such opportunity once the race has begun. I look about me, waiting for the signal to begin. The men in the crowd are laying last-minute bets, the younger women are giggling over certain names: the riders with the best camels, the best saddles, the best eyes… my eyes fix on the race master, a burly man currently shoving a camel away who has come too close to him, overstepping its mark.

He shouts and for one brief instant the crowd is silent. Then his arm waves and I kick my legs hard into Thiyya's sides. Her neck has already lengthened and now her usual swaying gait becomes a jolting run and then a smooth gallop.

The crowd roars as we leave them behind us. The older women clap and cheer on their sons and laugh at their husbands' wild yells, occasionally grabbing at a younger child and warning them to keep out of the way – the camels will be turning back in moments and they might find themselves trampled by a whirl of long, strong legs. A painful way to end your life, for sure.

I feel as though I am flying, like the desert spirits of the old times. Thiyya's neck reaches out ahead of her as though yearning for even greater speed. Though the dust rises all around the riders we are too far ahead of the pack for it to reach us, faster than the very wind, faster than the swirls of sand.

"On! On!" I shout at Thiyya, though she does not need my command. I shout again and again, a wordless scream of joy and hunger for the win.

Some of the best camels are gaining on us now, for a few improve in a longer race. I look over my shoulder and Thiyya can feel me tense, for she strains forward with her long neck, wanting to be further ahead. But the halfway point has come and I pull hard to make her wheel about, her long legs almost caught up in themselves. As soon as we turn the choking sand surrounds us. I can barely see, can barely gasp for air, even though the cloth pulled tight across my mouth protects me from the worst of it. I do not know how Thiyya can still breathe but she thunders on, the shadowy shapes of the slowest camels passing us in the cloud as we head back towards the screaming crowd. I look back once and see only the blue robes of the other riders, floating above the camel-coloured clouds of sand like some strange vision in the heat of the day.

The screams grow louder and louder until they are all about me and I raise my arm and punch the air. I am the winner. My breath comes hard in my throat and I look down on all the uplifted faces surrounding me, the hands slapping at my legs in praise and feel my face stretched in a hidden grin.

Shouted praises and boasts are all about me. In the crowd, possessions and sometimes even coins trade hands as bets are won and lost. Backs are thumped and hands clasped. The younger boys and older girls gaze adoringly up at me.

I remain on Thiyya, acknowledging comments and praise with a wave before turning her away from the crowd. I cannot let my identity be known and so I never linger once a race is won. Let the glory go to the second and third places, the riders who wish to boast and brag. I want only the wild freedom of the ride, the fierce joy of winning. That, I can best savour alone.

I spot my eldest brother who rolls his eyes at me and comes closer, pulling at my bridle. "Do you have to win *every* time, Kella?" he mutters. "It draws attention to you."

I laugh down at him. "To race without winning is not to race at all!" I say, my voice still elated. He shakes his head, but lets me go.

I make my way to our camp, set up on the outskirts. Here, among the one hundred or more camels of our caravan, I leap down from Thiyya and put on my sandals. I give her water and caress her, croon to her before I leave her to rest. Then I make my way into the main tent, pulling at my headdress as I do so, loosening its folds, then flinging it to one side.

Inside it is dark and cool. I reach for a cup and dip it into the water jar, greedily gulping down the cold water.

"Daughter."

I freeze, then carefully replace the wooden cup before I turn round, my face composing itself into an unworried smile. "Father. I thought you were speaking with the salt trader."

"I was. Then I went to see the camel races."

"Who won?" I try to keep my voice light as I seat myself on the foot of the low bed and kick off my sandals again, feigning a lack of interest while my heart thuds in my chest.

"I believe you did. On Thiyya. No-one else here has a white camel with blue eyes."

"One of my brothers – " I try but my father's eyes tell me not to bother. My shoulders slump.

My father settles himself at the head of the bed and sighs. He looks older than usual. "I know you are a good rider, daughter. And I turn my face away when you race against your brothers. You work hard, after all, and what is a little fun between siblings? In the desert no-one but our family and the slaves will see you. Amongst others you have always passed well enough for a boy."

I seize on this, my only excuse. "No-one here knows I am a girl. Everyone thinks I am your youngest son. No-one would suspect."

"You think not? When your hands are still so slender and your voice so light? No. I believe the time is coming very soon when I will have to return you to the main camp, to live with your aunt."

I feel as though I have received a blow to the stomach. I twist round to face him, appalled. "Aunt Tizemt?"

He laughs. "You need not look so upset. Your aunt is a good woman and she has the heart of a lion. She will teach you to be a fine woman."

"It is her voice that is like a lion," I spit.

"No need to sulk. She is a kind woman beneath her

roars. I will not have my daughter dishonoured. You will no longer race."

"But – "

"No buts. No more racing. You will remain disguised as a boy until I can take you back to your aunt. If you are very, very well behaved I may keep you with me a little longer. You are a good trader, after all, I will be sorry to lose your skills in the markets. I believe you secured us a bargain with the salt trader, he was as meek as a lamb when I saw him just now. We will have a camel's load of salt to trade at the next market."

I jump up, my mind racing to find a reason to stay that he will accept. "You cannot send me back to the main camp! I am a trader. I travel with you – with my brothers! What would I do at the camp?"

My father smiles. "Get married?"

"*Married*?"

He laughs at my horrified face. "Have you never thought of that possibility? Your eldest brother is married, two of your other brothers are already betrothed. Did you not consider it might be your turn soon? What, no young man caught your eye yet? No-one beaten you at camel racing?"

I snatch up the swathes of indigo cloth that make up my headdress and glare at him through the narrow eye slit as I wrap it tightly about my face. "No-one beats me at camel racing. And I am not getting married. I am staying with you, with the caravan. I am a trader. Now I am going to the salt trader. He promised me more than a camel's load of salt for that price."

"Your mother would have wanted you happily married," says my father sadly.

13

I walk so fast to the salt trader's encampment that I am breathing heavily by the time I reach it. The great slabs of salt lashed to saddles are piled up around his main tent, then surrounded by the prickly thorn bush branches placed to discourage every camel for miles around from sneaking up to get a free lick of salt. Camels will do anything for salt. The trader comes out to greet me, warily offering tea and a place in the shade to do business when he sees my glare. My only chance to escape being sent back to my aunt is surely to trade and to trade well. My father cannot send me away if I make myself valuable to him as a great trader.

The moon grows full and wanes twice over and still there is no mention of my Aunt Tizemt. I begin to hope that my good trading efforts have made my father forget his threats. I stay away from the camel races.

We reach an important centre on the caravan routes. A mayhem of a souk. Stretched out over a vast area and yet still crowded.

Its camel souk is beyond compare, and it is here that frantic bids are commonly made for the lovely blue-eyed, white-furred Thiyya, a rarity even here among thousands of camels. She picks her way daintily through the crowds, enjoying the caresses, soft words and sometimes handfuls of fruits that come her way. Seated comfortably on her back, above the crowd, I laugh and joke with all those who make offers for her.

"I'll trade you three fine camels for her," says one,

gesturing to what look like three ancient crones, wizened dun-brown, spitting this way and that.

I laugh. "I'd need a hundred of those for this one," I tell him. "One of those will fall over dead before I can even get them to stand up."

"I'll trade you my wife," says one man dourly and there's a shout of laughter.

"I'm sure my camel's prettier than your wife," I tease him.

"She is," he says mournfully and wanders off into the crowd.

More serious offers are made but I shake my head and with a gentle nudge from my feet Thiyya moves on. Grunts and roars are all around us, from baby camels, untrained camels and wise veteran camels. Almost-black camels rub haunches with the rare pure whites, golden sand camels with date-brown camels. Sweet cajoling, shrugged shoulders and moral outrage make up the bulk of the bartering, which may go on for days and is a sport in itself. On the busiest days, of course, there will be camel races and the traders' sons boast of their skills in advance, some louder than other, safe in the knowledge that their fathers plan to move on before the next race and their airy boasts will not have to be made flesh.

Everything is traded here. Some merchants are free to roam and do not have to barter, for they are about to go to the dark south. There they will expend all their energies and all their trade goods to return with precious gold for princes and dark-skinned slaves. They make their fortunes or die alone in the blistering sun, far away from their loved ones and any merciful shade, on the long, long routes where bandits may steal their goods and their lives. Others have already come from those lands and their relief at having come thus far makes them bold and free with their words. They eat and drink more than others and enjoy the company of their friends, while trading good-natured insults with their competitors.

They reserve their sweet words for certain women who make it their business to attend all such gatherings, whose faces are pretty and whose clothes hint at the goods for sale underneath the shining threads and tinkling bangles. As a young child I thought their lives delightful, for they wore pretty clothes and ate sweet foods all day and laughed a great deal. As I've grown older I've heard comments, here and there, from my brothers and the traders I frequent, and now I am all too aware of what they trade in. The women toss their long dark hair and call out in many different tongues, for they have learnt that a few words in a man's own language can tempt him to take a second look as he walks by, especially if his wife is far away and he is homesick. The women sit in comfort in highly decorated open-sided tents on soft cushions and play with their jewellery, gifts from many men. They drink fresh water and suck on oranges in the heat of the day. They offer honeyed drinks, dried fruits and promises of other sweet things to the men who stray a little too close to their warm rugs and the soft lanterns that will be lit when night comes.

"Come, my handsome friend," they call out as I pass. "Will you not take some – ah – *refreshment* with me?" and they giggle.

I make a mock bow in their direction and try to keep

my voice low. "Ah, ladies, if only I could," I call back. "But I must trade or go hungry."

"Surely you are hungry for more than food?" they call.

I laugh and walk on.

The older merchants are known friends by now and often sit with the women during the day, telling lewd jokes, relishing the shrieks of laughter as the younger traders relish the shrieks of feigned delight in closed tents a little way off.

This is my world and I swagger through it in my man's robes, my heart light. My relief at being reprieved and able to stay on the trading routes makes it seems as though I see all of this life anew. My eyes, the only part of my face visible, dart in all directions, taking in every colour, shape and size. I stop sometimes; a quick rub of my fingers establishing quality without a word. The old traders know me and nod without trying to woo me with sweet words. They know their quality will bring me back later when there is serious bargaining to be done. The newer ones offer teas, dates, sweet cakes dripping with honey, a soft seat in the shade, a cool drink of water, the finest goods in the souk – in the world, even! To these my quickly disappearing soles are an instant dismissal.

Oh how I love these moments! Surrounded by the world and all it has to offer, my every sense assailed with wonders. Knowing my own skills, the respect I command for my knowledge and my skills in bargaining, knowing that somewhere here are all the marvellous things that will soon be hoisted onto our camels.

My first stop is the slave souk. I need a new slave; a strong man, for one of our slaves has grown old and weak. He carries out the smaller tasks now, but he is no longer fit for the heavier work. I wait at the back of the crowd while the slave trader calls his wares. We are old friends and he knows that I will spot quality for myself, so he addresses the rest of his audience.

"A little boy here – you may think him small but I assure you he is strong already and can only grow stronger. My wisest clients know it is worth buying them young!"

The boy can hardly be more than ten, although his scrawny body makes me wonder if he is even younger. He stands still and miserable in the heat, till someone pokes him and nods grudgingly at a price that changes hands.

Spices float through the air from the cooking fires where fat spits, sizzles and drips. I am hungry. The slaves for sale stand, heads down in the sun, hoping to be sold quickly to someone who will find it in their heart to offer them water and some shade. Their teeth are examined, their eyelids pulled down and their arms squeezed. The tall and broad ones go quickly; the thinner or scrawnier ones must wait longer in the heat, along with the ill-favoured women who do not quickly catch someone's eye. Sometimes one faints, only to be slapped back to their feet by an irate merchant. I am impatient at waiting while the slight men and the unprepossessing women are offered for sale. But I have been promised that there is one worth waiting for. We are in need of a strong male slave and his time has finally come.

"You will not see a finer man! From the Dark Kingdom,

the land of gold! See his height and his shoulders. He can carry as much as a camel and his legs are like those of a fine racing stallion – see their elegance, ladies!" This last is directed towards two women passing by. They take a startled second look and then hurry on, giggling.

I lean against a scrap of a tree, which gives me a little shade, to watch. The slave is very tall; he would tower over me if we were to stand side by side. He is wearing only a loincloth and I look over his body, assessing it for strength and endurance while shaking my head at the foolishness of putting any man in this sun with no protection, whatever his colour. A few customers prod at him, one even punches him in the stomach to assess either his peaceable nature or the strength of his muscles, but he stays silent and unmoving, head up in the hot sun. He will faint for sure, however big and strong he is. Often the big ones go down first. The trader is a fool to risk damaging his goods like that. A fainting slave can forget being sold for the day; it makes them seem weak and prone to illness, no matter their height and breadth.

The trader has almost finished the bidding. A good price is being offered for the man, but I make a small gesture and the trader notes it at once.

"Come, come, step forward. That is your new master and you had better behave for he is one of my best customers. Move!"

The slave slowly steps down from the raised platform and makes his way to me. I nod to him and turn away, expecting him to follow. After a few steps I realise he has not done so and turn back. The slave is standing looking back at the platform, where the trader has brought on a woman.

"This one is fit for a caliph's harem! A joy, a beauty. See how smooth her skin is, how dark like the precious woods of her land. Her face is very fine – lift your face up, girl! – see! Now, what man would not wish to have such a face by his side in the morning? And such breasts!" He pulls at her simple robe, exposing a breast and tweaks her nipple, while eyeing up his audience to spot interest. If he can make a buyer desire the woman as a companion for his bed, he will get a better price for her than as a mere slave for domestic chores. "You, sir?"

The bidding starts but my eyes are drawn to my new acquisition. He is looking at the slave girl with an expression of abject misery and she is looking back at him instead of at her bidders, as the trader points out sharply, jerking her roughly back to face towards the crowd. Slow, silent tears fall down her face and although she obediently faces the bidders, her eyes slide sideways to catch a last glimpse of the man I have just bought.

I have no need for unnecessary slaves. Women especially are of less use to us than the men, for they cannot carry such heavy loads. I click my fingers at the slave to get his attention and prepare to tell him sharply to come along with me. But there is something about the woman's silence, about the tears that never stop falling. I hesitate and then reluctantly raise a hand. The trader blinks at me, puzzled.

"The pretty slave is sold to the gentleman, it seems," he says. There are some protests but he waves them away and pushes the woman towards me. She stumbles down the steps, almost shaking with relief. She tries a few words of gratitude, although she struggles with our language. I wave her away. It must be the heat, I cannot imagine what else it could be, nor why, in a fit of sunstroke, I have seen fit to buy a female slave only because of a few tears. But it is too late now, the trader will not take her back.

"Follow," I say. I turn away from them and make my way back to our tent, hardly caring whether they are following me or not. I curse under my breath. What was I thinking, to buy a female slave? It is exactly the sort of foolish decision that will have my father sending me home, camel racing or no camel racing.

Back at the tents of our caravan I wave them towards the water jar and they both drink gratefully and then turn to face me.

I take a seat and drink from a water cup. I look them over and then speak slowly, hoping they will understand. "Names?"

This much at least they know.

"Ekon." This from the man, who has a soft voice for such a large frame.

I look at the woman. She is nothing special; I hope she will be useful but she is hardly worth what I paid for her. I have to lean forward as she all but whispers her name.

"Adeola."

I nod, turning the names over in my mind. Slaves often come from the Dark Kingdom, very far away in the south. Still, the names sit strangely on our tongues.

"You will be part of our caravan. We are traders. We have other slaves. Some of them come from your own country. You can speak together. Join them now." I point towards two of our older slaves who have been with us for many years and have been watching with great curiosity while their hands keep moving, churning milk to make butter, shaking the goatskin bags back and forth to a smooth rhythm.

Adeola turns obediently to join the others. Ekon stands still and then approaches me. I draw back a little and put my hand to my belt where I keep a sharp dagger. He is very tall and I have a quick moment of fear. What if he attacks me? Some slaves do. I have heard of such madness, when for one brief moment a slave finds their own dignity again and the anger that comes with it.

But Ekon ignores my gesture and comes still closer. Then in one smooth movement, he kneels before me and touches his face to the ground, first one cheek, then the other. He looks up and I see tears in his eyes. He does not speak but rises slowly to his feet, looking down on me again for a moment. His dark lips still have a few grains of golden sand stuck to them from the floor but he does not brush them away. He turns slowly and joins the others who have been watching, breathless.

I feel my own breath release, although I hadn't realised I was holding it.

My trading is good in the days that follow. My father raises his eyes at the slave woman's presence but cannot fault my other purchases. While I negotiate my way from the first glass of tea to the last honeyed cake, my parcels, packages and heaps of skins grow ever larger and our caravan prepares for the next journey.

The camels rest, licking salt and enjoying the luxury

of sitting slowly chewing the cud rather than the constant walking under heavy loads. They drink water daily and enjoy passing treats given by children, graciously permitting them to play at riding them in return.

The slaves milk goats and churn butter as well as making cheese. They kill the male kids. There is time to roll finely ground grains of barley to make buttery soft couscous, to prepare mouth-watering marinades of goat's milk and spices that bring tenderness and subtlety to the meats. Time to slice oranges and serve them with cinnamon and rosewater rather than quickly munching them and spitting out the bitter skins between one day's journey and the next. Cracked wooden spoons and metal pots are replaced. The new carvings and patterns are appraised and give added pleasure to the dishes.

We eat well and invite many guests to our fire, other traders and sometimes their families. Among them is Winitran, an old trader I have known since my brothers and I were little children. He is a kindly man and an excellent jeweller, although his eyes are growing tired and he no longer does the finer work. Yet we make sure to trade with him whenever we pass by here.

"You'll be back at the usual time next year?" he asks my father.

"Of course," says my father. He thinks for a moment. "Although perhaps my youngest will soon join our village rather than continuing to trade. My sister is growing older and so he may be a help to her." He is careful, always, not to use my name; not to let slip that I am a girl.

I sit bolt upright, seething. I've traded well and yet my father is still talking of sending me back to Aunt Tizemt!

I scowl but under my veil no-one can see me. I hope that by next year, when we are due back here, he will have forgotten. It's a long way off. I might still change his mind.

Winitran turns to his attention to me as the others talk of trading. "I have something for you," he says. "Something to remember me by." From his robes he pulls out a little leather pouch and shakes out its contents into his hand.

It's a *tchirot*, a man's silver amulet. A simple silver square, intricately engraved, hanging below a small scroll-shaped silver box. Between the two is a hinge, allowing the two parts of the pendant to move back and forth independently.

Winitran holds it out to me. "It contains the sand from the entrance to my house and my blessing for your own journey, that you may always find your way safely home."

I bow my head, keeping my voice low as I answer. I'm fond of the old man and he's been good to me over the years. But I wish he didn't feel the need to say goodbye to me as though he will never see me again. "My thanks for the amulet. And for your blessings."

Winitran lays his hand gently on my arm. "Blessings, daughter," he says very softly, so that none of the other guests can hear him.

I pull my arm back quickly. "How did you know? No-one ever guesses."

Winitran chuckles. "I am an old man and have seen many things. But I should tell you that a *tchirot* is a man's jewel, you know, not a woman's."

"I know. May I keep it anyway?"

Winitran smiles. "Of course. I think you may be more of a man than many young men who think themselves most manly." He pats my arm and then turns back to the others, joining in their laughter and talk while I finger the *tchirot*. I can't help feeling a little pride in his praise of me.

We prepare to move on. The tent must be taken down and made into bundles that can be quickly and easily pulled from a camel to reassemble into a living space wherever we might be. The slaves curse under their breath when old straps will not come undone but work fast and soon the tent crumples to the ground, sections already being taken away. The camels are loaded up and stand blinking haughtily, shuffling from one leg to the other, pushing out their stomachs as the men tighten their saddles. A quick poke to the belly and they blow out, disgusted at the failure of their cunning plan as the straps are pulled tighter. The lead camel, my father's, is a very dark brown female of great docility when dealing with her master and utter viciousness when approached in any way by anyone else. She values her place in the lead, however, as it enables her to ever-so-subtly adjust her position when walking and reach out her thick lips for the leaves of passing poplars and willows. My father allows her to get away with it when he is in a good mood. When he is not he corrects her direction and she rolls her eyes back at him and glowers at the titbit passing her by.

Each camel receives its due – a saddle and then a range of burdens are meted out. The lucky ones get a single rider; perhaps an inexperienced slave, easy to fool into allowing it a stop or a nibble of passing food. The less lucky ones get heavier people; the strong male slaves, or piles of trading goods and the party's cooking pots and provisions. They droop their heads and try to look hard done by but their efforts are in vain as more goods come their way. At last they give up all pretence of delicacy and stand, blowing their warm breath into the cold air, bored and sulky by turns.

A new city and its souk. One known for its camel races.

The young men boast and show off their saddles; some new and some old but polished so hard that their colours shine, almost reflecting their owners in the wood and leather. The riders introduce their camels as they might a well-favoured bride, boasting of her beauty, her good breeding and wondrous abilities. Meanwhile they pour scorn on their rivals' beasts, pointing out bucked, yellowed and missing teeth, straggly coats, an old saddle that will be bound to break under any strain.

"I don't care for your camel's knees," one says, winking at his friends while shaking his head in sadness at his rivals' grave misfortune. "Too knobbly, as you can see. Not like my camel's – now she's a beauty!"

One camel is given particular care, although mostly in secret. Thiyya grunts as I examine her pads and brush her coat. She sighs when the old worn tack is exchanged for new, stiffer reins and a halter that rubs her face a little at first. She groans when the straps of the saddle pull her stomach in a little tighter. But she makes contented sounds when she is offered a little more salt than the others, a few handfuls of dates and even some whey left over from the cheesemaking. I whisper endearments and praise into her soft ears for her long legs, her speed, her strength. Thiyya blinks her spidery white eyelashes and takes all such praise as her due.

It is months since I have raced and I can bear it no longer. I have avoided all the races in minor souks and trading cities, turned my face away, allowed my brothers to ride Thiyya without a murmur. But this race... this is the one where the champions compete, where the very best stretch their mounts and themselves to the limit; where just last year Thiyya came second by only a muzzle-length and I know that she could win. If I could just spur her on a little more, just the length of her neck and we would win. I can taste the glory of it. Not the prizes or bets, for I have never cared about them. But the elation, the thunder of feet followed by the fierce joyful moment of triumph. Briefly, I consider riding a different camel, to hide my intentions from my father, but I know in my heart that Thiyya will make me a winner, that none of our other camels can win.

I beg my youngest brother to aid me.

"But if our father – " he begins.

I shake my head. "No, no. You will stand close to me all the time in the crowd. When I mount Thiyya, who will know for sure which of us did so? And when I win – "

"*When* you win?"

"*When* I win," I say firmly. "When I win you must be at my side again, as soon as you are able. Then I will slip down and you can take Thiyya's reins. Parade around, show her off, make a fuss, strut a little. People will forget which of us exactly they saw. And with any luck father will only see you. I will be back in our tent, well-behaved and irreproachable."

"Kella..."

"Please," I beg him. "Please."

"Very well," he says. "But if this goes wrong it falls on your head."

"How can it go wrong?" I ask.

The early evening grows cooler as the crowds gather for the race. Those riding arrive with their camels walking proudly behind them. The spectators fight over good positions, some little boys even attempting to watch from palm trees for a better view; their elders laugh at them as their grip begins to falter before the last of the riders has even arrived.

My father is safely in another part of the city; I saw him set off with my own eyes before I crept out of our tent, my younger brother already well ahead of me, leading Thiyya by the reins to the race track. I arrive just before the race begins. Envious looks are cast.

"Azrur's two youngest sons. They are excellent riders and win often. I would not bet against them if I were you!"

"They've been working hard this week though, out every day and half the night trading. Maybe they are a little weary by now. Might be worth a small wager against one of them."

"Don't say I didn't warn you – I've lost a dagger and a belt because of them!"

The crowd jostle, excited as the race grows nearer. Children are hoisted onto shoulders. The women begin their ululation, the shrill trilling echoing out across the dunes, making the younger camels sidestep, ears pricked. The more experienced camels tense. Soon they will be racing and they are keen. After days of good feeding and drinking they are rested and full of strength. They want to run, to feel the heat of the other camels all around them, the sand and wind in their ears, their riders' feet and voice urging them on.

I squat down to take off my shoes. I prefer to ride barefoot. My brother crouches beside me, the better to maintain our deception.

"Are you riding in the race?" An eager little boy is standing behind me. He tugs at my veil, tightly wrapped about my head, hoping for my attention.

"Let go," I snap, feeling the veil loosen.

He makes a face at me and retreats. I fumble with the veil, trying to tighten it again. It is difficult to do; it takes several moments each day to wrap it about my head as a turban and then tuck in the last part as a veil around my face. To adjust it here, in a crowd, is taking too long and I cannot simply remove it and start again.

"Mount," hisses my brother. "The signal will come at any moment."

Quickly I mount Thiyya and move her into the starting place, alongside the orders.

A hush falls. Our eyes look for nothing but the signal and when it comes there is a slow pounding, growing faster and faster. The crowd yells and once again the riders' blue robes float as though we are spirits of the air.

I am lost in the moment, in the rise and fall, the air clear around me as we pass the other riders. I have missed this. The freedom of the wind rushing past my face, the strength and power of Thiyya. A raw scream rises from my lungs as we pass the leading camel. I look back to see the narrowed eyes of its rider, angry at being passed already, well before the halfway mark. I hear the *crack* of his whip but there is nothing he can do. I am flying. Thiyya turns as though she is dancing, twirling, and now I face all my competitors, their heads lowered against the rising sand and the taste of defeat. I am already looking for the finish line, somewhere ahead of me in the whirling sand. Now I hear the ground shaking as the other riders head back, still comfortably behind me but drawing closer and I turn for a brief moment to see them, shimmering blue shapes against the gold of sand and camels. Looking ahead again I see the crowd trying to draw back as we reach them although there is nowhere for them to draw back to. Their screams of excitement are mixed with fear, yet no-one would miss this moment. I raise my arm in triumph when suddenly something blue flutters before my eyes and my whole headwrap falls, falls even as I try to catch it but Thiyya is still running and my clutching is too late, I hear the gasps before it has even fallen to the ground.

For I might be dressed in a man's blue robes, and have cropped hair. But I am no man. The winner of the camel race is a young woman! People jostle forward to take a better look, children ask excited questions of their unhearing parents and the runners-up begin to hurl insults, made more fierce by their shame at having just been beaten by a woman.

I look desperately this way and that, Thiyya's head jerking up nervously at all the excitement and at my shaking hands on the reins. I try to use part of my robes to cover my exposed face and then my head drops as I try to shield it from the gaze of hundreds of people, all staring at me in aghast amazement.

The reins are suddenly pulled from my hands, the leather burning my palms. The crowd falls back around my father as he tugs at Thiyya, who follows meekly as though she feels his anger and fears its redirection towards herself.

People begin to follow as he leads Thiyya back to our tent, but the look he throws at them makes them fall back. They rejoin their friends to gossip and speculate.

"Was it always her then? On that white camel?"

"Must have been."

"It's a disgrace. A girl! Racing!"

When they catch sight of my brothers in the crowd they surround them, asking questions, some outraged, some teasing.

"What kind of man lets his sister ride in the camel races?"

"So – any more beautiful young women under those veils, eh? Perhaps your father has six daughters, not six sons as we were led to believe!"

My five brothers push past in silence, their eyes cast down.

I stand sobbing outside our tent. Thiyya noses me, her moist huffing breath meant as a comfort. All around us is chaos as the slaves hurry about, dismantling our tent, packing up the caravan. They've been given no warning and everything is in disorder.

My eldest brother steps towards me, his face concerned. "Sister –" he begins.

I wave him frantically away, still crying. "Father says I'm not to speak to any of you. He says I'm a disgrace." My shoulders shake uncontrollably before I burst out again. "I didn't mean to unveil! It got caught and came off, I tied it badly and it was loose from the race! He is so angry! He says we are going back to the village, right now. He says I will be left with Aunt Tizemt and never trade again!"

"Where is he?" My youngest brother's voice trembles. He hates angry scenes. He holds out a length of cloth so that I can veil my face again.

I shake my head. "In the tent. He won't let me veil my face again. He said I am a woman and I'd better get used to dressing like one!"

We stand helplessly around the tent. The slaves lower their eyes and speak between themselves in tiny whispers while they hurry to get the camels loaded up. My brothers try to avoid looking at my face with its cropped hair, my skin sun-darkened around the eyes and pale everywhere else.

Our father strides out of the main tent. Behind him the slaves rush to dismantle it, the last item standing.

My father gestures for our riding camels to be brought forward and then yells: "Kneel!"

The camels can feel anger and each of them sinks without protest to their knees. My brothers and father mount, the slaves behind them just managing to prepare the last camel in time before taking their places.

I stand by Thiyya, tears trickling down my exposed face. I feel like a fool. I have lost my freedom and for what? For a race? I look at my father. His eyes tell me there will be no reprieve, no way back.

"Get on Thiyya at once." His voice is tight with anger.
"Father – "

"At once!"

I climb onto Thiyya's back and sit, waiting awkwardly, clasping my waterbag as though it is some magic charm against my current disgrace, not daring to give the command to rise myself.

"Rise!"

More than one hundred camels stand in unison, ready for the long journey home.

Celebra — A Woman's Necklace

*T*HE WATER IN MY GOATSKIN bag is unpleasantly warm and tastes of goat. We have been travelling since dawn today but now the sun's heat is beginning to seep into us. We should stop and seek shade but we are very close to the camp now, so we press on.

My eyes are fixed on my father's silent back, up ahead of me. His camel, the colour of dried dates, is particularly good at mirroring her master's moods and at this moment she is walking with her head held very high and a majestically haughty look to her slowly swaying hindquarters. Neither of them wants to listen to my repeated pleas to turn back.

I drink again, grimacing.

The camp seems smaller than my memories of it. It's been a few years since our last visit.

The children playing at the top of the dunes spot us from a distance and run to escort us with whoops of excitement and endless questions. My younger brothers smile at them and lift a few of the smaller ones up to join them on their saddles. These lucky ones cling on tightly and make faces at their lowly comrades. As we approach the camp's mud walls the men and women come to greet us with wide smiles as soon as they recognise us, exclaiming over how much older we are, pretending mock-horror over my man's robes.

Aunt Tizemt is waiting, hands on her hips, trying to hide a smile. "I suppose this is one of your brief visits, brother?"

My father grins as he jumps down from his camel. "Sister, you will love me more than ever. My daughter is coming to live with you at long last. I do listen to you, you see?" They embrace. When my father steps aside Aunt Tizemt is engulfed beneath a mass of blue robes as my brothers reach her.

When she emerges, ruffled but smiling, she makes her way to me. I'm still mounted on my camel. I set my jaw. I have been forced to come here, I will not pretend good humour.

Aunt Tizemt looks around as though confused. "My brother said he had a daughter, but I see he is mistaken – he has a sixth son! What do men know, eh?" She smiles and holds up a hand to me. "Take that look off your face, anyone would think you liked being a man!"

I ignore her hand. "I do."

"And you don't want to come and live with your Aunt Tizemt? When she is a poor old thing with all her own children married off and her husband dead so many years and no-one left to keep her company?"

"I want to trade. I'm a good trader." I lift my chin and look upwards to keep my tears from falling.

My aunt lowers her offered hand. Her voice has lost its

humour. "You think a woman's skills are not as important? Not as hard to learn?"

"I didn't say that."

"No need. Your voice said it." Aunt Tizemt turns and walks away. No backward glances or coaxing. My aunt is a fearsome woman.

My father comes towards me. I stiffen, waiting for the order to dismount, but instead he stands in front of Thiyya and strokes her nose without looking at me, as though thinking.

Thiyya is impatient. The other camels are free of their burdens, why is she made to stand here in the heat with a slumped, angry rider who keeps pulling sharply at the reins if she stretches out her nose towards the other camels, who are being fed and watered? She drops briskly to her knees, nearly causing me to fall off at the sudden and unexpected movement, thrown fully forwards and then back. Despite my angry urgings, Thiyya sits, uncaring, on the ground and rises again only when I dismount, muttering rude words under my breath and threatening her with a dire fate involving tasty herbs, rock salt and a very hot fire.

My father is trying not to laugh which only makes me more angry. I stand, head down, wanting to walk away but knowing that I am already in enough trouble.

At last I feel his hand on my arm. "Come and sit with me in the shade," he says.

I follow him reluctantly to the first tent which the slaves have managed to erect. There is fresh water and I drink it greedily, relishing its clean taste, devoid of goat.

When I look up my father is holding out a small pouch of soft yellow leather. "Open it."

It's heavy for its size. I pull open the leather strings that hold it shut and cautiously tip the contents into my hand. It's a necklace. A simple thread of small black beads, with a pendant almost the size of my palm made up of five silver rectangles, with pointed ends, which between them create a deep v-shape at the base of the pendant. Each silver strip is intricately engraved with tiny symbols.

I look up, confused, to find that my father is slowly unwrapping the veil round his face. He sighs comfortably as the cool air takes away some of the heat in his cheeks, stained blue in places from the indigo dye of his robes. He closes his eyes and leans back on the cushions for a few moments.

When he opens his eyes again he gives me a weary smile. "There was once a trading caravan in the Tenere desert, between Bilma and Agadez. In the blinding heat and on an unfamiliar trade route, they lost their way."

I frown. "Father – "

"They wandered in the desert, growing ever more tired and thirsty. They were close to death, even their camels' knees trembling with the heat, when suddenly before them appeared a young woman of great beauty, wearing a magnificent necklace with many engravings."

I sit back on the cushions opposite him, unsure where this story is going. This does not seem like an appropriate time and place to be telling old tales.

My father smiles and continues. "The beautiful young woman showed them to a well nearby. The men hurried to drink and then gave water to their camels. When they were sated, they turned to thank the woman, but she had disappeared. When they reached Agadez, the men told their amazing story of how they had been saved from certain death by a beautiful young woman. An old jeweller, hearing their story, set to and made a necklace that matched the men's description of the young woman's ornament. Upon it he carved symbols of stars and dunes, trails and tents. He called it '*celebra*'. This necklace carries memories of the trade routes through the desert and night travel guided only by the stars above."

I sit in silence, a cold certainty in my belly, and wait for what I know is coming.

"The necklace is yours. You are a beautiful girl and it is a fine piece of jewellery. But I chose it because it speaks of the trade routes – it will be a memory for you of all the days you have spent in the caravan. The trading, the desert, the goods we have bought and sold, the nights following the trails of the stars. You cannot continue on the trade routes with your brothers and I. I have been foolish and kept you too long by my side because I love you dearly." He pauses. "And for your mother's memory," he adds with a sigh. "But now it is time for you to stay here in the main camp. You will live with your Aunt Tizemt for a time. You will learn new skills from her. You will become a woman, as you should, instead of playing at being a man. Your time on the trade routes is ended."

I look down at the heavy silver pendant and feel the first tears falling, hot and shameful on my cheeks. I try to speak, clutching the *celebra* tightly in my hand as though about to throw it back at him, but manage only a swallowed sob, an ugly gulping noise that makes my tears fall faster.

My father rises slowly to his feet and silently puts his arms about me. My muffled voice produces more gulped noises, intended as flat refusals. He waits. When my sobs begin to slow, he speaks and his voice is kind but firm.

"Your Aunt Tizemt is a very kind woman – for all her loud voice and louder opinions. She will teach you many, many new things, and you will come to enjoy them and be proud of all you will have to show your brothers and I when we come to see you. And perhaps you would like to marry soon." He pauses to allow me to attempt another muffled refusal. "I am sure you will have more choice than you will know what to do with. And I am also sure that you will choose wisely, for having lived for so long with men you know what we are like better than any woman." I can hear him smile. "So, may I see your face again? If it is not too red and ugly after all that crying?"

My father's caravan stays only three days, enough time to share stories and gifts, for saddles and tents to be mended and all the goods to be sorted and re-loaded correctly. My father agrees to leave Thiyya with me, but only after I wept at the thought of losing her.

"No racing," he reminds me. "Thiyya will have to get used to a different life, just as you will."

Thiyya snorts in disgust when she is used to collect water but I cannot let her travel far away from me.

The slaves gather round to bid me farewell. Some of them have known me since I was a little girl and they stroke my face and murmur endearments. Adeola weeps and Ekon stands silent, his sad face echoing my own, but he puts out one large hand and pats my shoulder before my father approaches and the slaves move away, ready to mount.

"We will visit, daughter. We will return in a few months, have no fear."

I stand before him, silent and pale, unable and unwilling to speak.

"Now then." My father's voice becomes overly brisk. "Where are all those sons of mine? Come and bid farewell to your sister."

They are upon me in moments, a swirl of blue robes and five sets of arms hugging me from all directions. Jokes, laughter, my cheeks pinched and my shoulders pulled this way and that before suddenly, they are all on their camels. I stand alone, cold without their surrounding bodies, their smiling faces now far away on the camels high above me. I manage a trembling smile, my cheeks stretching unnaturally, then I wave and wave and wave.

As soon as they are too far for waving I run in the opposite direction, beyond the camp, where I fall to the ground and beat the sand with my fists, my mouth open in a silent scream of rage and unhappiness, my heart racing and my mind a huge black cloud of disappointment.

"It's not *that* bad being a woman, you know. My sisters and mother seem to enjoy their lives."

I look up, spitting sand out of my mouth and see a young man squatting beside me. His eyes are warm and merry.

"Go away."

"Not very friendly, are you?"

I spit out more sand in his direction, hoping some of it will land on him. "Who are you?"

"Amalu. I was a baby when your father left the village and began trading."

"So was I."

"I know. We are the same age. My mother suckled you when your mother died. She said I was a fat enough baby to be able to share some of my milk."

I sniff disdainfully. "You look skinny enough to me."

He pretends to be insulted. "Skinny? Look at my arms! Are they not mighty?"

I shrug but have to hide a smile. "I have seen mightier."

He laughs out loud and makes himself comfortable. "I am sure you have. Tell me."

Talking seems to help a little. We sit together for more than an hour and I tell him stories of the trading routes. He makes a good audience, widening his eyes, shaking his head in disbelief and begging for more whenever I draw breath. By the time my aunt finds me I am sitting upright and laughing.

Aunt Tizemt is not laughing as we enter her tent, my new home.

"Sitting around while still dressed in a man's robes, giggling with some boy you have never met! It's a good thing your father brought you to me. I can see you have never learnt how to behave like a woman. Take off those robes at once. I have poured some water in that bowl. Here is a cloth. Clean yourself and then dress in a more becoming manner." She throws down a cloth and marches out of the tent, closing the flaps behind her. The sound of her grinding stone outside is fierce.

I am alone. And unused to it. On the trade routes there were always people. Slaves, my brothers, other traders, even my quiet father. Here there is no-one but me in the tent, and the camp outside is small and peaceful, not like the hot swarming cities I have been used to. Slowly I take off my robes and begin to wash. My thick black hair has begun to grow out. Now, for the first time in my life that I can recall, it is past my shoulders. I try to tie it back, catching my hands in it and finally succeeding in making it into a tangled knot at the base of my neck.

Once clean I look around. There are some clothes lying on the bed but I am unsure of whether they are the right ones. They look gaudy after my plain blue robes. A long red cloth and a smaller orange cloth, all decorated with little silver discs here and there. A couple of brooches, designed to hold the fabrics together in a becoming way when wrapped around the body. A multi-coloured shawl for my shoulders and a wrap for my hair, although my face will remain uncovered now that I am to be dressed as a woman. The wrap is woven in reds, oranges, yellows and covered with symbols and patterns. A pair of simple leather slippers are the only things that look familiar so I put them on and then stand, uncertain. How to fold the cloth correctly to make my woman's clothes? Oh, for a simple blue robe, dropped over my head in moments and then tied at the waist!

My aunt must have heard the silence that fell after the slow washing sounds had stopped. She appears inside the tent.

"Why are you not dressed? Do you intend to wear only shoes? You'll find a husband a lot quicker like that but I am not sure he's the sort of husband you'd like to have."

She looks me over approvingly as I stand naked before her, as though inspecting a goat for sale. Only seventeen, I have a slender body the colour of golden sand, except for my forearms and feet, the skin around my eyes and a small part of my neck, all burnt walnut-brown from the sun. My tangled hair has already fallen out of its badly-made knot and although it is not smooth, it is at least thick, dark and glossy. My breasts are small but shapely and I have a wiry strength that can be seen in my thighs, belly and arms as I shift nervously from one leg to the other and attempt to cover myself from her unrelenting gaze with my hands.

"I didn't know what to wear."

"What's wrong with the clothes I've laid out for you?"

"They're very…" I falter.

"Very?"

"Bright."

"And your blue robes are not? Bright enough, I think. Now put those clothes on."

I stumble over the clothes until my aunt has to step in to pin them correctly. The wrap for my head is worse.

"Let's start by combing your hair. You look like a wild thing. I can see your hair is new to you – did you keep it cut short before?"

"Yes."

"Well it will grow longer and you had better get used to it. It will be very fine once it has grown to a good length; your mother always had good hair. Come here. The knots in this! It will hurt but you will just have to bear it. It will

43

be a lesson to you to brush it every day." She drags a wooden comb through the tangled mass, taking no notice of the way my head jerks back with every stroke and disregarding my yelps of pain. By the time she has finished the comb has a broken tooth and my tangles have become soft dark waves.

"Better," says my aunt. "Now for your headdress." In a few quick twists she wraps up all my hair, piling up the bright fabric into a high turban. A few folds hang down at the sides and back, but my face, still darker round the eyes than the rest of my face, is fully visible.

"There! You look like a beautiful young woman instead of a skulking boy. And lift your head up. I know you are not accustomed to having your face on display but you must get used to it. Now then, you are properly dressed and your hair is brushed. Do you have any jewellery?"

I nod, my scalp still smarting from her attentions. "I have a *celebra*," I say, clasping the heavy necklace round my neck. Aunt Tizemt gives an approving nod. "And my *tchirot*." I pull out my square silver amulet from the old jeweller Winitran.

My aunt frowns. "A *tchirot* is a man's jewel."

I close a hand over it protectively. "It is mine and I will wear it."

She shrugs. "As you wish. You do not have a lot of jewellery. That will change when you have a husband. If you are lucky he will bring you many gifts, as your father did for your mother. He spoilt her. He was a good husband, though," she adds, grudgingly giving him his due. "You would be lucky to find such a man."

"I am not sure I want a husband."

"What, you with all your giggling with strange young

men? Huh. I will see you married within one month at that pace."

"Is that what I am here for? To be married off?"

"Now, now, no need to get angry. You are here to learn some women's skills, for your father tells me you have not learnt them from anyone."

"I have plenty of skills."

"Really? Can you use herbs for healing as well as cooking? Can you spin? Weave? Sew? Do you know where to find the wild grains and how to make a milk porridge? Cheese? Butter? Or did your slaves do all the work? Can you sing? Dance? Play music?"

"No…"

"Can you read and write the *tinfinagh* alphabet? I would wager that your father and brothers have not taught you. The boys learn it but they do not pass it on, it falls to us women to do that. No, niece, you must admit to being ignorant of many things. It will be my job to teach you. And if you meet a young man that pleases you before I am finished – well, you will have to learn even quicker, for no man will want a woman who can trade but not cook." She gives a rare smile at my dejected face. "Come, it is not so bad. We will sit together and we will talk as we work. I will tell you about your mother and your father when they were children. We can gossip and you will meet girls your own age and find out that it can be fun being a woman. It is not all work."

"It sounds like it is."

"Well, for now you are right. I have a bowl of grains out there and they will not grind themselves. You will learn to grind the grain and roll it to make couscous while I make you some more clothes, for you have nothing but your old blue robes and what you have on. A good thing your father left me with a generous quantity of new cloth for you from his stores. Come."

The women's skills are every bit as dull as I had feared. What skill is there in the washing of sweaty greasy sheep's wool in the little water available, hauled one laborious bucket at a time? The dyeing, staining my hands a multitude of colours. My arms ache with the endless carding, using the big wooden combs studded with metal spikes to make the wool soft and ready for spinning. The spinning! Never-ending fruitless attempts to make the spindle twirl without stopping, one hand holding the distaff, the other frantically pulling at the wool, trying to produce a regular, even thread. And after all that work, the tedium of weaving! Back and forth, back and forth and the cloth growing barely at all. Hours of work for no visible reward. What skills are these? Where is the quick banter, the knowledgeable eye cast over goods, seeing the quality at a single glance, sweeping aside the unimaginative engravings, the shoddy dyes, the badly cut stones. Reaching out for the sparkling gemstones, the soft bright leather, the fine clay pots and when the bartering is done, the pride of the war waged and won. And the greater prizes. The shining bars of salt. The gleam of gold. The rippling muscles under black skin. These were my skills and now they are deemed worthless.

The days come and go. My mind feels slow and dull, its

once fast-moving spirit searching across the dunes to find the trade routes and the caravan that has left me here. I wonder about my mother. Did she wish to travel as well or did she stay in the camp willingly? Did she feel her spirit grow heavy with each child that kept her tied to the camp or did she enjoy this life? I cannot find the pleasure in it.

Sometimes when I sit gazing at the dunes, having escaped my aunt's many chores for a moment, Amalu finds me and we talk.

"Enough, enough!" he cries, as five children chase him across the dunes to where I am sitting. "I have no breath left!"

They fall on him as he reaches me, climb all over him while he laughs and succumbs to their insistence that he play the camel and allow them to ride on his back.

"I beg you to save me," he gasps and I cannot help laughing.

"I am afraid not," I say. "If you are a camel then you must endure your burden in life. Otherwise I will have to sell you off for meat."

"Alas, have pity on a poor exhausted camel," he says, lying on the ground. The children thump him and yell that he must continue but he will not and at last they leave him be, tempted by rolling down the sand dunes towards the encampment.

"I think you are safe now," I suggest.

He sits up with exaggerated caution, then re-adjusts his wrap, which has almost revealed most of his smiling face. "I am truly exhausted."

"They are not even yours," I tease. "What will you do when you have children of your own to contend with all day?"

"Ah well," he says, easing himself onto one elbow at my feet. "I will have a wonderful wife who will save me from them."

"Will you, indeed?" I ask.

"Yes," he says confidently, his eyes on mine. "Now tell me what you are doing up here all alone."

I shrug.

"Ah come now, Kella," he says. "I know you miss the trading life. But are you so unhappy here?"

I smile a little. "Not when you make me laugh. But I do miss it."

"Tell me about the trading life," he says. "I would like to be a trader myself one day."

"What do you want to know?"

"Tell me about the jewellers, the leatherworkers, the carvers," he says. He has already learnt that I need little prompting. Just the names of the craftsmen will have me talking for hours.

I gaze across the dunes. "The jewellers have steady hands. They can tell so many stories on a tiny circlet of silver. They spend hours turning over gemstones to find the perfect matches of size and colour for a string of beads or a pair of earrings. You can ask them for magic amulets and they will whisper prayers over jewels for fertility, for luck, for wealth. Some of them roll up tiny scraps of parchment containing verses of the Qur'an, prayers and blessings that will be kept close to the skin within a tiny box of silver."

Amalu nods, touching his own silver amulet, dangling from his neck.

I sit up a little straighter, gesture at my yellow leather slippers. "The leatherworkers buy whole dyed hides from the tanneries and sit in the shade of their tents with all manner of colours spread out before them. The pure whites fetch the highest price. The mixtures used to make them can rip the skin off a man's hands at the tanneries. The yellows are dyed with the stamens of the crocus flower. Aunt Tizemt only needs a tiny pinch of saffron for a meat stew, but a lot more is required for a full hide. They cut out small pieces for shoes and use the bigger pieces for saddles."

I pause for a moment, thinking of the races in which I used to take part.

Amalu sees my face lose its brightness and interrupts my thoughts. "The carvers – you forget to tell me about them."

I nod, distracted from my regretful thoughts by his enthusiasm. "The carvers work precious woods but also ivory. They make such wonders – the tiniest shapes, the most delicate markings. One false move and the work would be ruined."

"No spoons and cups, then?"

I smile. "Those too and in far greater quantity. They are not treated with such care. I used to buy so many replacements just for our own family and everywhere we went we could always sell such goods."

Amalu's eyes are bright. "I will go to all the places you have been," he says. "And see such things for myself."

I want to say *take me with you*, but that would be too forward. Already I know there are whispers about us in the camp, but although Amalu looks at me with loving eyes I am unsure of my own feelings. Still, he is a friend to me and I feel the need for someone who will let me speak of my trading days.

"Kella! Kella!"

I roll my eyes. "Aunt Tizemt is looking for me again."

"I will hide you behind a bush," offers Amalu mischievously. "And tell her you have run away."

I shake my head. "Your life would not be worth living when she found you out," I tell him and together we make our way back to the camp.

Back and forth, back and forth. Buckets from the well, thread on the loom, this grindstone, crushing the wild grains gathered one by one. I refocus my eyes from the horizon and catch sight of Aunt Tizemt, who has paused in her weaving and is looking over her shoulder at me. She smiles encouragingly. Waving her hand at the bowl of grains by my side that are yet to be ground, she begins a story.

"There were once some children lost in the desert. They were hungry and could find nothing to eat. They were surrounded by vile-tasting beetles, beautiful but poisonous oleander bushes, and sand. Sand everywhere, rocks and sand."

I break in impatiently, rudely interrupting her story, which I have heard once too often. "Then one small boy caught sight of a column of ants. Back and forth, they scurried, back and forth, each ant carrying but one grain on its back. The children took the grains of the sand from the ants, one by one, and so they were saved from starvation until they were found." I gesture angrily towards the bowl of grains. "You can tell all the stories you like, Aunt, but there is nothing interesting about the gathering or the grinding of grains. In the great souks I could buy my couscous ready ground and rolled by slaves. Street vendors made great basins of hot milk porridge to be eaten by those who had coins. I traded. I was quick, I knew the gemstones, the quality of skins. I chose the strongest slaves, the finest jewellery, the softest leather shoes. I spent my days seeing all there was to see, bartering for goods from all over the world. I felt the weight of cold gold in my hands and felt its softness against my teeth. I threw coins to the street vendors and they served me fresh bread and roasted meats, cool drinks and sweets to please the tongue and eye. I did not stoop to collect one grain at a time, nor did my hands chafe with the distaff. My hands were tough because of the reins of my camel, the bundles of goods I lifted to the pack animals. I was better than this."

Aunt Tizemt is unmoved by my outburst. She keeps weaving, her broad back firm and upright. She speaks without turning round. "You think you have seen everything the world can offer. I think you have not. You think too highly of yourself."

"What have I not seen? I have seen more than you!"

I cannot goad her. She keeps her back turned and her voice is calm.

"Have you seen a child come slithering out of its mother's womb, covered in blood and slippery to the touch? Have you heard its first cry and seen the joy in its mother's eyes and the pride in its father's? Have you caught a dead child in your hands and seen its shriveled body fall limply without breath to the floor? Have you seen the tears of its mother and the cold hurt of its father? Have you seen the man of your dreams and heard him whisper your name? Have you stood naked before a man and seen his face turn to yours? Have you held a man in your arms and loved him throughout the night? Have you held your dying father and wept your heart away as he leaves you alone and unprotected in this world? Have you held your first child in your arms and prayed that every one of your days would be so happy?" She turns, smiling, to face me. "I think not. I think you have seen a great deal and lived very little. I think you have been so busy seeing everything that you have not experienced the moment when every grain you grind is food for your child and brings warmth to your heart. I think your eyes have been so filled with the wonders made by man that you have not seen the glory of the sunset and sunrise, the rise and fall of the dunes, the tiny ant and the mighty wind. You have seen everything and nothing at all. That will change. But sometimes you must be very, very bored before you can see something wonderful that is right in front of you." She gets to her feet, hands on the base of her back, stretching out her cramped muscles after many hours at the loom. "Now finish those grains. A child of ten would have finished them by now and I need them for our evening meal. Tomorrow I will take you to Tanemghurt."

"Remember to call her *Lalla*," says my aunt in a whisper as we make our way to her tent, which is large and well situated, for she is held in great esteem.

Tanemghurt is our camp's healer and wise woman. There is not a child here who was not born into her hands, as were most of the adults. Tanemghurt has lived longer than anyone can recall.

I roll my eyes. I am hardly in need of lessons on

basic manners, of course I would use a term of respect for Tanemghurt. "Why am I going to her at all?" I ask ungraciously.

"She will teach you the uses of herbs," says Aunt Tizemt.

I bite back my rejoinder: that I have seen more herbs and spices on my travels than Tanemghurt can ever have seen, since she has spent her whole life here, in a tent in the middle of the desert.

The tent flap draw back suddenly and Tanemghurt stands before us. Her face is a wrinkled mass of lines, but she stands erect, taller than I am by a good hand's breadth.

"Tizemt," she says to my aunt, nodding her head as though to an equal.

"*Lalla*," says my aunt. "This is Kella."

Tanemghurt turns her dark eyes on me and says nothing.

"*Lalla*," I say.

She holds the tent flap aside. "Enter."

I hesitate, then step inside, the flaps closing behind me on my aunt.

Tanemghurt's tent is very different from my aunt's and I look around it with interest. I have not seen her tent inside, for few people are invited into it unless they have an ailment, and often Tanemghurt will choose to take her herbs and spells to the sick person's tent. It seems larger than most for it is family-sized, but Tanemghurt has never had either children or a husband, so it is for her alone. The space that would have been set aside for her husband's possessions is full of her little pouches and her mixing and measuring bowls, stacked by size and sometimes by colour. She has spoons of every size, not just the big ones for stirring and the smaller ones for eating, but tiny ones for measuring small doses of the powerful herbs she uses. Some are stained strange colours and some, I see, are kept apart from others. They hang on small loops of string sewn onto the wall. Below them and facing the wall is a large seat, something like a saddle but made for her to sit on, for Tanemghurt is now very old and she finds it hard to sit or squat low on the ground as the rest of us do. The large seat has a small ledge on it where she can rest her mixing bowls or mortar and pestle when she prepares her medicines. All around this seat are pots, many containing water, some containing strange substances that I cannot identify. The tent smells of herbs and perfumes.

"Do you miss the trading life?"

I turn towards Tanemghurt. No-one has ever asked this except for Amalu and the question brings a sudden sting to my eyes. She stands, watching me.

I swallow. "I have no choice," I say.

She lowers herself cautiously onto her seat, one bony arm supporting herself as she does so. "There is always a choice," she says.

"What is my choice?" I ask, my tone disrespectful enough that Aunt Tizemt would cuff my head for it.

She smiles. "That is not for me to say. It is for you to make."

"What would you do in my place?" I ask, my voice still too sharp.

"I would be honoured to learn women's skills from a woman as accomplished as your aunt," says Tanemghurt, unperturbed.

I stay silent.

"So," says Tanemghurt. "You wish me to teach you about the uses of herbs?"

I nearly say I want no such thing, but even I know that would be going too far. "Yes, *Lalla*," I say.

And so she teaches me the herbs to drink when I wish to bear a child as well as those to avoid bringing life to the womb. She shows me how to deliver a child, should I ever be called upon to do so. She tests me on my knowledge of the *tinfinagh* alphabet, which only women pass on. She has me recite large tracts of our legends, our songs, the right ways to live. I stay in her tent for many days, leaving only to relieve myself. At night she shows me the stars and nods with approval when I can name the constellations and know how to navigate by them.

"We are done," she announces one day.

I look at her.

"You may go," she says, as though we have only been conversing a few moments.

I stand, awkward. "Thank you," I manage, unsure of what else to say.

She nods. I turn towards the door of the tent.

"Kella."

I turn back to her. "Yes, *Lalla*?"

"Treasure your aunt. She has more to teach than I."

"I have learnt what she had to teach," I say, a little confused. "She said I should come to you."

Tanemghurt looks at me. "Skills are not the only thing to learn," she says. "Your aunt is both fierce and full of love. She lost her husband and yet still she has a great love within her, no matter what her life brings. Perhaps you still have something to learn."

I try to think what to say in return but Tanemghurt has turned away, looking through her herbs. I am dismissed.

I resent her words at first. But as the days come and go and the moon grows and wanes over and over again, I begin to take some small pride in my new life and the skills I am learning. I grow accustomed to my new clothes and even sew myself some new ones, adding decorative panels to the red and orange lengths of cloth I wear, learning to tie my headdresses more elaborately and without help. The blue dye fades from my skin, the rest of my face grows brown and I begin to lose my former long, swaggering strides and take on a slower walk, my hips gently swaying.

"Keep walking like that and your friend Amalu will be falling off his camel when you go by. Perhaps a crack to the skull will bring his mind back," jokes Aunt Tizemt. But she is proud of me and my new skills, developed under her tutelage.

I can cook a good meal now, for I have always had a fine palate for spices and herbs. I know the quality of spices from my time trading.

"Well, at least you learnt something useful in all those years," my aunt teases when she sees how well I judge quality and quantity, allowing the subtle and strong tastes to emerge, scenting and spicing the food I make – the milk porridge sweetened with cinnamon, the kid meat rubbed with cumin. I make fresh-smelling herbal teas, steeped mint for the evenings after a heavy meal, ground almonds for a sweet milk, a dipping sauce of rich argan oil and honey to scoop up with fresh flat breads cooked on a hot stone over the coals of the fire. My aunt has seen how Amalu watches me walk by, follows my newly-graceful walk with his eyes, then licks his lips when he smells the good food I make.

"Men love soft hips but they love good food even more," she says and laughs.

But still I miss my freedom. Traders pass by sometimes. I sit with an arm around Thiyya's neck and watch them with envy when they leave, their camels swaying them onwards to other places, other worlds from here. I wonder whether Amalu, if he does become a trader, would take me with him and my cheeks grow a little flushed at the thought, though I am still unsure whether it is Amalu or the trading that brings colour to them.

He does not wait long to make his move. "*Lalla*?"

My aunt looks up from her work. "What do you want, Amalu?"

"May your niece accompany me to the *ahal*?"

Aunt Tizemt stops her work on the stretched-out goatskin. She is rubbing it with a thick butter to soften it. She sits back on her heels and considers the young man. Nearby, I sit very upright, pretending all innocence. My hands keep moving, carding thick matted wool into soft clouds that drift down onto the carpet where I sit. My ears, meanwhile, strain to catch every word that passes between them.

"How many are going?"

"Perhaps a dozen of us."

"She has never been before. I doubt she would know what to do."

"There are other girls there, *Lalla*. They can show her."

"I'm sure. Show her how to dance and sing and show off in front of you boys."

"I will take good care of her."

My aunt laughs. "You will spend all your time making up poems in her honour and insults for all the other boys to make her think better of you and worse of them. I know your reputation as a fine crafter of words."

He waits, casting quick looks at me from under his dark lashes.

Aunt Tizemt relents. "Oh, very well then. She has to have some fun. I admit she has worked hard and learnt a great deal in a short time. Perhaps she had better learn some new skills from young people instead of a grumpy old woman like me."

"Yes, *Lalla*."

"Yes, what? I *am* a grumpy old woman?"

He shakes his head at having fallen into her trap and makes his escape, winking at me as he flees. Aunt Tizemt laughs to herself and turns her attention back to the skin. After a few moments' work she speaks to me over her shoulder.

"Tonight you may go to the *ahal*. It is in the small oasis half an hour from here. Nothing there but oleanders and palm trees, but I am told the oleander flowers are out at the moment – every colour you can imagine. Don't drink the water there though, the oleander poison may have tainted the water. Take a waterbag. And you can take my *amzad* with you if you wish. About time you learnt to play it. I have too many other things to be teaching you. Someone else can be your teacher."

I want to know more. "I have never been to the *ahal*. What happens there?"

Tizemt sighs. "You *have* missed out. I spent all my evenings there when I was a young girl. I was a very fine dancer. I know you think I have thick ankles and wide hips, but my sturdy ankles kept me dancing long after the other girls had tired – and then the boys had only me left to look at." She chuckles to herself, remembering her youth. "The *ahal* is a place close to the main camp, chosen for its charm, where young men and young women can meet, talk, joke. The boys will make up all sorts of insults for each other and recite love poems to you girls. You girls will play music, sing, dance. About time you learnt to dance as well. Can you sing? I have never heard you sing at your work."

I make a disbelieving face. "What is there to sing about?"

She reaches over and slaps at my ankles. "Stubborn girl. Well, you will start learning tonight. That Amalu cannot wait to recite his love poems to you after all your chattering about your travels around half the world. And the girls will show you how to dance and play the *amzad*."

I hurry inside the tent and come out holding the single-stringed instrument. "How do you play it?"

She waves me away. "Go, go. Better to learn such things from your friends than your elderly relatives. I could not repeat the bawdy songs without making you blush." She grins and returns to her goatskin, growing soft under her strong hands.

The oasis is beautiful in the light of the setting sun. The

heat of the day gives way to the welcome cool of the evening. The palms are very tall but some of the boys risk the climb to pluck fresh ripe dates, pale gold in colour, crisply juicy within. The oleander flowers range from palest white to dark purples. The light makes the surrounding sands glow and the well's water is fresh and sweet, with none of the promised taint of oleander poison detectable.

We sit, seven girls and five boys, eating the sweet dates and drinking the fresh water. Amalu begins a soft beat on a small drum and a boisterous girl named Tanamart begins a comedy dance; a small palm tree her solid and dependable, if uninspired, dance partner. We laugh and cheer her on. Tanamart winks and holds out her hands to me. "Come now! The newest member of our *ahal*! You must learn to dance. Come and dance with me."

I demur, embarrassed, but am coaxed to my feet and hand in hand with Tanamart I learn my first dance steps, how to move my hands and sway my hips. The sand is warm under my bare feet and the cool air caresses my arms as I move them. I am conscious of Amalu's smiling face and the beat of his drum that guides my steps.

The rest of the evening is spent teaching me more steps, with much laughter over my very poor attempt at playing my aunt's instrument and applauding of the boys' poems, which range from romantic to insulting depending on their intended recipient. Amalu is quieter than usual, his friends teasing him for shyness in front of his lady-love but he only smiles and spends his time improvising rhythms on the drum for the others to dance or recite to.

It grows late and cold. Slowly we begin to depart. Amalu

holds down his hand from his seat on his sand-coloured camel. "Will you ride back with me?"

I hesitate but the other girls nudge me forward, giggling. I smile and hold out my hand to be helped up onto the camel. He pulls me up to sit behind him. I try to settle myself. I have not ridden behind anyone since I was a tiny child behind my father. It feels strange not to hold the camel's reins, not to see where we are going. Instead I hesitantly put my arms about Amalu's waist and feel his warm hand cover mine.

The others clap and laugh. "We will accompany you home," calls out Tanamart.

"You will do no such thing," retorts Amalu and he spurs on the camel so that we quickly outstrip them. It is a strange feeling to be on the back of a camel galloping without having control over it and I hold Amalu more tightly.

Once we are comfortably ahead of the others he slackens the reins and allows his camel to walk. We are all alone in the darkness and for a few moments I rest my head against his back and hear his heart beating, feel our bodies slowly rock together with the pace of the camel.

He peers round at me. "Have you nothing to say to me?"

"What would you like me to say?"

He sighs. "I would like you to say that your heart beats faster when you are close to me. That you like to ride together like this. That you would ride with me always."

My heart beats a little faster. "Would you be a trader?"

"I would."

"And I would travel with you?"

He laughs. "You would be here, in the camp. With our children."

I am silent.

"I would come home often," he assures me. "I would not be able to stay away from you for long. You are too lovely."

I stay quiet and still.

He speaks again, more cautiously. "Would you not like that? Do you not favour me? I hoped you might look kindly on me."

When I speak my voice is low. "I loved the trade routes and our life there. But most women must stay at home and weave and bear children." I stop, for my voice is wavering.

"And you would not be happy to do so?" asks Amalu.

My voice is so low I am not sure he can hear me. "I want to travel the trade routes again."

"Alone?"

My face is growing warm. "With a husband and my children," I say. "I would be happy to travel alongside a husband, to trade together."

Amalu is quiet. "It is not a life for a woman," he says at last. "Women stay in the camp. Would you not be content, if you were my bride?"

I am silent. I feel the warmth of his back, think of his gentle way of speaking, of his good nature. I try to weigh what I feel for him against the desire to travel again, to trade. To be free. I was a trader once, but I am uncertain about this trade. I am not sure if it is weighted in my favour.

Amalu speaks again, very soft and low, his head tilted back towards me. "Will you be my bride, Kella?"

My heart is full but I do not answer. I am distracted by

the sight of the main camp. The fires should be burning low, families finishing their evening meals and beginning to think about sleep. But as we approach there is the sound of music, of people talking and laughing. The fires are burning brightly and there is a smell of roasting meat. The children are awake and excited. As soon as they catch sight of us they run shrieking in our direction.

"They're here! They're here!"

Amalu looks up, startled. "Who is here?"

"Kella's father and brothers! And they have such news!"

I let go of Amalu's waist and slide quickly down from the camel, running towards the camp, leaving him alone.

My father looks up with a warm smile as I run towards him. My five noisy brothers whoop and leap up to hug me, before delivering me to my father's side by the fire. All the camp is gathered to hear the news and see them after many months' absence.

My father hugs me tightly and then leans back to get a good look at me. He speaks over my head to my aunt, who is beaming. "Tizemt, I congratulate you. I see a grown woman, not the half-man I brought you! She is most beautiful and I am sure most accomplished. Can she weave? Sew? Cook?"

"All of that and much more besides." My aunt is proud.

"I am in your debt, sister."

I interrupt, tugging at his arm like a child. "They said you have news."

My father nods. "I have, exciting news. Sit by me and I will tell you everything."

The camp makes itself comfortable, the older children as keen to hear the whole story as the adults. The smaller children sit in their parent's laps but doze, the words meaningless to them. My father waits until everyone is ready and then begins.

"Ten years ago the Almoravid army captured the city of Sijilmasa in the north from the Zanata tribe, and then went on to sack the trading city in the oasis of Awdaghast, in the south. In this way they controlled the two ends of one of the great trade roads. But when a few years later they tried to cross the High Atlas to fight the Barghawata tribe and take control of a wider part of the country, their leader Abdallah was killed and the Almoravids were forced to retreat. His general and second-in command, Abu-Bakr bin Umar, took over the leadership. Now Abu Bakr is ready to attempt the crossing of the High Atlas again. His army is far larger and stronger than it was before. They have had a few years to build up their strength and develop their plans. His cousin is Yusuf bin Tashfin, and he is now the second-in-command. A very strong and pious man, so they say – I have spoken more with Abu Bakr but have seen Yusuf also. Together they lead the army. I have met Abu Bakr over the years through my trading, and now they have asked me to help them plan their attack, as I have been to many of the trading cities across the High Atlas. They want to take Taroundannt and then the merchant city of Aghmat, which is very rich. Abu Bakr, Yusuf and some of their men will come here tomorrow, and we will talk. There may be young men from our camp who wish to join their army – many men from local tribes have joined them. My own sons wish to go but they cannot be spared for now – perhaps later on they may join Abu Bakr and his men. Also," he winks at Aunt Tizemt, "I do not believe my sons have the discipline to train and pray so hard whilst eating only meat, water and fruit as the Almoravids do – I think they are too fond of their aunt's good cooking."

My aunt laughs. "I will feed up your boys while they are here. They will be able to taste their sister's fine cooking, too. Tomorrow we will have a feast to honour our visitors when they arrive here. For now, it is very late and time for everyone to get some sleep."

The camp disperses, although I can hear everyone talking long into the night, excited and curious about the news. The young men are probably dreaming of glory, their mothers hoping to persuade them to stay safely at home.

I wake at dawn, nudged into sleepy consciousness by Aunt Tizemt. We creep out of the tent, past my brothers and father sleeping just outside the tent. Wrapped in thick blankets they are indistinguishable from one another.

The goats are milked and herded away from the main camp for pasturing by the slaves before the men wake. They rub the sleep from their eyes and drink hot tea and eat handfuls of fresh dates with bread from the night before. The boys tease me when they see their breakfast. "What, no fresh breads with honey and butter? No soft porridge? No fine meats and stews cooked to perfection? We were promised fine cooking from our oh-so-grown-up sister!"

I laugh and chase them away. "Go and fill the water bags and pots. We are planning a great feast for tonight. This morning you eat leftovers. It will whet your appetite for later."

My youngest brother makes a despairing face. "I am still a growing boy! I cannot survive on such meager fare!"

"Still growing?" I poke at him with my wool carders as I tidy the tent, looping up the sides to let the cool air flow through. The sharp metal spikes make him squawk and leap out of my way. "I think you are only growing fatter, brother, not taller! Now go with the others, I need plenty of water! When you return there are goat kids to be slaughtered so that I can begin to marinate the meat."

When I step outside Amalu is waiting.

"Kella – "

"I cannot talk now, Amalu," I say. "Aunt Tizemt will have plenty to say if she catches me loitering."

"I asked you a question," he says. He is rarely so serious.

"I know," I say.

"And?"

"And I cannot think on it when I am being pulled every which way by work," I tell him. "I need to think carefully before I answer you."

"Do you?"

"Yes," I say.

He nods, his eyes a little sad. "Very well," he says. "When there is a quiet moment, think on what I asked you."

I nod, serious enough that he seems satisfied.

It is not until the afternoon that one of the children comes running to tell my father that our visitors have been spotted. A party of twenty men, all on horseback, "And such horses! Not like ours but grey stallions, their legs so fine and such fast racers!" They are followed by another sixty men variously mounted on camels and horses.

The men gather to welcome the guests. The children peep from behind tents and the women cluster a little further back as they approach. Abu Bakr, at their head, is a stocky man with a broad smile. He slips quickly down from his horse and steps forward to take my father's hands and exchange greetings. Next to dismount is his general.

"Yusuf bin Tashfin," murmurs my aunt, always well informed. "They say he has an even greater vision for the future than Abu Bakr. The whole of the Maghreb united under one rule, a mighty empire."

I watch. Suddenly the camp feels small and dull. I had thought I had grown somewhat used to my life here, but these visitors, bold on their fine steeds with grand visions for the future, about to travel far away from our little camp, have made me jealous already. Something in me I thought had been tamed is tugging to be set free.

Chachat — An Engagement Necklace

I AM DRAWN TO YUSUF. ABU Bakr is gruff but pleasant. He seems like a practical general rather than a visionary leader. That role, oddly, seems to belong to his second-in-command.

Yusuf's voluminous black robes, turban and veil hide his body and most of his face, but his forearms, where they are visible, ripple with strength. He has a sharp face, all angles. A long straight nose, high cheekbones and a pronounced browline. His eyebrows are thick and well defined. I find out that he is forty-eight years old but I think that he could pass for a much younger man for his skin is still smooth, his hair dark and his body upright and powerful. He has arrived on a very fine silver-grey horse, which he rides easily, poised and confident on his saddle. Although the fineness of his horse should demand an elaborately decorated saddle, his is entirely plain, made of simple brown leather. It is good quality, my trader's eye tells me that, but it is plainer than a slave's saddle.

When he dismounts to greet the men of our camp he walks briskly. He is of no great height but the other men straighten as he approaches as though attempting to reach a physical height demanded by his presence.

The men gather in one of the larger tents and my aunt and I serve tea. The other men drink and eat, but I see that Yusuf has his tea unsweetened and does not touch the sweet sticky dates we offer.

"Someone needs to stay here with the men and look after them," says my aunt, looking about for a likely candidate. "Make sure they have water and food if they ask for it."

"I will do it," I say before she has even finished speaking. I cannot be stuck over some fire, poking at the coals and seasoning stews when there are people here talking of wars, of trading routes, of great new possibilities. I want to be close to them, to hear what they have to say, to taste my old life, even second-hand.

Aunt Tizemt huffs. "I have enough to do without losing you as a helper."

"But they are our honoured guests," I say desperately. "We cannot leave just anyone to look after them."

"Oh, very well," she says and hurries away, chivvying her other helpers.

I try to be discreet, to keep myself to one side. I speak or move only when someone needs something. I do not want to be dismissed, for one of them to say that they will manage by themselves. I want to hear their plans, about the challenging adventure that lies before them.

They talk until it grows dark, my father sharing information about routes, cities, the terrain that he knows well on the other side of the mountains. Abu Bakr and Yusuf talk about their plans: how many men, how many horses and camels, the weapons they have amassed, their battle tactics. Yusuf is respectful towards Abu Bakr, but not deferential. He speaks when required and falls silent when he has nothing of value to add. His words are measured and certain. He speaks without pause or hesitation. When he is silent he listens with great care to those who speak, considering their words one by one, nodding slightly when an important point is made. He does not become distracted, even when the talks continue for some time. Other men in the group look around with natural curiosity at the camp or smile at the children who peek shyly at them from the folds of the tent, overawed by their weapons. Yusuf seems to notice nothing except the people with whom he is speaking.

Abu Bakr pulls out maps and they all pore over them, tracing possible routes across the mountains. Sources of water are important, along with an understanding of which tribes they may encounter along the way, whether they may show resistance or could be encouraged to join the army.

As cousins, Abu Bakr and Yusuf seem to have an easiness between them, occasionally filling in the words of the other one, comfortable with taking over from one another when necessary. Their military time together must have given them a deep understanding of one another's strengths and weaknesses and the ability to work together closely without needing to question the other's decisions. Yusuf speaks of the army's training, their strict discipline. He wants to try new formations, better strategies. Abu Bakr, for now, wants to talk about routes and recruitment, hence this meeting with my father, whose local knowledge, both of tribes nearby who might be persuaded to join the army and of the possibilities for attack once they crossed the mountains, is invaluable to them. Yusuf's face lights up when my father talks of a possible route through the mountains that would hide much of their progress as they make their way closer to the point of attack. But my own interest comes when they stop talking of fighting formations and instead Yusuf begins to talk with enthusiasm of what will come after.

"We will command the trading routes. We will create a new city, a great city from which we will control the whole of the Maghreb. We will be better able to protect the traders, in return for their taxes. The trade will benefit all. There will be great souks, larger than those in place now. We can trade further and in greater quantities than before, for we will be the central point between the countries of the north, across the sea via Al-Andalus, and all of the Dark Kingdom in the south. It will be a great new time."

I edge closer. I think of what it would be to have all of the Maghreb under one ruler, to encourage trade from distant countries. The souks would grow and flourish. And a new city! A gathering point of the greatest traders, where north and south would meet and trade. I can feel the excitement growing in me of the trading possibilities, of what could be done. The longing I thought I had buried for the trade routes rises up in me so sharply it is all I can do not throw myself on my knees and beg Yusuf to take me with him there and then.

I feel a sharp dig in the ribs and Aunt Tizemt hisses in my ear. "When you've finished staring, I need your help. They are fine by themselves."

"They might need me," I begin.

"They are wrapped up in their plans," says my aunt. "They don't even know you exist. Come on."

I follow, reluctantly, looking back over my shoulder. "But I…" my voice trails off as my aunt laughs. "What?"

"I think you were staring at the Commander's general. A very fine man, I'll grant you that. But a little old for you, isn't he?"

I feel heat rising through me and know my cheeks are flushed. How to explain it is not the man I am interested in, it is his vision for the Maghreb? Aunt Tizemt will only laugh even more. And perhaps I have to admit that there is something about this man, so fierce-looking but so eloquent, so driven for a life of adventure, that does draw me a little to him. I grab at the dough that has been rising in an earthenware dish nearby and begin to knead it. Aunt Tizemt laughs even more when she sees how violently I press and pound it.

"They say you should knead bread when you are angry. Perhaps you should knead it when you are in love as well. All that new-found passion has to go somewhere." She looks over at the men in the tent, heads bowed over their maps and plans. "Especially when the object of your affections is oblivious to you. Too busy thinking of fighting and glory. Typical man." She bustles off, carrying a whole goat kid's carcass high in one hand, a bowl of spiced yoghurt in the other for marinating. Her voice can be heard as she makes her way across the camp, exhorting any men, women, slaves or children who cross her path to work harder – build up fires, bring water, cut up more meat, grind the grains finer. My aunt can turn a whole camp into her own personal army when she needs to.

By evening a magnificent feast has been prepared. There is meat in abundance, marinated, spiced, baked, roasted and cooked in rich stews. There are soft warm flat breads, bowls with dips and flavoured oils, butters, cheeses and then fresh fruits and little cakes, soaked in honey and dripping with spiced sweetness. There are olives, figs and dates in great bowls to be passed from hand to hand.

The children are half-mad with hunger, their mothers having denied them anything but simple foods. Perhaps a little congealed porridge, a few dates, scraps of meat and stale bread for the lucky ones. All day long they have smelt glorious foods being prepared, tantalizingly faint at first, then growing stronger as the sun fades. They have been kept busy fetching and carrying, chopping and pounding, shelling and mixing. Any straying fingers have earned them a quick slap, knocking their hands away from temptation. Now that satisfaction and satiety lie only moments away they grow shrill and restless with no chores left to steady them, hopping from one leg to another, begging their mothers and more especially their fathers to say blessings over the food and let them eat.

At last the food is served and the children watch in agony while the guests are offered the choicest morsels. While Abu Bakr and most of his men give thanks and eat heartily, praising the fineness of the food, the wide-eyed children see to their disbelief that Yusuf bin Tashfin, although he also gives thanks, hardly eats at all. He accepts a piece of plain roast meat, a small hunk of bread, and a handful of dried figs. The other food he waves away politely but firmly, or passes it swiftly to the next person. He eats slowly and with apparent enjoyment, but finishes long before everyone else, for he eats far less than the other men.

I find myself almost angry. "Why did I bother to learn all those cooking skills you said were so important?" I hiss to Aunt Tizemt, as we sit side by side, eating the good food, which tastes like dust to me after a day of endless cooking. I feel strangely awake and feverish.

She frowns. "What are you talking about? Look how much everyone is enjoying the food we have prepared. Look at your brothers – I believe they have become camels after living with them so long – it doesn't seem possible that a mere man could eat so much in one sitting." She chuckles and reaches out for another cake. My aunt loves the little spiced honey-soaked cakes and considers no feast complete without them.

"Well, he has barely touched the food."

She raises her eyebrows. "*He*?"

"The second-in command."

"What, you don't know his name yet?"

"Yusuf bin Tashfin." It comes out too quickly because I have whispered it to myself all day.

Aunt Tizemt grins as she takes another bite and speaks with her mouth full. "Oh, so you are offended because Yusuf does not cram his belly like your brothers?"

I shrug, embarrassed. "Perhaps there is something wrong with the food."

"I do not think so – look at everyone else here, eating until they groan. He is known for being a very disciplined man. He follows a very strict diet, so they say."

"What else do they say?"

My aunt smiles. "There is not much to say. He does

not care for filling his belly with rich foods and drink. He drinks water and eats but little. He prays to God. He plans for a country united and obedient to the will of God. This is his mission, his dream."

As the night draws on there is dancing and singing, much discussion of the visitors' plans as well as general gossip. The children begin to sit by their parents rather than chase around.

The old storyteller Aghbalu makes his way slowly to the main fire where the meat was roasted. By now the flames are dying down a little but the children, seeing him make his way there, revive and dash about to gather up more firewood. They like the flames to be high when he tells his stories, for then his gnarled old body and his sun-faded robes take on movement and make his stories come alive as his arms wave and his feet take on some old-remembered nimbleness as he plays every part – handsome young men, terrible djinns, beautiful maidens and their fearsome mothers.

Now the flames rise higher and the children shelter by their parents, who lie back on their elbows or squat comfortably to hear the story. Suggestions are shouted out.

"The moon lady!"

"No, no, the terrible djinn of the desert!"

"Aghbalu! The courting of the camel-girl!"

Aghbalu smiles and claps his hands loudly. There is silence. "Some of us are too old to need to be reminded of our origins." He points at my father and nods at the roars of laughter as my father good-humouredly bends his strong lithe body and imitates the shufflings of an old man.

"Some are too young." He points at a baby, asleep in the golden firelight and the women coo.

"But these ones," says Aghbalu, and he points at the young men of our tribe who have chosen to join Abu Bakr's Almoravids. "These ones must be told once again a great and wondrous story so that they will not forget where they have journeyed from, however far they travel on their mission."

The crowd waits. Aghbalu smiles. He knows how to build up the tension. He claps his hands again. "Tonight, I tell the story of Tin Hinan and the goatherd."

There is a murmur of approval and the crowd makes itself comfortable.

Aghbalu waits a moment and then gradually sinks to his knees on the sand. He stretches out his arms and looks into the distance of the night.

"What do I, a poor goatherd boy, see? What is this sight that comes towards me? It seems to me that I see two camels approaching but this surely cannot be, for there is no-one who lives nearby but my own poor family and none of us has such fine camels. One is very pale, indeed as it comes closer I believe it is white."

There are nods. A white camel like my own Thiyya is a sought-after rarity.

Aghbalu peers far away. "The camels are coming ever closer. And what do I see on these two camels? Two women. All alone in this great desert, far away from anywhere. Their long robes move in the breeze. One is a small woman, strong and wiry. She is a fierce one, a fighter for sure, loyal and kind. She wears robes of black with much embroidery.

Her camel is a fine beast, sturdy like her. They could go a long way without succour."

More nods. But everyone is waiting for the description of the other woman.

"Closer they come to me and still closer. My goats are restless and curious. Some scatter but I do not chase after them. I am too curious about this mirage. Is it a many-headed desert djinn, come to claim me for its own? Should I run? But I cannot bring myself to run for I have never seen such a woman as this one who leads. Her camel is white, and it has blue eyes. Such a rare camel! Such a camel would be fit for a princess. I look slowly further up and I see long red robes of great fineness, and then…"

In the firelight he slowly stands and in doing so transforms into a tall and wondrously beautiful woman, graceful and queenly in her bearing, her robes shifting shades of red in the flames. Her face is handsome, framed with long dark hair and high cheekbones. Aghbalu's voice grows higher and stronger as he bends his head graciously towards a small boy sitting by his father.

"Who are you, child?"

Under the gaze of the entire camp only one answer can come from the boy. "I – I am a poor goatherd, lady."

The lady-Aghbalu nods slowly. "And where do I find myself, goatherd?"

The answer is on every person's lips. "You are near the Oasis of Abalessa, lady."

"Is it far?"

"No, lady, but one more day's journey. My family gathers dates from the palms that grow there and our flocks drink from the waters. But there is no one who lives there."

"Then it will do very well. And you and your family may always come and gather dates from the oasis and bring your flocks to water. Thank you, child."

The lady bends her head again and turns away. But the goatherd cannot resist asking a question.

"Lady?"

Her profile comes back into view before she continues her journey.

"What is your name, lady?"

The camp waits for the great name to be spoken.

"My name is Tin Hinan."

The camp settles back, satisfied. The boy hugs his father in delight at having been part of history.

Aghbalu allows him a majestic smile before he gently squats back to the ground, somehow losing the woman's shape as he does so and taking back his own form. "Yes, she was Tin Hinan. A tall woman, of great beauty and strength. She was a noble woman. She set out from the Oasis of Tafilet and went across the desert with her faithful servant, Takama. The country they travelled across was empty but when they came to the Oasis of Abalessa Tin Hinan established herself there. She had a daughter, Kella," he nods in my direction, acknowledging the importance of the name I was given at birth, "from whom came the noble tribe of Kel Rela. Takama had two daughters – from one descended the tribe of Ihadanaren, from the other the tribes of Dag Rali and Ait Loaien. Tin Hinan gave the oases of Silet and Ennedid to the two daughters of Takama, and their descendants have them still today." Aghbalu pauses. "She died a great queen, and when she was buried she was placed on a bed of leather and adorned with her finest robes.

On her right arm she wore seven bracelets of silver. On her left, she wore seven bracelets of gold. Beside her were laid fine drinking vessels. Many songs were sung for her and many stories are told of our great Queen Tin Hinan, the mother of all our tribes. This story is but one: the day when Tin Hinan heard tell of the Oasis of Abalessa from a poor goatherd boy."

Whistles and applause break out, along with shouts of praise, before the camp begins to disperse, bellies and minds replete. The younger children are taken to the tents, a few adults still linger, talking amongst themselves. Here and there some of the young women are still dancing but they are growing tired. I see Yusuf turn away from the sight of them, devout even in this. He is sat near my father and now they begin to talk together. I edge closer to them, walking softly and slowly, hoping not to be noticed.

"Kella."

"Amalu," I say, one eye still on my father and Yusuf.

"I came to your tent but could not find you," he begins.

"I am very tired," I say, moving back a little.

"I wanted to give you something," he says.

The men nod between themselves. I wonder what they are speaking of, if I can find out more about Yusuf's plans for the Maghreb.

"Kella?"

I drag my attention back to Amalu. "What is it?" I ask, impatient.

"Nothing," he says and walks away.

I feel bad for a moment but now my chance has come. I manage to step closer to where my father sits and sink to the ground behind him. My heart beats so fast and loud inside me that I think everyone nearby must hear it, but the men are oblivious to me and continue to talk amongst themselves. I have to steady my breathing to stop the pounding in my ears when Yusuf speaks, his voice clear and slow.

"Your help has been invaluable. The information you have given us will make our journey smoother and our chances of success greater. We have trespassed too long on your hospitality and our mission must begin. We will leave tomorrow."

My father nods. "Yusuf, Abu Bakr, I thank you for your faith and trust in me. I am but a humble man and if I have helped your mission, then I am glad. It is my duty before God to help you in your mission. I will ask Allah to bless you in my prayers."

I stand, legs shaking. I sway for a moment and then walk slowly towards my tent. They are leaving. The excitement that has surrounded their visit will go, everything will return to how it was: the daily monotony of rolling couscous, spinning, weaving and whatever other tasks and skills Aunt Tizemt can conjure up. I can hardly bear the thought of it. While Yusuf and his army will travel across the whole of the Maghreb, creating new cities and forging a new empire, I will stay here forever, eventually married to a man who will expect me to be happy caring for his children and no more. My eyes well up at the idea.

"Kella?"

Amalu is standing outside the tent.

"Go away," I say sharply.

"What is wrong?"

I face him. "Will you take me on the trade routes with you?"

"What?"

"Answer me."

He frowns. "Kella – "

I push past him, closing the tent flaps behind me.

"Kella!" calls Amalu outside.

"Leave me be!" I shout back. I fall down on the bed fully clothed and lie still and silent, unable to cry or move.

I am listless the next day. Aunt Tizemt chides me several times for foolish mistakes. I burn the milk porridge and refuse point-blank to serve the men, leaving the task to my aunt while I sit carding and spinning wool. She is appalled at the poor quality of my spinning.

"Anyone looking at that would think it was the first day that you had picked up a tuft of wool! What sort of poor rug will that make?" She tuts and walks away, muttering about young girls and their flighty, sulky ways.

I pay no attention to her comments. Yusuf has just walked past me. I leave my spinning to one side and follow him. He walks a little way outside the camp and then kneels to say his prayers. From behind one of the outer tents I catch a glimpse of his face as he lifts it up to the heavens. His expression is not fierce nor solemn, but calm and full of trust in God. As he prostrates himself his body is graceful and pliant, not sternly upright as he holds himself the rest of the time. He seems at ease with Allah – he offers his prayers as a small child might offer a humble gift to a loving parent, confident in a kindly response. It is a different side to him. I thought Amalu might relent and take me with him when he becomes a trader, if I married him, but he has refused more than once. Now my thoughts turn towards Yusuf. I wonder if I could marry such a man, if he would have me. If I married him, I think, I could travel with him, however dangerous the journey or the battles I would not be afraid.

I would be in the army's camp and taste freedom again. Would my father give permission for such a marriage? How could I draw Yusuf's attention to me as a possible bride? But he is engaged in a holy war, he is hardly about to stop and get married while his army amasses. I duck out of sight as he stands and return to the darkness of my aunt's tent, where I fling myself down on the bed and weep in rage and despair.

After a while, when my cushions are wet with tears, I turn onto my back and stare up at the ceiling. As I do so my hair, which has tumbled out of my headdress, catches in something that has been under my head while I wept. I had not felt it then, for it was only small and my feelings are too overwhelming. But now this thing, whatever it is, is tangled up in my locks of hair. With some mutterings under my breath and much fumbling, I eventually untangle it and sit up to look at it.

I drop it immediately and have to bend to pick it up from the rugs on the floor. I hold it up again. It is a very simple necklace, alternating tiny black beads with beads in the form of hollow silver tubes. At regular intervals there dangle small silver triangles, each with delicate engravings.

My first instinct was correct. It is a *chachat*, an engagement necklace.

I let it drop into my lap and then fall back on the bed, the tears slowly coming again. A *chachat*. It is from Amalu, of course. He must have sneaked into the tent when no-one was looking and laid it here on my bed so that I would find it. He asked me to be his bride and I never answered him, what with the excitement of my father returning and then all the preparations for the last few days, attending to our unexpected guests. Despite my snapping at him he smiled at me more than once and gestured helplessly at all the work we are all burdened with. There has been no time to talk. But now our guests are about to leave and the camp will grow quiet. Amalu must think the time is right to broach the subject again.

I sigh heavily and roll onto my side, one arm lifted to dangle the *chachat* in front of me. It is pretty. Amalu is a good man. He is friendly, caring and my own age. He will not let me trade alongside him, but there is no man who will let me do that. Why am I foolishly supposing that I might find one? Certainly pinning my hopes on an older man who may well be about to get killed is even more foolish than begging Amalu to take me trading.

Slowly I sit up and move my hair to one side, then fasten the necklace round my neck. Amalu is a good match for me. My family will be happy. I will go and find him and tell him.

But Amalu is nowhere to be found. Keeping the necklace hidden until I can speak with him I walk all over the camp but cannot see him anywhere. Meanwhile Abu Bakr's men are amassing, ready to leave. I steadfastly ignore them, turning away from the crowd of men, horses and camels, saddles being lifted into place and harnesses tightened. There are perhaps one hundred men in all. My chance to leave has gone. Yusuf would have to stay in the camp a great deal longer if I were to somehow woo him. Not that I have any idea how to do such a thing and anyway, he is devoted to his mission. He is not interested in a woman.

Not a woman.

I run.

My two youngest brothers are nowhere to be seen. No doubt they are bidding farewell to the soldiers. I know they have asked my father more than once if they may join the army, but he has refused. He needs their skills on the trade routes and he is afraid for their safety. Their tent is empty.

I do not waste time by undressing. I take one of my brother's blue robes and pull it on as quickly as possible. My hair wrap has to come off, for it is too bulky to hide beneath a face veil. I hide it in a large chest. I fasten a belt, take a dagger and my youngest brother's sword, pull at my veil to be certain that my face cannot be seen. If Yusuf bin Tashfin is not interested in taking a wife then I will join his army. Many young men of our camp and others of our tribe have joined him in the past few days. I will not be noticed.

Thiyya watches me as I saddle one of our sand-coloured camels.

"I am sorry," I tell her. "You are too noticeable. My father will take one look and know who is riding you."

She huffs and turns her face away when I try to stroke her, insulted.

"I will send for you one day," I tell her, a lump in my throat. "I cannot stay here."

I join the crowd of men and make sure to keep my distance from my father and brothers, whom I can see a little way off. Instead I mount the camel and join those who are ready to depart. I watch as Abu Bakr and Yusuf bid farewell to my father and other important men and bless the people of the camp for their help and support. Once they mount their horses the signal to move comes quickly. I make sure to be away from the officers, taking up a position within the crowd where I will ride side by side with the men who accompanied Yusuf here and will not know the young men of my camp. I do not speak to those around me and look only ahead, my veil tight around my eyes, my heart hammering in my chest.

We travel through the night to avoid the heat of the day and as the moon rises my heartbeats slow a little. We are moving ever further from the camp. It is many days' journey to the main army encampment and once we arrive there will be many hundreds, even thousands, of men, making it far easier to take my place among them unnoticed. For now I must only stay quiet and be noticed as little as possible. We will travel by night, sleep by day, thus aiding my disguise. I am a little afraid of what will happen when I am expected to train to fight and then join an army. But the thrill of being on a camel again, riding freely towards adventure is too great a pull. With every pace away from the camp my spirits rise. Beneath my veil my mouth is stretched in a grin.

There are no tents. The men wrap themselves in blankets and sleep on the sand under some scraggly trees, hoping to benefit from a little shade when the sun rises. My blanket smells of my brothers and suddenly I am afraid. I should have left them a message so that they know I am safe, for they will be searching for me if I am not seen tomorrow morning at the very latest. They may even have spotted my absence in the evening. How keen-eyed will my brothers be, how quickly will my father see what has been taken and understand what I have done? They will come after me for sure. But I am too tired. The dawn will be here soon and I must sleep; it will be harder to do so once the sun rises and we will ride on come the cool of the early evening.

I wake with a start as the man near me pokes me with his foot.

"Commander says we must be on our way," he says. I put my hand to my face to make sure it is hidden but I am safe. I struggle to my feet and roll up my blanket, kneeling to fasten the strap holding it in place.

"You."

I look up over my shoulder. A man stands behind me.

"Yes?"

"The General asks for you."

I swallow. "The General? What for?"

"How would I know? Don't keep him waiting."

I stand, stumbling over my blanket and then follow the man's pointed finger towards a solitary figure some way away from the men. Yusuf. I hesitate but I have no choice. I make my way over to him. He is sitting calmly, one knee pulled up, his hands wrapped around it while he gazes across the dunes. When I reach him I stop at a distance and wait for him to notice me. I hope he will not ask me to come any nearer to him.

"Come closer," he says, without turning his head.

Reluctantly, I take a few steps forward.

He doesn't move for a moment, then slowly turns his head and looks up at me. His black eyes stay fixed on me for an unnervingly long time. I try to stand like a man, head up, feet planted a little apart, my shoulders thrust back. Still he says nothing.

"Sir," I say, keeping my voice as deep as I can. "You asked to see me."

"Indeed," he says. "Take off your veil."

I swallow. "Sir?"

"Remove your veil," he says.

I try to bluster my way out of it. "It is not seemly..." I begin.

His shoulders shake a little and I see laughter in his eyes. "Not seemly for a man," he says. "Remove your veil."

My shoulders drop. I remove the veil as well as my whole headdress, letting the cloth drop to the ground. My hair tumbles down my back and the wind blows it into my face. I don't move.

Yusuf looks away from me, back across the dunes, nods to himself. "What is a young woman doing amongst my men?" he asks, as though to himself.

"How did you know?"

He looks back at me. "I know every one of my men," he says, his eyes serious. "We have an army of many thousands and I make it my business to know every one of them. They fight by my side, they would die for me. I should at least know their names, their faces, how they move. Do you not think?"

I say nothing.

"Well, you had better tie your hair up again," he says. "And then fetch your camel."

"I won't go home," I say. "I won't go back to the camp."

"No," he agrees. "I thought you might say that. I will take you there myself."

"What?"

"I will accompany you," he says. "Your honour is in my hands. I would not allow any other man to escort an unmarried woman back to her father and explain what she was doing out in the desert with a hundred men, none of them her own family."

"Please," I begin, but he has already stood up and is walking back to the men. He speaks with Abu Bakr, before turning to wait for me.

Horribly aware of a hundred pairs of eyes on me, I use the veil to wrap my hair up into a woman's headdress and walk back to Yusuf, my face flushed with humiliation and anger. I wait for the men to speak, for lewd comments or outrage, but they stand silent under Yusuf's gaze.

Abu Bakr looks me over. "Yusuf will accompany you home," he says. "With an escort. We will ride on to the garrison. Goodbye, Kella. I hope your return will be a comfort to your father."

I wonder that he even knows my name. I stand and watch as Yusuf and Abu Bakr embrace one another and then most of the men ride away. We are left with a dozen men, Yusuf and myself. All of us will be riding camels; Yusuf's fine grey stallion has been sent on ahead.

"Kneel," says Yusuf.

The camels kneel and the men mount their steeds.

I stand unmoving.

Yusuf looks at me. "You are in the middle of the desert, Kella," he says, his voice utterly calm. "You cannot hope to survive alone, even if I left you the camel. Mount." He slaps my camel on the rump and it kneels obediently.

As slowly as I dare, I mount the camel.

"Rise," he orders.

The men riding behind us occasionally talk to one another but their voices are low. Yusuf and I ride side by side as though we are friends but we are silent for a long time. When he does speak, I startle.

"Why did you run away?"

I don't answer; I don't know how to. Where to start and how to explain?

"Were you badly treated by your family?" He sounds concerned. "Beaten?"

"No," I say quickly.

"Promised in marriage to someone you dislike?"

"No," I say. I wonder what Amalu is doing now, whether he has joined in the search for me or thinks that he is well rid of such an ungrateful woman.

He looks amused. "I don't suppose you actually want to fight?"

"N-no," I confess.

"So why are you, a young woman *not* ill-treated by her family and with no desire to fight, running away with an army, dressed as a man? I think you owe me some sort of explanation, since you are wasting my time."

"I used to travel with my brothers and my father when he traded," I say slowly.

"Not a life for a woman, perhaps," he comments. "Not very safe."

"I was dressed as a boy," I say.

"Dressed as a boy?" he asks. I am not sure if he sounds disapproving or just surprised.

"Yes," I say.

He raises his eyebrows.

"I was a good trader," I say defensively. "And an excellent camel racer."

Now he laughs out loud. "You rode in camel races?"

"Yes," I say. "And I won," I can't help adding.

"I see," he says. Suddenly he brings down a whip on his camel, who begins to run. "Race me, then," he calls back to me.

I gape at him but the sight of his back ahead of me brings out my stubborn side. If he wishes to make fun of me, he will find out for himself what I am made of. I do not have Thiyya, more's the pity, but these camels have been chosen for warriors and already I can feel my own mount's power gathering beneath me. I urge it on, lean forward and note exultantly that we are already gaining on Yusuf a little.

He is an excellent rider and I do not manage to beat him. But I am very close to him, only a few strides separate us when he finally reins in his camel.

He is bent over laughing. His men are still a way off, they have not raced with us. "Truly a descendant of Tin Hinan herself," he says, his eyes amused.

I can't help but smile.

"Ah, a happy face at last," he says.

I frown.

"And gone again," he notes. He waits for his men to join us, looks me over. "You miss your trading days so badly?"

"Yes," I say and then swallow, so that I will not cry. I do not want to cry in front of him when he has seen me race well.

"And you thought – what? That you would run away in my army and then slip away unnoticed in some city, set up by yourself as a trader?"

I shake my head. "I don't know," I say. "Time was running out, you were leaving and I had no time for plans."

"Why run away with us? You could have waited."

"You had such a vision for the future," I say and then feel myself blushing, heat traveling up my neck into my cheeks. I sound as though I am flattering him.

"Vision?"

"For after the war is over," I say. "When you win."

"If Allah wills it," he reminds me.

I nod. "If He wills it," I repeat. "But you spoke of the whole of the Maghreb united under one rule. That great cities could flourish, that after the battles would come building: mosques, souks, caravanserai, bath-houses. That the trade routes would be made greater than ever before and traders could travel further and bring back wonders from all parts of the world. That the people would live in peace."

His head on one side, he watches me. "Go on."

"I – I would want to help make that happen," I say. "To plan which routes could be made safer and faster, in return for taxes. To show where cities could best grow because of their position on the trade trails. To build caravanserai large enough for many traders and their beasts to rest. There is so much that could be done."

His men have reached us. Yusuf only nods at what I have said and then falls silent. I turn over what else I could say but all of it sounds foolish in the silence and so we travel back to the camp without speaking again.

My father's eyes are grim. I am afraid to dismount for fear he will drag me back to the tent by my hair, he looks so angry. Instead I sit very quietly and wait.

"I humbly beg your pardon," begins Yusuf. "I have behaved very ill towards you, sir. I must speak with you."

My father looks as confused as I feel. What is Yusuf apologising for?

"In private?" asks Yusuf politely, dismounting.

My father walks away with Yusuf, looking back once over his shoulder at me, frowning.

They are gone some time. Half the camp has gathered to watch. Their silence is unnerving. Aunt Tizemt's lips are pressed so tightly together they have disappeared into a thin line. I look down. If Aunt Tizemt is not roaring then things are very bad. Behind her stands Tanemghurt, who looks amused. I dare not smile back at her. I look away and spot Amalu. His face is pale with suppressed rage, his hands in fists by his side. I have never seen good-natured Amalu look like this. I look back down at my reins.

"Kella."

My father and Yusuf have returned. My father still seems confused but no longer angry. I risk meeting his gaze.

He blinks a couple of times, as though he does not quite believe what he is about to say.

"Kella, I understand from Yusuf that he desires to marry you."

I gape. I look to Yusuf, who raises his eyebrows at me, his eyes quite serious.

"Yusuf has apologised for the dishonour risked by allowing you to run away with him but tells me it was only because of your great love for one another. He has now formally asked for your hand and if you are content, the wedding will be arranged with all due haste. After which you may accompany your husband on his onward journey to fulfill his great mission."

I look at my father and then at Yusuf again. There is utter silence all around me. I dare not look at Amalu. Aunt Tizemt's mouth is open.

"Is this true? You wish to marry Yusuf?" repeats my father.

I think of my freedom. I am being offered my freedom if I will marry a man with whom I have only spoken today. I am being offered a chance to leave the camp as a married woman and to follow my husband on a great adventure.

"Yes," I say and my voice comes out so quietly and huskily that I have to say it again. "Yes. I wish to marry Yusuf." It comes out too loud this time.

My father nods, still baffled by all that has happened. "Very well," he says and walks away. The rest of the camp scatters to make ready for the riders and no doubt to gossip amongst themselves. Tanemghurt says something quietly to Aunt Tizemt, who stares at me one more time and then follows. I look towards where Amalu was standing but he is already walking away, towards the dunes, no doubt to be alone as I did on the day my father left me here.

The riders dismount and begin to set up camp. Yusuf walks over to me and holds up his hand to help me down from the camel. I do so ungracefully, half-twisting my ankle. When I have recovered myself I look around. My father is out of sight. I turn to Yusuf. He seems serene, as though he has done nothing worthy of note.

"Why?" I say, blurting out the word.

He looks down at me and chuckles at the expression on my face. "Are you unwilling after all?"

"No," I say, feeling the heat in my cheeks rise again.

"Very well," he says with satisfaction, looking ahead again.

"But *why?*" I ask again.

He looks at me again, his eyes grown serious. He pauses, as though collecting his thoughts. "For many years now I have been set on my path by Allah. I have a mission to undertake and I swore to stop for nothing and no one. But when I made my promise I thought of warriors and armies seeking to cut down my body, of unbelievers seeking to cast doubts in my mind. I did not think a young woman would stand in my path and make me pause in my journey. Abu Bakr thinks only of battles. But I think of what the war will achieve. I want to create a land of peace and prosperity, of holiness and righteousness. And this is not done only through war. It is done through building and prayer, through treaties and trading. And then I hear my own thoughts spoken aloud by a young woman, a woman bold enough to ride away from her family, hidden within an army." He thinks for a moment. "I think Allah has sent you to me for some purpose. You will be at my side, you will help me create an empire when the battles are won." He lowers his voice until it is barely a whisper, we are so close he could touch me. "Perhaps you will be the mother of a son who will continue my work when I am gone."

If I am breathless it is surely only because Yusuf's face is only a hand's breadth away, his lips close enough to touch mine.

Houmeyni — Wedding Necklace

A UNT TIZEMT IS ON THE warpath. "What kind of wedding can be adequately prepared for in so short a time? Allah, give this poor humble woman strength to carry out your will!"

Yusuf has insisted to my father that we must be married with all speed for his mission cannot wait, and yet he will not leave me behind. So there is much to do in a very short time, and Yusuf's insistence on speed has thrown the camp into turmoil.

Children flee before Aunt Tizemt as she stamps across the camp, each of them knowing that to be caught will mean hours of tedious work as she commandeers everyone who crosses her path to help her prepare for the wedding. Already the young men have been sent off on the best camels in every direction, to invite kin from neighbouring tribes to attend. Relatives that no-one has seen for many years will be on their way shortly, much food and drink must be prepared. The older children are set to gathering thorn bush branches to make temporary enclosures for any animals that the guests might have with them. The work is difficult and painful, for the bushes have to be sought out and then branches cut with sharp axes, while fighting off the vicious thorns that stick out in every direction. No-one can escape without painful red scratches, which my aunt dismisses airily, and they sting for hours afterwards as a reminder to each child to avoid her in future. The younger children have to build up heaps of dried camel dung, which burns well and is a good substitute for hard-to-find wood in a landscape where trees are a rarity and only bushes and shrubs offer sufficient opportunity for fuel. The camel dung, at least, has no thorns.

For those children who have successfully escaped my aunt's eagle eye, Aghbalu the storyteller is a focal point. He sits in the shade and rehearses his stories for the bridal feast, finding himself surrounded by an eager audience of small upturned faces, which have the disconcerting habit of disappearing suddenly before his very eyes like a many-bodied djinn whenever Aunt Tizemt's heavy tread can be heard approaching.

The older women are preparing their stocks of spices and discussing recipes for the wedding feast, counting how many mouths they will have to feed. The younger women and the craftsmen are set to preparing items for my future. I will no longer use my aunt's cooking pots and musical instruments, her waterbags and rugs. I will have my own possessions.

"And you need your own tent, of course," says my aunt. "I had thought we would have more time before you found a husband. But the time is upon us now and we must prepare everything quickly. Come with me."

I follow obediently, glad to be let off the weaving of a huge rug that will cover the floor of my tent. The other girls wink at me behind her back as I walk by, miming exhaustion and other, ruder, signals that, thankfully, my aunt does not catch. I suppress my giggles and bend to follow her into the cool darkness of the tent.

Inside it is hard to see after the glare of the sun. I narrow my eyes as my aunt searches for something and then sits on the bed.

"Sit."

I sit by her and watch as a large triangle of thick rough cloth, embroidered with once bold but now faded red and yellow symbols is unfolded on the bed between us. I look up questioningly at my aunt.

"Do you know what this is?"

"No."

"It is a piece of your mother's tent. I cut it out after her death, before you all left the camp to trade when you were still a baby." She smoothes the fabric with her hands.

"The tent and everything in it belongs to the woman. When she marries, her husband comes to her tent. If he divorces her, he will leave her tent." She gestures towards the camp outside. "Everyone is preparing your goods – your bowls and spoons, your rugs, blankets and waterbags, even your musical instruments. Your saddles and your husband's weapons will also be kept in the tent. Your brothers and father are preparing you a marriage bed. But you must have a tent to house all of your goods and your family. It is traditional, when you marry, for your mother to cut a piece from her tent and for that piece to form part of your own tent. When your mother died and your father decided to take you far away, I cut a piece of the tent to keep against the day when you would be married. Now that day is coming, and this is the piece of your mother's tent around which we will make your own tent. Every slave in the camp will be working on it to make it in time for the ceremony."

I reach out a hand and touch the strong yellow cloth that once sheltered my mother, father and brothers, and which will now provide shelter for Yusuf and myself. Tears spring to my eyes as I trace the symbols for protection and fertility. Aunt Tizemt smiles and places her rough warm hand over mine.

"Your mother was a most kind and loving woman. She loved your father and was loved by him. She bore six children, five of them sons. She was blessed by Allah before she left this world. You will also be blessed with sons, I am sure. Your husband-to-be must love you deeply. You drew his eye even while he was set on the path of his holy mission. He loves you enough to stop in his path – even though he has insisted that you must be married quickly so that he can continue along that path. You are a Tuareg woman, a free woman. He seems happy to give you much freedom, a rare thing amongst some men today. I hope your marriage will be most happy. May Allah bless you."

I throw my arms around my aunt, the closest thing to a mother I have ever known. She responds with a strong warm hug and then becomes brisk and business-like again.

"There are forty slaves who will be working on this tent. The men are finding strong poles. The women are sewing the cloth and skins together to make the coverings. I will be overseeing the embroideries. I would like them to match your mother's tent." She smoothes the triangle of cloth again and stands. "We have a lot to do in only a few days. Yusuf is an impatient man. Come."

With so many slaves working on it, the tent quickly takes shape. With Aunt Tizemt's urgings, oaths and threats about what will happen to anyone who slows down its progress, it is finished the day before the wedding.

Now it can be erected. A wide, flat sandy area near to the main camp has been chosen for the festivities, and the children have been charged with clearing the space; removing more of the dreaded thorn bushes, keeping the animals away and removing any particularly sharp rocks. The relatives, as they arrive, are shown places to set up their tents by the main camp, close to the area set aside for the marriage.

Within this space is now heaped up a mound of sand, packed down firmly until it resembles a large cushion, wide enough for two people to sit side by side. Over this my new tent is loosely erected, but it is not put up properly, for that will come later when it takes up its permanent location within the camp. The poles are not firmly planted, so that the cloth and skin folds sag and make a small dark enclosure barely big enough for two instead of a wide airy space made to contain a family. I try to peek at the tent but am shooed away by Aunt Tizemt and the other women, who hustle me back to the main camp.

"You have to be prepared! What will your bridegroom think of you if he sees you in that state?"

I have to laugh. I am dressed in my plainest clothes and am unwashed. My hair has not been combed for days as I have toiled away at all the tasks that my aunt has decreed must be done in a short time. Now, the night before my wedding, I am to be pampered.

I am taken to Tanemghurt's tent. She appears in the doorway and looks me over. I stand before her, suddenly conscious of the rank odour of my sweat and the dirt which seems ingrained in my very skin.

"You should be in your mother's tent, of course. She would have prepared you for your wedding. But you were born into my hands and so I have taken on her role at this time."

I step inside. The tent is heavily scented with two perfumes. One is incense, which Tanemghurt has just lit and which has now begun to smoke as its flame dies out. The other is henna powder, which Tanemghurt will later mix with a little hot water to make a paste to decorate my hands, feet and face. She sets the bowl aside and gestures brusquely.

"Take off your clothes."

I obey, looking around for somewhere to put them as I remove each item. Tanemghurt holds out her hand and I deposit the old worn clothes with her. She flings them casually but accurately into a corner of the tent, where they make a neat and insignificant pile.

Once I am naked Tanemghurt sits in her wooden seat and looks me over. I stand silently under her gaze, feeling like a slave at market, fearing to be found lacking in some way. I have grown in all directions since returning to the camp. I am a little taller, my hair now reaches down to my waist, while my breasts and hips have grown rounder, first with my aunt's and now my own good cooking to fatten me up. My calloused skin has grown smoother now that my aunt has shown me how rubbing butter and oils into the skin makes it glow like the warm sands as the sun falls. Still, at this moment I am sweaty and dirty from days of working with no time for washing and I feel unfit to be a beautiful bride.

Tanemghurt finishes her inspection of me without either condoning or condemning my current state. She calls out, startling me, and one of her slave girls appears, carrying hot water from the fire outside. She pours it into a great basin on the floor, then brings more until the basin and three more large pots are full. Tanemghurt tells her to keep the fire going and more water heating, and then stands. She makes her way to the basin and then slowly kneels, her knees letting out a loud cracking noise that alarms me. I try to help her but she gestures impatiently at me and I step back, rebuffed.

She picks up a cloth, wets it in the hot water and begins to pat my body with it. I nearly cry out, for the water is almost boiling. Tanemghurt, however, seems able to immerse the cloth without flinching, her hands hardened after many years. She ignores my whimpers and wets me thoroughly all over, by which time my body is flushed pink.

When I think she has finished she takes a small cloth, woven with rough wool. Aunt Tizemt would scold me for producing such coarse work, but I quickly realise its purpose. Tanemghurt dips it in the burning water and begins to rub me ferociously all over, using small circles, working her way up from my feet. I stand first on one leg and then the other as she scrubs viciously at the soles of my feet, then works her way up without pause except to dip the cloth back into the water. I look down, whimpering quietly, and see my skin being scraped off me in little rolls, layer upon layer. I protest weakly but Tanemghurt has suddenly and conveniently become deaf. Only when every part of me has been scrubbed and I am scarlet from head to toe does she gesture to me to kneel and dips the cloth yet again. She kneels opposite me and pushes back my hair. I close my eyes and steel myself for the assault on my face, the skin so much more tender than the rest of my body, but when the cloth touches my face it is pleasantly warm rather than burning hot and the strokes are suddenly soft as a caress as she gently wipes each part of my face.

This unexpected gentleness lasts as long as it takes to finish my face and then Tanemghurt gets back to her work with a vengeance. My head is all but submerged under water in her largest pot, filled with hot water. I feel as if I might be cooked and briefly wonder what spice she might serve my head with, letting out a hysterical giggle at the thought which is instantly stopped as hot water enters both my nose and mouth. Having dunked me, she begins to rub a thick paste into my hair while I try to get my breath back. The paste smells of herbs and rose petals and she seems determined that it should penetrate my very skull. I grit my teeth and wait for this torture to be over, for there is no arguing with Tanemghurt. Certainly, I muse to myself as my head is violently jerked about under her strong hands, I will never be so clean again, no, not even if I spent whole days in the *hammams*, the great steam baths of the cities.

"Has your aunt instructed you on what happens between a man and a woman?" asks Tanemghurt matter-of-factly.

"Oh yes," I say quickly, seeking to sound mature enough to be a wife although in truth I have not received any instruction on this topic. Aunt Tizemt probably thought there was plenty of time for such things.

Tanemghurt only raises her eyebrows without challenging me.

At last she seems to have finished with me, for I can think of no other part of me that can be cleaned. She has even cleaned my ears with a small stick carved with a curve at the end and has removed not just a few but all of my bodily hairs. I tried not to shriek when she did this but I could hear small children outside, giggling between themselves and know that my howls of pain have most certainly been heard by others.

But I still have the thick paste in my hair and my body is covered with stray plucked hairs and little rolls of grimy skin which is an entirely different colour from my new skin, as though I am a serpent and my skin has been shed to bake in the sun, leaving me with a new glossy set of scales. How am I to remove all of this debris? I think perhaps I could immerse sections of myself into the large pot of water – my head, an arm, a leg, although how to manage my torso is beyond me. But Tanemghurt has bolder ideas. "Go outside," she commands as though I were not entirely naked and there was not a whole camp of people outside, including my father, brothers and future husband, all nearby. I do not move.

"Are you deaf?"

"*Lalla*, I am not going outside naked!" I exclaim.

She laughs as though she had expected me to say this and thinks I am a simpleton. "No-one will see you. Outside. Now." Her tone does not invite refusal. She yanks back the flaps that covered the entrance to the tent and draws back to let me see what she has done.

Outside stand many slave girls in a circle. Between them they hold up bright, fluttering lengths of cloth, making a new tent with no roof, outside. If I step out of the tent now, no-one will see me. I step out cautiously, noticing too late that Tanemghurt has remained in the tent, then gasp as out of nowhere more slave girls appear on the other side of the bright cloths and each pours, in rapid succession, a big pot of cold water over my head. I stand, shaking and choking out some of the water I have accidentally breathed in when I gasped in surprise. Before I can even raise my hands to my face to wipe the water away, Tanemghurt is by my side and has wrapped me tightly in a large cloth. She is shaking with laughter, her few teeth exposed and the wrinkles of her face so creased I can barely see her eyes. She quickly pulls me back inside the tent as the slave girls, smiling at my shocked face, lower the cloths and go about their business as though what had just happened is a daily occurrence.

Back inside the tent, Tanemghurt has lost her fierceness. She seats me, still wrapped in my cloth, on the bed and then kneels before me and begins to rub warm perfumed oil over every part of my body.

"Did you like the waterfall?" she asks, smiling.

I wriggle my toes in her hands and relax as the warmth creeps back into my body, inhaling the smell of roses that fills the tent. "I have never seen such a thing before, *Lalla*," I say honestly.

She chuckles, pleased with her work. "It is hard to bathe out here – water has to be carried so far, and we cannot build the great steam baths of the cities. But I have heard tell of them, how the skin is steamed so that the old skin will fall away and open up to receive softening oils, how great buckets of water are thrown over the women who go there. It is a gift I make, for brides of our camp. Our brides are the cleanest and most perfumed of all the tribes. I have had women come and beg me to do this for them from tribes far, far away!" She is proud of her reputation as a wise woman, one who can manage not only the hard things, like a childbirth gone wrong, but also the joyful things of life, such as the honour of preparing a bride for her husband. Tonight I will sleep in her tent and tomorrow she will send me out as a bride to my husband, for the first day of celebrations.

All day long the guests have been arriving. They are offered hot tea and all manner of good things to eat. They set up their tents and settle down to the best part of a wedding – the gossiping, the catching up with family and friends and enjoying good food and drink. In the afternoon the young men race their camels while the women ululate and praise them with shrill cheers and songs. From Tanemghurt's tent, as I sit still, waiting for the henna to dry, I smile when I think about my camel racing days.

"What are you smiling at?" asks Tanemghurt.

I shake my head. "I used to race camels," I confess. "I pretended to be one of my brothers but it was always me. I won so many races," I add a little wistfully.

I think that Tanemghurt will frown, or tell me that it is high time I set aside such nonsense, but to my surprise she chuckles and then pulls at my foot. With her henna stick she quickly draws a tiny camel on my ankle, hidden from all but there for me and me alone. I look down and smile at its shape.

"Thank you," I say.

She smiles. "We all have our memories," she says.

I am unrecognisable. My hair is brushed and perfumed with rosewater, then draped with many loops of silver circlets, which cover all but every strand. I wear my *tchirot* under my new, brightly coloured wraps made of the finest cloths my aunt can find at such short notice, helped by my father's stores of trading goods. My *celebra* and an engagement *chachat* from Yusuf are round my neck. I have more new jewellery from Yusuf. He has sent the traditional set of wedding gifts to Tanemghurt's tent. I wear a pair of large earrings, multiple pendants, then another necklace with a cross pendant. The final item is a headpiece, which is added to my already crowded head. It is a triangular carnelian stone jutting out of a square of silver, which adds height and elegance to my already elaborate hair. I feel weighted down with silver and stones, but my aunt and Tanemghurt only nod at each other with satisfaction when they look at me. My hands, face and feet are marked with henna paste. I had to sit still for a very long time watching as it dried crustily, like scabs on a wound on my newly washed and oiled skin. But it was worth it, for the patterns are very pleasing to the eye. The whirlwind of the past few days is settling and I am about to marry Yusuf. What at first felt like some strange dream is now becoming real. I am a bride and I am about to be married.

As darkness falls, there is music, singing and dancing. Somewhere on the other side of the camp Yusuf is in another tent, heavily veiled as I will be when I finally emerge.

At last, the women come to fetch me. It is almost midnight, and they are very merry as they encircle me and we begin to walk slowly to my newly-made tent, erected outside the camp over the pile of packed sand that will serve as our seat for a few hours.

We arrive together, the men leading Yusuf, the women leading me, and we are shown into our tiny, misshapen tent. There is only room for the two of us, each swathed in our layers of robes, mine strewn with jewellery, his plain as ever. Outside our tent everyone sings and dances, the drums wild and the singing rippling over their persistent pulse. Even if we had spoken in the darkness, we would not hear one another. Under our many robes Yusuf reaches for my hand. It is a strange feeling, to clasp hands with a man I barely know. I have not yet grown used to it when they come back to return us to our own tents, Yusuf holding a sword and I a knife, for iron is lucky at a wedding.

As we slowly make our way back to our separate tents, behind us my new tent is being pulled down, the mound of sand left in place, to be gradually dispersed across the vast desert by the slow winds of time.

It is almost dawn, but I have time to sleep while the men properly erect my tent. I will not join Yusuf there until later today. At first I cannot sleep, my head too full of the songs and rhythms and the touch of Yusuf's hand. But Tanemghurt bends over me to hold a cup of sweet warm milk to my lips and soon I am asleep, my body a loose heap of twisted cloth and silver.

It is late morning when I open my eyes again, prodded awake by Tanemghurt and my aunt, who stand over me, smiling.

"Yusuf has already gone to your tent," says Tanemghurt.

Aunt Tizemt chimes in. "They are finishing the camel rides in front of the tent. It will be time for you to join him soon. Come, sit up and sip some tea. Not too much. Remember, once you are in the tent you cannot leave till nightfall, not even to relieve yourself."

I sit up and drink a little mint tea to freshen my mouth. The women are gathering again. This time we walk within the camp to my new tent. It is beautiful now that it is fully erected and bathed by the sun's rays. The embroideries shine out and I put up one hand to touch the old worn triangle that belonged to my mother's tent, before I enter.

All my new possessions have been laid out and the tent is now a real home. Rugs cover the floor and cushions are scattered everywhere, inviting comfort. At the centre is my marriage bed, again spread with blankets woven with bright symbols for fertility and good luck. Seated on the bed is Yusuf.

I pause in the doorway. Here I am alone with a man I barely know, a man I chose to marry in a fit of boldness, challenged by him to accept in front of my whole family and encampment. I chose him – why? For a moment I feel panic rising in me. Why did I not spend more time with Amalu, perhaps persuade him to take me trading with him? Why did I think I could marry this stranger and follow him on a terrifying mission to conquer the Maghreb, a mission which has failed once before? If he dies and then I am left alone or worse, taken as a captive and…

Yusuf is watching me. "Will you sit by me, Kella?" he asks gently.

I swallow and step forward, then almost trip and land ungracefully by his side.

He laughs as I struggle to regain my composure. "Your eagerness to be near me bodes well for our marriage bed, I think."

I blush and try to smile, my heart thudding as I think of our 'marriage bed'. How easily he says the words! Does he have no doubts? He is far older than I, does he not think I am a foolish girl who knows nothing and will now be a burden to him? Does he not have any regrets as to his hastily-made choice of a bride – and indeed to marry at all?

The tent folds at the entrance are still open, for now all the guests will dance and sing in front of our dwelling to wish us well and give us their blessings. We have many hours yet before we will close the tent door and be alone. I try to make myself a little more comfortable on the bed. Yusuf offers me additional cushions, which I accept. When I have stopped nervously adjusting my position he reaches out and takes my hand in his, then turns his face back towards the guests, now engaged in good-natured jesting.

I sit still, watching the dancers and singers while trying to grow used to the sensation of holding hands with him. I try to think of something to say but I cannot think of anything and he seems happy in silence, so after a while I stop trying.

At last, as dusk falls, the guests begin to leave. I am certain that all of Allah's ninety-nine names have been invoked as each of them finds a new way to bless us and wish us well. Then they say their goodbyes to one another. The tents are folded down and loaded onto camels before people begin to drift away in every direction from our camp.

By the time it is fully dark the hubbub around our tent has subsided and Tanemghurt comes and shuts all the sides so that we can be alone. "Do not forget," she says as she leaves us, "You are to stay in this tent for seven days and seven nights. You may leave only to relieve yourselves, and that only at night. I will bring you food each day."

We have been given bowls with soft dates and herbed olives, roasted meats, fresh flat breads and dipping sauces to eat with them. There are two large waterbags propped up by the tent.

I clear my throat, as though about to say something and Yusuf looks at me questioningly. I shake my head, feeling myself blush against my will. I have never felt so useless. Surely a new bride should be more comfortable in her new husband's company?

Yusuf interrupts my train of thought by reaching for something in his robes. It makes a clinking sound as he pulls it out and I look to see what it is. He holds it out to me in the flickering light of the fire.

"My gift to you on our wedding day."

It is a *houmeyni*. A leather thong, with a large silver

111

articulated pendant, carved all over with tiny symbols and shapes. A traditional wedding gift, given by grooms to their brides. He should have given it to me at the ceremony earlier, but I am glad he has chosen this moment for it seems more intimate and is a more important gift than the many other items of jewellery he had sent to me in Tanemghurt's tent before the wedding and which I have worn all day. The *houmeyni* is associated with courtship, with moonlit encounters, with romance and even those sexual encounters that sometimes take place before a wedding. I lift off all my other items of jewellery, letting each fall onto the carpet at our feet and allow him to place the necklace round my neck.

When he has done so he sinks to his knees before me and begins to unfasten my clothes. I stand very still, looking down on him nervously, but he takes his time, his fingers do not stumble over the clasps and ties which hold my many layers of finery together. As he undoes each item he places it to one side without looking to see how it falls, never taking his eyes from my gradually exposed body, my outlines slowly becoming clearer in the half-light. When I am naked he sits back on his heels but rather than look at my body his eyes come upwards to my face and when they meet my blushing gaze he smiles. He reaches up to my waist and back, carefully lowering me down to the soft carpets and the furs that have been strewn there, in which he lays me down and covers me. Then he rises to his feet and begins to undress himself.

I am entirely naked except for my *houmeyni* necklace, the silver cold on my skin. I tremble. Not from cold, for I am wrapped in fine blankets and even have furs which feel soft as they shimmer against my bare skin with every tremor. I am trembling because I know very little of what will happen next. I wish earnestly that Tanemghurt had challenged my airy claim to know what goes on between a man and a woman. My erotic instruction comes down to everything I have seen animals do, none of which seems very romantic or alluring; matter of fact information from Aunt Tizemt, which mostly consisted of her view that we are not much better than animals; and hints from girls of my own age and the women of pleasure from the souks, which were nothing but a mass of unlikely-sounding fantasies. None of this is what I need now. I lie silent as Yusuf undresses and I see all of him for the first time.

His skin is very smooth and also very pale, something like a fine golden sand rather than the dark brown of his forearms and feet, for it is always sheltered from the sun under his heavy robes. I shrink back a little in my furs, for it now becomes evident to me for the first time that I have married a warrior. Every part of his body is a weapon. His muscles are large and well-defined and I have no doubt at all that any man facing him on the field of battle would think twice before approaching him. He undresses quickly and efficiently, like a soldier stripping down armour, and as he does so I watch as his muscles ripple and play in the flickering light and shadows. Last of all he unwraps his veil, so that I can see his face. His expression is kind and calm and although I am still nervous, he is gentle with me as he begins to touch me and after a little while I cease to tremble.

Our days are spent in the colourful tent in the camp, where we can hear passers-by and the giggles of the children as they try to peek in at us. Unlike his usual fierce bearing and passionate commitment to his cause, I find that Yusuf can also be humorous. He will suddenly grab at the children's questing fingers and cause high pitched shrieks of surprise, at which he roars with laughter. The tent grows hot in the heat of the day and we laze in each other's arms, sleeping and waking. We play games when we are awake, with pebbles or bones and rough marks in the sand of the floor. We try to cheat and demand forfeits when we catch each other out.

We eat together. Tanemghurt's food is surprisingly good, for I have never seen her cook with the other women. She has her own work, and it is not cooking and caring for children, weaving, or any of the other skills women possess. Her skills are valued highly enough that she has more offers of food, cloth or utensils than she will ever need, from those who have received her healing in the past and know that the day will come when they will need to call on her again. So I have never seen her cook. But all the food brought to us now comes from her hands. She uses herbs and spices better than anyone I know. Her sweet cakes are soaked in honey and then coloured with spices to make them pleasing to the eye as well as the mouth. Her stews warm the heart as well as the body and some of the drinks she leaves for us do more than warm the heart. We feed each other with our fingers, sometimes giving each other the very best morsels, sometimes playing little tricks on each other, such as when I feed him fine cakes which he says are too rich for him, or when he chooses a particularly spicy morsel for me and laughs when I flush with the heat of it.

We pray. As each of the five prayers of the day come and go I grow to care for him more, for his prayers are more sincere than any I have heard before. Many of the tribesmen that I know pray rarely and some still cling to the old ways. Amongst the tribes there are those who are very pious, but even they seem to pray by rote, as if by command. But Yusuf prays with every part of his heart and soul. His eyes are lit as if from within with a soft and gentle light, a true flame of faith. When his body sways, so too does his voice as he murmurs his prayers. At these moments I am certain that my choice was the right one. This is a man who will achieve great things and I wish to be by his side when he does so. I am afraid of the battles yet to come but I know that if he is successful afterwards there will be a time of peace when I can prove my worth.

In the darkness we wrap thick blankets round us and sit outside, braving the cold to gaze at the stars and talk. I hear of his childhood, his friends, his parents and siblings. I hear of how he and his cousin Abu Bakr began by playing at war as children and are now engaged in a true war. Abu Bakr is a dedicated leader, but Yusuf has a vision that Abu Bakr sometimes struggles to comprehend.

"He is a great commander," says Yusuf, as we sit eating dates and bread and gazing at the stars. "He cares for his men. He trains them to be the best that they can be, not only their bodies like any commander, but their minds also. He reads the Qur'an with them daily, he asks them about their families, their hopes for the future. Their prayers are his prayers. He is a good man." He shakes his head as though at an unsettling thought, then repeats his words. "A good man. I would hope to always serve under him. But he may not wish to continue as the commander."

I know nothing of the politics of commanding and armies. I know only that Yusuf's body is warm next to mine and that his voice is soft and soothing, even now, when he is serious. "Why would he not be the commander?"

Yusuf shrugs. "Sometimes he looks at me in wonder when I speak of all of this country united under Allah, under one commander. I think perhaps he does not think it is possible. That the tribes are too many and will not swear allegiance to one commander. That there will always be fighting and squabbling. He knows the tribes well, he speaks easily with them. I do not have that gift. The heads of each tribe always speak more easily with Abu Bakr than with me." He raises his head and his voice grows a little stronger. "But I have something he does not have. I look into the future and I see a great land, united under Allah, with one commander. It could be done. We could do it. But we must keep that vision before our very eyes."

I yawn a little. It is very late. "I am sure you will succeed, husband." I say, warmly. It is the truth. I cannot imagine him wanting something and not succeeding in getting it. Men from all the tribes are willing to join him in his holy war. He can accomplish anything.

He hears me yawn and chuckles. "My poor sleepy wife. Am I boring you with talk of war again? I am sorry. But you are married to a warrior, I am afraid. You will hear much more of war before you are an old woman."

"Old woman?" I feign indignance. "How long do you intend this war to last?"

So our seven days and nights pass, and on the morning of the eighth day we say the dawn prayers together and leave our tent as husband and wife.

Trik — Bridle Ornaments

*T*RADITION DICTATES THAT WE SHOULD now live in my own camp for at least a year before leaving to go to my new husband's camp.

But tradition cannot be obeyed. Yusuf is anxious to get back to Abu Bakr and the army of men, who are only waiting for our wedding rituals to be completed before they can begin their first great challenge: crossing the High Atlas mountains. It will be an exhausting journey, but the men have been well trained and are strong. They will fare better than most travellers who attempt to cross the steep and rocky mountain paths, where a simple misstep can result in immediate death. Their strength and stamina will be tested however and once over the Atlas mountains they may be called on to fight at any moment. This will prove a harsh test for men who have only just scaled a mountain range and come safely down the other side, carrying heavy weapons and leading their mounts.

Yusuf suggests to me that I should stay at the camp and he will send for me later on.

"I did not marry you to stay at home!"

He laughs out loud at my appalled face. "I would keep you safe," he says.

"I did not run away with your men in disguise because I valued my safety," I say.

He nods. "Very well. I should not allow it, but I know it is not in your nature to stay here. If I refuse to take you, no doubt I will find you at my side in the heat of battle, wielding a sword."

I have to laugh. "You would indeed," I tell him with mock fierceness.

"It is agreed then," he says. "Tell your slaves to pack your belongings."

I have to decide what to take with me. Thiyya, of course. I must have my tent and its contents in order to provide us with a home. My father says I need slaves to accompany me, but I am reluctant to take too many with me. At last we agree that I will have only two. I can have more later when we are more settled and know where we will be based. My father offers me two young slaves, hardworking and healthy as a gift, and I agree gladly.

But that evening, as I oversee the cooking, the slave woman Adeola comes to me and asks me to come to one side, by my tent. Here I find her man Ekon. When he sees me arrive he kneels before me, as does Adeola.

"What is the meaning of this?" I ask. "Do you have a boon to ask of me?"

They nod, and Adeola speaks, for she has learnt more of our tongue than her man, although her words are still slow and careful. "We want… be your slaves."

I frown. "You are already my family's slaves."

They shake their heads together. "We be *your* slaves,

your father's… gift. We go with you when you leave with husband." They both look at me earnestly, waiting for my reply.

"Are you not well treated here that you wish to leave?"

Again they shake their heads. Adeola tries to explain herself more clearly. "You bought us. We would have been…" she struggles for the word.

"Separated." I give her the word and nods. I am moved by their loyalty to me for an action from what feels like a long time ago, something which I had chosen to do on the spur of the moment, yet which has meant so much to their lives. Now they want to come with me, to serve me themselves, out of this devotion. I try to dissuade them.

"There will be long travels over rough ground, through the mountains. There will be much work, for I will have only two slaves, perhaps for a long time. It will be hard. And we will be part of an army. There may be danger."

They look up at me and then Ekon speaks. I am unaccustomed to hear his voice, for he is a quiet man. "We are not afraid. We work hard. We come." It is not a request, it is a simple fact. I hear the finality of his tone and smile at them both. I know that I could not have two more loyal slaves with me. My father will understand my reasons for taking them.

"Then you had better plan what you will take with you. You will each ride a camel and you will have one camel for your tent and your possessions. We leave in a few days."

Too soon everything is ready. The camels are saddled and most are piled high with my belongings. Yusuf's men are already mounted, as are my two slaves. Only Yusuf's camel and Thiyya stand without riders, each slowly chewing and enjoying their last few moments of freedom as Yusuf and I make our farewells. Tanemghurt says little, giving me a few spices and herbs, then touches my cheek and smiles before walking slowly back to her own tent, with no superfluous tears or words. I notice that she moves a little more slowly than usual and wonder how much longer she will walk in this world.

The children cluster around, full of questions for Yusuf. They cannot wait for the day when they too can be bold warriors and they fight amongst each other now to stand closer to him, touching his weapons with awe.

Aunt Tizemt pours out a string of instructions for my future life as a married woman, everything that is to come and which she will be unable to tell me when the time comes. Foods to please a man's upset stomach, how to bathe a baby, the proper way to dress my hair now that I am married, how to address the grandfather of my children, what gifts to give to my mother in law, should I ever meet her. The list goes on and on, and becomes more broken and confused as she begins to cry, an unheard-of weakness from my fearsome aunt. She is devastated to be losing me now. Only the day before I confided to her that I have not bled, and that perhaps I am carrying Yusuf's child, which made her very happy until she remembered that I was about to leave her and go away and that she is unlikely to see any child of mine for a very long time, if ever. I cannot put together the words to thank her for all she has done for me. Instead I embrace her tightly and bury my face in her shoulder. She smells of all her womanly skills – wool, good food and woodsmoke. I inhale her scent and force back the tears that sting my eyes.

My father speaks mostly with Yusuf, but when he turns to me there are tears standing in his eyes and his voice is a little hoarse as he gives me his blessing and promises he will see me very soon.

It is time to get into the saddle. For the first time in my life I will ride on a woman's saddle, a giant throne of twisted cloth laid over the leather and wooden harness. I will sit in this like some great queen, my feet resting on Thiyya's neck straight ahead of me. Thiyya screws up her nose at the ungainly weight, so different from the racing saddles she has been used to. It will be more comfortable for me for long journeys, but it feels strange to sit there so lazily, as though I am not in full command of my own mount, and the saddle rules out any racing across the dunes for my balance will not be as good; the saddle sways more than the ones I am used to.

Thiyya is made to kneel. I climb into my new seat. As she rises to her feet the saddle sways perilously and I can do nothing but cling to the arms of my throne and hope for the best.

Now my brothers gather round me. Each of them brings out from behind his back a *trik*, a small silver ornament for Thiyya's harness. They attach these to the harness and reins and tears spill from my eyes as I see that each of them bears a letter denoting my brother's names amongst the other symbols etched on them. The symbols are for fertility, long life, good luck and many other blessings. When they are all attached I shake the reins and the *triks* tinkle softly together. My brothers are delighted.

"Ah, see sister, you will not miss us now, for listen to all that noise – it will be as if we are by your side at all times."

"That noise is as the sound of a flower bending in the breeze compared to the noise you boys make," I retort, laughing through my tears.

The camels shift beneath us, made impatient by all these drawn-out farewells. I look at the crowd of men whom I am about to join, Adeola and I the only women. I frown when I catch sight of Amalu, mounted and armed. I guide Thiyya towards him.

"What are you doing?"

"Joining the Almoravid army," he says, looking ahead, away from me.

I move Thiyya so that I am almost face-to-face with him. "Joining the army? Have you gone mad? You never wanted to be a warrior."

"I wanted you," he says.

I lower my voice. "I am married," I remind him.

"And it will go wrong," he says.

"Are you cursing my marriage?" I ask, offended.

He shakes his head.

"Well then?"

"You do not know this man," he says. "All you wanted was your freedom."

He is uncomfortably near the truth but I fight back anyway. "He and I see what the future could be," I say.

"And I will be there when it goes wrong," he says.

"It will not go wrong," I say, angry now.

He turns his face away.

"Amalu!"

He looks back at me. "You do not know what love is yet," he says more quietly. "When you do, I will be waiting."

123

"And if I never come to you?"

"Then I will be happy for you," he says. "Because I love you."

"You could die," I warn him.

Amalu shrugs. "We all of us will die one day," he says. "Better to die for love than cowardice."

I want to say something else, but while I try to think how to dissuade him Yusuf rides up to us.

"Are you ready?" he asks me.

I nod.

He makes a gesture with his arm and the men fall in behind us, Amalu swept into the crowd where I can no longer see him. Instead I look back to my family, to their waving arms and try not to let sudden tears fall.

Our journey will take us first to the garrison basecamp where the men are being trained, in the foothills of the Atlas Mountains, ready to cross the mountains and begin their planned conquest.

We move off, twisting back to wave at all the people of the camp, gathered to bid us farewell. My brothers, father and aunt wave to us until we are out of sight.

I did not know then that I would never see any of them again.

We travel for many days and I am now sure that I am carrying Yusuf's child, although I do not tell him yet, for it is still very early. But my bleeding should have come many days ago, and it is not yet here. I hold my secret to me as I sway along on Thiyya's back, and I walk gently when I am set down. I am not entirely certain how I feel about a child. I meant to be free, to be a right hand to Yusuf, to help him build a peaceful future and I am nervous that a baby will mean that I am kept back, for my safety and that of our child, that I will be kept out of decision-making. But I comfort myself that Yusuf married me because he liked my vision for the future, that he wanted a child. And I think that perhaps a child coming so quickly is a blessing from Allah on our marriage and mission, that it points the way to a time of peace and plenty. I will have a baby. Yusuf will leave me reluctantly and only for a short while and then he will send for me. I will join him with a healthy infant in my arms and we will have our own little family. I hum as we ride and Yusuf teases me for singing lullabies and asks whether I think he is a little child that needs to be sung to in order to travel quietly. I only laugh back at him and try to sing other songs, although the lullabies return to me day after day.

And so we travel onwards. I have only rare moments alone with Yusuf and I begin to realise the reality of his life, which now is my own. He comes to my tent, but often it is so late that I have fallen asleep, and I wake for dawn prayers to find he has already left the tent and gone to pray, or is training or making plans with some of his men, earnestly discussing tactics, weapons or which animals will make better mounts in the heat of battle. The camels allow the rider to see far but provide an all-too-easy target for the enemy to cut down mid-battle. The swift horses can come closer to the foot soldiers in the enemy's ranks, allowing the rider to strike them from a vantage point. But their swift hooves can also slip at a crucial moment and a tumble would be fatal.

Occasionally I catch sight of Amalu but he never speaks to me. Sometimes I catch him looking my way but when I face him he turns his gaze away and will not meet my eye.

I also hear about the cities they plan to attack. The most important will be Aghmat, a rich trading city, well-guarded by walls and mercenaries as well as the amir's own guards. It is a fine city, with a busy souk through which many treasures pass from trader to trader, hot bath houses that all can visit and water brought by canals to the very heart of the city itself. Aghmat has become the capital of the Sous region under the leadership of the Idrisids. The amir of the city now is the leader of the Maghrawa tribe. Luqut al-Maghrawi is a noble man, so they say, and a fierce warrior. It will be a challenge to take Aghmat, for the amir and his men will defend it to the death and the Maghrawa are not to be taken lightly. But it must be done if the army is to take the region and stand a chance of continuing their progress throughout the rest of the country, heading north. The Almoravids's holy war will come to a stumbling halt if they cannot take key cities, and Aghmat is the first of these that they will encounter. To take Aghmat will be to send a strong message to all the tribes that here is a force to be reckoned with, that a new era is coming.

I hear their words in the still heat of the day or blown to me on the cooling wind of the evenings. Talk of weapons, mounts, men, training, the cities they hope to take easily, those that are better fortified. Sometimes I listen intently, desirous of knowing everything about what the future holds for my husband and therefore for me also, as though knowing every detail will make their plans successful.

Often, though, I turn my head away and watch the soft sand sinking under the camels' feet, see horned vipers slide away at our approach, or fat green lizards clinging to rocks. I close my eyes to enjoy what little breeze blows across my face. I still cannot believe that I have left the camp, that I am journeying again. The sense of freedom it brings me is a joyous thing, my mouth stretches into a smile without my even realising.

Sometimes I seek Yusuf out, looking for a glimpse of his rarely-seen humour and mischievous side, which he shows only when we are alone. Travelling with the men he has been serious again, intent on the plans for the future and the many things to be done at the main camp before they will be ready to face their first real battles. Abu Bakr will be impatient for his arrival, for together they are a formidable pair, their strengths complementing one another. Together they will be able to make plans, to see that all is ready, to encourage the men before the real hardships began. Their training will have prepared them for war, of course, strengthening their muscles and bringing bravery to their hearts, but no training can truly take the place of war. No man who has not fought against a man who wishes him dead can say that he is ready for a battle. Most of the men until now will have fought only each other, where the weapons are handled with caution and no real harm will come to them.

I catch sight of Amalu one day and hurry towards him. "Amalu."

"Kella," he says without emotion.

"I wish you would return home," I tell him. "I am afraid for you."

"You doubt I can fight?"

I sigh. "I do not doubt your manliness, Amalu. I doubt your desire to be a soldier."

"That is no longer your concern," he says and walks away.

I sit with Yusuf one evening, sharing a few dates together, away from the others so that we can be alone. We talk of small things only; the jackals we heard the night before and whether they will be bold enough to approach again tonight, the shapes of clouds, our camels' demeanour. But after a while the talk drifts to his plans, as it always does. He wants to have drummers with him when they go into battle, as their strong rhythm will not only give courage to his own men and unite them but bring fear to their opponents, for only a confident army can have drums beating for them in the thick of battle. He describes the heat of a battle, how they will keep tight formations, no falling back, nor even advancing, allowing the enemy to come to them and then realize their error when they find out how strong the army is, how well-trained its men and beasts, how they can be caught up in the fervour of drums and be merciless in their fighting, leading inevitably to success.

I grip Yusuf's arm, unable to keep my fears to myself.

"What if you are not successful? What if your men fail, and you are driven back?"

He strokes my hair. "It is a risk that we must take," he says simply. "We cannot succeed if we do not fight. God is with us, I feel His hand upon us and we cannot fail if it is His will."

I cannot let it rest so simply. "And if it is not His will?"

He smiles sadly at my anxious face. "Then we will die."

"You cannot die!" My voice grows louder and Yusuf puts one finger gently against my lips. I push his hand away and go on, unthinking. "How can I raise a child with no father?"

He looks closely at me. "What?"

I shake my head and lower my eyes. "Nothing. I only meant…" I am suddenly crushed into a breathtaking hug.

"You are with child!"

I cannot deny his hope. I lower my eyes, suddenly shy. "I believe I have your child within me," I say softly.

His face is full of great joy, and he holds me very tenderly. We had been about to sleep, but now he is wide awake. "He will be called Ali," he says firmly. "He will be a brave and noble warrior, and he will follow me to war in God's name."

I shake my head. "There will be no need for war when he is grown. For his father will have won all the wars there are to win. My son will live in peace, caring for his father's people and building a new country."

Yusuf likes this idea. "Yes," he says eagerly, pulling me close to him as we settle into our blankets to sleep. "He will build a great mosque, to honour God. He will ensure that the people of our land live by His word and that they are fairly treated. There will be no unlawful taxes, there will be great cities built and all will be done to praise His name." He continues to talk in this vein, while I fall asleep, happy in his arms, the murmurings of my son's great future still being whispered in my sleeping ears.

From then on Yusuf worries about my health, insisting that we travel only in the cool of the days and that I should sleep well at night, thus making our journey much longer, for we had been riding for many more hours each day than Yusuf will now allow. The men grumble a little, in a good-natured way, about men becoming fathers for the first time and how they turn into old hens, fussing and clucking and wasting time over a healthy young woman who has been riding every day with no ill effects so far. I agree with them and try to convince Yusuf to let me continue as before, for I feel well and happy, but he will have none of it. So we travel only in the cool, and each day he ensures that I am delicately placed in my saddle and that I am well rested before we ride out each day. The long hot days are spent in the shade, which means that we have to find places of shelter or erect my tent, which wastes a great deal of time for it is large and not meant to be moved quite so frequently. Ekon and Adeola erect and dismantle it almost every day, and they work hard, but they do not complain. Adeola smiles at me and points at my still-flat belly and imitates how I will soon look, with a great round stomach like a giant melon, staggering along under the weight of my huge son, which makes me laugh until I see Amalu's expression, his eyes full of pain.

In the heat of the day we sit, the men sometimes playing games with pebbles and bones, or praying with Yusuf. Sometimes they will train, although the fierce heat is not conducive to this and they drink so much water that the water bags need refilling over and over again. We always fill them whenever we have the chance to do so and when we make camp a few of the men will go and find water, for they know all the sources along our route, having travelled it once already.

In these quiet moments I sit with Adeola and spin wool, or embroider cloth for clothes. We cannot chatter to each other as she does not know enough words, but she can make herself understood through gestures and mimicry, and her speaking begins to improve. Ekon is quiet, but he watches over us with interest and smiles sometimes when we laugh. He takes our small flock of goats to find pasture when there is some to find, and milks them with great speed and skill, bringing the milk to us to cook with or sometimes for Adeola to churn by shaking it in a goatskin bag. Our progress is certainly far slower than before, but we enjoy the journey more and it gives me time with Yusuf before I have to relinquish him to his mission.

When he has finished praying or training or talking with his men, he will come and sit with me, and Adeola will move away a little so that we may sit close to one another.

He pats my belly. "My son," he says. "Do you hear me?"

I laugh and make a tiny voice. "I hear you, Father," I say.

"Are you well, son?"

"I am well," I reply. "My mother's womb is a fine dwelling place."

Yusuf chuckles and begins to talk of his great plans for this unborn child while I lie back on my elbows in the shade of my hastily-erected tent and listen lazily, warmed by more than by the sun.

The garrison camp is like nothing I could have ever dreamt of. No matter where I turn my eyes there are soldiers. Some are our own people, some paler, from the land across the sea to the north, Al-Andalus. Some are black-skinned from the kingdoms in the south. All are fearsome to my eyes.

Not to Yusuf's eyes, for they are like water to a dying man in the desert to him.

"At last we are here," he says when he sees the camp and I hear the smile in his voice.

We are surrounded in moments, his men chanting out his name, seeking to touch his shoulder or take his hand as he passes each of them.

"My cousin, we have missed you," says Abu Bakr and they embrace as though they had thought never to see one another again.

"My wife," Yusuf says, bringing me forward. "I believe you remember her," he adds mischievously.

"You are welcome here, Kella," says Abu Bakr. "You must have made quite an impression on Yusuf. No man could have stopped him in his mission and yet his gaze fell on you."

The men tease Yusuf for his long absence but are kind to me, their smiles and nods courteous and welcoming. In their eagerness to welcome me and show their devotion to their general our camels are quickly unloaded by many hands and my tent is erected in a quiet spot where I will be out of sight should I wish not to be seen. Ekon and Adeola's smaller tent is pitched alongside mine. They have nothing to do but seek out water and turn our tents back into homes; Adeola beating the sand from the rugs and blankets and learning where to fetch water while Ekon finds places to graze our sheep and goats. That night I eat alone for Yusuf has much to do, but I sleep well.

The next day I walk around the garrison. I have never seen such a sight, a whole army gathered in one place, ready for battle.

I cannot count how many men there are, but they are many, many hundreds. To see them pray together is awe-inspiring, rows upon rows of strong men on their knees to their God, praising His name together.

They eat sparingly: camel or goat's meat, milk, dried fruits. I smile when I see how they eat, for Yusuf likes to eat like this and now I see why. Their diet is simple, but they are brothers and they share the hardships of their life for the greater glory of God. They dress in plain woollen robes and simple shoes. They are of many skin colours and of all sizes, tall, short, thin or large, but all are heavily muscled and all are ready to fight to the death.

I watch some of the training, and am struck by the formations they use. They move seamlessly into tight, closed ranks, with foot soldiers at the front, then the mounted soldiers behind them. Most ride camels, for they are better mounts in the desert, but Yusuf has plans for more horses once they reach the other side of the Atlas mountains. The ground there is harder underfoot and horses are faster, able to turn more easily and quickly. For now, though, there are hundreds of camels, and they are mostly bad-tempered and fast. Yusuf warns me to be careful of them, and I walk cautiously when I approach them, for they can bite or kick. Unlike most camels chosen for riding, they are male camels, and they are less docile than females like my own Thiyya. They fight amongst themselves, too, and sometimes the men have to beat them with sticks to break them apart from one another when they are enraged. I keep Thiyya well away, for she is of great interest to them all.

The closed ranks of the army are unlike any soldiers I have seen or heard tell of. I thought armies used loose, long lines, which allow for greater flexibility in battle. I mention this to Yusuf but he explains to me that those long lines allow the enemy to attack one part, cutting men off from their fellow soldiers and leaving them to be slaughtered alone. The Qur'an itself, Yusuf tells me, says that fighting should instead be done in these closed ranks, so that all the men are protected by their fellow soldiers. He has studied closely how that might work, training his men for many months until they have mastered the technique. He believes that this way of fighting will serve them best.

The training is an amazing sight. They practice daily with javelins, daggers and swords. They have great shields covered with strong hides, many made of ostrich or antelope, some of other beasts; all thick, heavy and very strong, protecting the men from the deadly weapons of their enemies. They have drummers, who beat a strong rhythm for the men to move to, but Yusuf wants even more drummers in the future. He talks often of how the army might be made stronger, larger, better. I cannot imagine it. It seems so vast to me already.

I see Amalu joining the men in their training, wielding a vicious-looking sword. I feel guilty. He wanted a peaceful trading life and now he is learning to be a warrior. He looks fierce but I am afraid it is only his anger at my marrying Yusuf instead of choosing him. I feel responsible for him being here and my heart sinks at the idea that he may be harmed in battle, even killed. It will be my fault if anything bad happens to him.

There is a camel fight one night, and I hear the shouts of the men and the hard thumps of blows delivered to break up the camels. Yusuf goes out to investigate and when he returns he tells me all is well and holds me softly in his arms as I drift back to sleep.

There are meetings among the leaders, made up of great men from the Sanhaja confederation of tribes – the Lamtuna, the Musaffa, the Djudalla. These tribes have all contributed their men, weapons, and their support to Abu Bakr. He presides over these meetings, his gruff good-natured manner easing any tensions and his firm belief in their success comforting any nervous doubters. Meanwhile Yusuf will slip away from these meetings when they grow dull and endless, and come back to his men, training alongside them, urging them on, eating and praying with them. They love him; he is their general. While they respect and obey Abu Bakr in all things, still they turn to Yusuf for their inspiration and to find their courage.

I take to watching the men training, for they are an awe-inspiring sight. No-one can fail to be inspired by their courage and fierce faces, they make me truly believe this great war may be a triumph, no matter what happened in the past.

One morning my path is blocked by a group of camels. I skirt around them but as I watch the men training I forget about them and do not notice when they move closer. One sniffs at my hair and I, startled, turn and cry out, which makes the beast panic. In a moment all is chaos. The group begins to fight, biting and roaring at each other, and I, seeking to escape that frightening place, suddenly receive a kick in the belly and find myself lying on the ground, crying out with pain. I hear men come running and Adeola's shrieks. I hear a howl of rage from Yusuf's voice though I barely recognise his voice, for I have never heard him truly angry. I lie very still and clasp my belly. When I open my eyes for one brief moment I see a glint of metal before a spray of red blood appears on my sleeve. I hear a dying groan from the camel who kicked me as Yusuf slits its throat. I close my eyes and am lifted tenderly by strong hands and taken to my tent.

Inside Adeola, her face tight with worry, sits with me. She tries to feed me broth and sweet dates, but I turn my face away.

"All be well," she says, over and over again, as though it is a charm. "All be well."

But my belly cramps. I slip a hand beneath the blankets and pull it back covered in blood. Adeola repeats her charm faster and faster, but even she has to admit defeat when she sees the blood trickling steadily down my legs. Her eyes fill with tears as I begin to sob. When she has done all she can for me she dispatches Ekon to Yusuf and then sits with me, her small calloused hand tightly clutching mine.

Adeola never leaves my side but it takes three days before Yusuf comes to me. I grow sad – and then angry – at his absence from me, but Adeola whispers in her broken way that Yusuf has been beside himself, that he ranted and raved about our loss and that even his strongest and most-trusted men dared not approach him. He spent the past three days sat alone, not eating or drinking, until Abu Bakr went to him and spoke softly.

Now he comes to me, his face full of misery. I know he killed the camel to try and assuage some of our grief, so I take his hands and thank him for it, although one camel or another means nothing to me, for I have lost my baby and nothing else matters. Then I hold Yusuf while he sobs. I had not thought I wanted a baby so much, after all it would have curtailed the freedom I craved, but now that it is gone I am crushed. Is it an ill omen? Will Yusuf think he should not have married me at all, that this is a punishment for delaying his mission?

"It is Allah's will and we do not question His will," says Yusuf, although his eyes say otherwise. "We will be blessed again if He looks on us with favour. In the meantime, it is my fault that you were hurt."

I open my mouth to argue but he gestures that I should be quiet so curtly that I stay silent. I know from his voice that I have no say in this matter. He is my husband and he has made a decision.

"I will not argue this with you, Kella," he says. "I should not have kept you here at all," he says. "An army is no place for a woman. In a few days we will leave this place to begin our journey across the mountains. I will leave behind only a small base camp. You will remain here and I will send for you when we have crossed the mountains and secured a safe city for you to come to."

I weep, for I do not want to leave Yusuf. How to explain that such an accident could have happened anywhere? That if he leaves he may never return, never send for me at all? But I have no choice. I spend time recovering, during which I am forbidden to leave my tent, although Yusuf comes to me often. The men are sorrowful, for behind their mighty shields and their great muscles are kind hearts and they mourn their general's loss of a son.

One tent after another is packed away. The weapons are sharpened and repaired. The great garrison is now nothing but a small base camp made up of a couple of dozen older men and their slaves, a few wives. The men left behind are grumpy at being left out of the adventure and excitement ahead, however dangerous it may be. When I come out of my tent and see what is to be left I am horrified. It is a tiny, dull camp, I would have been better off staying with Aunt Tizemt.

The night before they leave, Yusuf takes my hand and leads me away from the camp, lifts me onto a camel with him and rides a little way off, far enough that we can no longer see or hear the men. In the still-warm sand Yusuf lets the camel wander off a little way in search of tasty shrubs and we sit together watching the dying sun. Yusuf has brought some water, dates and flat stale bread, but it feels good to eat together, alone, without being surrounded by an army of fighting men. Although we have no fine food or a comfortable tent and furs, sitting together in the bare sand has about it a tenderness that I will miss.

I am afraid for Yusuf, of course. Tomorrow he will leave me and go to fight his holy war. Holy or not, I am afraid. The last time the Almoravids tried to cross the High Atlas their leader was killed and they were forced to retreat back to the desert. Now I try to speak of my fears to Yusuf, but he hushes me.

"Now is not the time to talk of fear, my jewel." He puts one arm around my shoulders as we sit and turns his head to smile comfortingly at me. "What will be will be. We are but Allah's servants and we win or lose according to His wisdom." He sees me begin to object and kisses me gently to stop the words in my mouth. Then he searches in his robes.

"I have a gift for you."

I cannot help smiling. "What is it?"

"Close your eyes and tell me."

I close my eyes and feel something cold and hard in my hands, dangling from above. It is jewellery, I can tell, and my smile broadens. "You have given me so many jewels, what more is there to give?"

He laughs. "A woman can never have too many jewels nor kind words, so a wise man once told me."

I laugh again and give up guessing, opening my eyes. "A *khomeissa*!"

The thick silver pendant is a triangle with an additional part below which has five parts to it, making it akin to the 'Hand of Fatima', giving the wearer protection against the evil eye. I slip it round my neck, feeling happy that Yusuf's protective gift will be with me even when he leaves me the next day.

He smiles mischievously. "I hear that women will rather go naked than without a *khomeissa*, is that true?"

I laugh. "Perhaps."

"A good thing I gave you it, then. I would not have you be naked when I am not there to enjoy it!"

We lie together under the stars and later tears come to me again for my lost child, but Yusuf holds me close and whispers kind words. Eventually I fall asleep in his arms and wake in the pale cold dawn to join him in prayer. Afterwards we sit together for a little while on our last day together, perhaps forever.

"You will join me soon," he promises. "Very soon."

"When?" I ask, wanting an answer that I know cannot be given. Who knows what the future holds? They may all be killed, driven back to the desert like their leader was ten years earlier. Or they may sweep victorious throughout the Maghreb, praising the word of God as they go. Only Allah knows, and He will reveal His plans when the time is right and not before.

Yusuf does not try to give me the answer I want to hear, only the answer that is true. "When it is safe for you to be by my side I will call you to me," he says simply. "I would give my own life willingly, but I will not risk yours."

He strokes my hair and face and looks at me for a long moment before he wraps his veil around his face and disappears beneath it. Only his eyes show, hiding the man I know and becoming once more a warrior and leader of men. I know I will not see his face again for a long time and I fight to not let my tears fall. I want him to remember my smile and to miss it so badly that he will call me to him quickly, danger or no danger.

I wrap my arms around him as we stand and hold him close to me, enjoying his warmth against me.

"Perhaps I am with child again," I say hopefully. "I was with child so quickly after we were married, perhaps when you call me to you I will bring you a child!"

Yusuf smiles tenderly at me. It is unlikely, and we both know it, but he nods, ready to believe in my tentative hopes for happiness. "When I send word for you I shall say to my men, 'Bring my beautiful jewel to me. And her little gemstone must come with her also, for he must meet his great rock-father at last.'"

I giggle at his make-believe family of rocks and embrace him again. Then we ride slowly back to the camp together.

I stand and watch Yusuf and his men as they leave the camp. I try to speak with Amalu, to tell him to be careful, but he does not ride close enough to me, whether on purpose or not I do not know. I wait to wave, but neither he nor Yusuf look back. Slowly their shapes disappear into the shimmering heat.

Assaru Ouanafer
— A Veil Key

1 LOOK AROUND ME THROUGH A haze of tears. The garrison camp is now smaller than my own. A wave of disappointment sweeps over me. I could have stayed at home. I could have been with Aunt Tizemt, who for all her roars is a kitten underneath. We could have spent the days together as equals rather than teacher and pupil. We could have cooked and woven together, sharing recipes and patterns, stories, jokes and gossip. I could have learnt skills from Tanemghurt, for she was always willing to teach, and understood the healing powers of plants. I would have been surrounded by my own people, my own kin. I wonder whether I should take my slaves and head back there now, but it is a long journey and Yusuf's men have been ordered to protect me here.

My mind offers up ever darker thoughts for me to consider. What if Yusuf is already tired of me and has chosen in his kindness not to humiliate me by divorcing me but simply to hide me away here?

As my spirits drop I feel a warm, calloused hand on my shoulder. Ekon is standing behind me, with Adeola at his side.

"We are here," he says and my tears fall at his kindness.

When Yusuf first left I hoped that he had left my womb filled again, for I know that he wants a son, and I also wish for a child of his; a part of him to keep by me until we can meet again. I have happy moments when I imagine him sending for me, and my longed-for arrival carrying his own son. I close my eyes and see his smile and his surprise, imagine our loving joy at being together again and our pride in the first of our many children. I want a child that he can love and raise, who will take his name and follow in his footsteps. But the moon grows bright and then dark and I have to resign myself to my fate – I will not be a mother until I see Yusuf again. There are two women in the camp whose bellies swell as the months pass by and I watch them with a fascinated envy.

Time passes quickly when every day is the same. Sometimes I cannot believe how long it has been since I last saw Yusuf. At first I am certain I will be sent for at any moment, but as the months pass my excitement becomes dull acceptance. It takes time but slowly we begin to settle into a daily routine. I take the opportunity to practice new styles of weaving from Adeola, which I enjoy. I share my own designs with her. We cook together and she learns from me as I do from her. Sometimes the other wives and slave women join us and we make enough to feed all of the camp, we eat together and have some sense of kinship, for we are all bound to this place until we are told otherwise.

Here there is much easier access to water than at my

own camp. When the rains come we even go into the rocky outcrops at the foot of the mountains and bath in the ice-cold water that falls over the rocks. It sweeps away the dirt and leaves us gasping with cold but our hearts racing with life. There are a few tiny villages close to us but they regard the camp with fear, having seen the size of the army that set out from here. They avoid us where possible, only occasionally trading with us, knowing we will buy what spare food they can grow.

The first news we hear about the army is that they have crossed the High Atlas. We hear little more than this, but I know that it will have been hard. So many men, so many animals, difficult and rocky roads in the mountains, the planning of battles yet to come whilst perhaps being attacked by local tribes who oppose their plans.

It is a long time before we hear of their progress again. I have nights when I toss and turn as though tormented by a thousand djinns. I know that unless they have some decisive victories and secure cities of importance, they will struggle and may well be wiped out.

I pray often and when I do my very heart is in my words and thoughts as I long to hear more news and to hear that Yusuf is safe. My days are mostly passed weaving, for I am skilled at this now and my work will one day adorn a new home. I sew tiny disks of silver onto my work and watch it glitter in the sunlight. When I am not weaving I talk with Adeola, or we sometimes play games together such as chess, moving our carved pieces across the board even as the army must be moving onwards.

One baby and then another is born and although I hold them and exclaim over their soft hair and tiny hands, although I gift their mothers blankets I have woven myself, I cannot help but wish that I, too, had a child.

At last we hear that they have captured Taroundannt in the south and, having left good men to hold it, are now heading north, towards the rich merchant city of Aghmat. That city's wealth could provide them with the riches they will need to feed so many men and animals, and send a message to all that these are not men to be trifled with. But the last time the Almoravid army attempted this it failed and was wiped out. We will not be sent for until Yusuf is certain he has a secure stronghold. Reluctantly, the men begin to make simple stone houses to protect us come the winter, for we cannot be sure that we will be sent for before then and here, so close to the mountains, the weather will be harsh.

I sit with Adeola. All my thoughts are on Aghmat and the army slowly approaching it. I can talk of nothing else, even when I try my words return to the same place.

"It is a trading city. I was there in the old days with my brothers and father. It is a city full of rich merchants and they will not wish to see it taken and sacked, all their profits going to some conquering army on a holy mission. They will pay for mercenaries to fight them if they think it will save their livelihoods."

She keeps her silence and lets me talk, nodding from time to time but not seeking to ally my fears, for she knows they are real.

I think back to the gossip I heard in my trading days as we passed through that city. "The Amir of Aghmat is Luqut al-Maghrawi. He is a great fighter and the richest man in all of Aghmat, which must make him one of the richest men in all the land. His queen is a woman called Zaynab, daughter of a merchant from Kairouan. They say there is none so beautiful. She told Luqut he would be a very great man, for it was foretold that she would marry the man who would rule all of the Maghreb." My voice trails off as I consider the implications of this prophecy. If the prophecy is true and Zaynab is married to the Amir of Aghmat, then he would be the man to rule all of the country.

Adeola sees where my thoughts were taking me and interrupts them. "Not everyone sees truly," she says gently. "Many prophecies are not understood. We cannot know our fates until they are revealed."

I bow my head but cannot control myself. "They say she is a sorceress! She could use magic against them in some way, to protect her own city and her husband the Amir!"

Adeola shakes her head and leaves me to my own turbulent and dark imaginings, which torment me by day and leave me sleepless at night. As time goes by, I grow to know every constellation of stars as though they were the creases of my own hand. I spend many nights wrapped in blankets sitting outside my tent at night when the camp is asleep, gazing upwards and praying for the army's success and Yusuf's safety.

When the news comes I am jubilant, but we are all shocked at the magnitude of their success.

Aghmat lies in ruins. The city has been taken and summarily sacked; all its riches plundered to support the holy army which has swept across it like the wrath of Allah and left it in tatters. A once rich city now humbled. The Amir is dead, his beautiful queen Zaynab has been taken in marriage by Abu Bakr. I try but cannot image the sturdy, earthy and friendly old Abu Bakr married to a beautiful young sorceress.

The decision has been taken to leave Aghmat in its ruined state and found a new city, which will be the base for the army as they carry out their holy war throughout the rest of the country and beyond. Abu Bakr has chosen a place, a little more to the North of Aghmat, close to the Wadi Tensift, providing them with ample water resources close by. Many men and animals will need a lot of water, and the thick snows of the Atlas mountains will provide the foundling city with water forever. Now the army will set up camp, a rough garrison, while the men regroup and their leaders make new plans.

Abu Bakr will take his new wife with him, forcing her to leave the comforts of her luxurious palace to live in a tent amongst soldiers and beasts.

I wonder about her. How must she feel now? Her husband and king is dead; she is now little better than a captured slave, to be taken to the bed of the Commander of a conquering army. She will have to lie in the arms of the man who has killed her husband. I feel sorry for her.

"No need to feel sorry for Queen Zaynab," says the man who brings us more news not long after. "She is a witch, that woman. Beautiful, but dangerous. They say she talks with djinns and can see visions."

"But still," I protest. "Her husband has been killed and

she is taken as a wife by the man who killed him. She has lost her love, her power…"

He laughs. "Queen Zaynab lost no time in making herself agreeable, I can assure you. She claimed that the prophecy that she would marry the man who would rule all of the country is coming true at last, that Abu Bakr is the man foretold, that she was meant for him from the very beginning, no matter that she was married to Luqut and another before him. She offered him all her wealth to aid his holy war."

I frown. "Surely all her wealth was at his disposal already? He sacked Aghmat – all its riches were his to take."

He shakes his head. "It is said that she had a great personal wealth, hidden where no-one knew of it. She went to Abu Bakr and promised him all her wealth to fulfil his destiny. She blindfolded him, then took him alone to a secret underground cave, where she took away his blindfold and lit a candle in the darkness. She showed him the greatest treasure ever known. Gold and pearls, rubies and silver – all his, her gift to him. 'All this is yours', she told him, then she tied the blindfold round his eyes again and led him away from that place." The man subsides, satisfied with the grandeur of his tale.

I narrow my eyes. "So he never knew where that place was and yet the treasure within it is his?"

The man frowns as he follows my logic, then laughs. "Just like a woman! Promises, promises, and then you must go with her in darkness that you may be tricked into believing the treasure is yours when it stays always within her gift to give!" He winks at Ekon who smiles and shakes his head. Then the messenger goes to be given food and beer by the camp slaves, who are keen to hear all the gory details of the battle, and of the legendary beauty of the Commander's new wife.

It is enough for me to know that Yusuf is safe and that his holy mission is smiled upon from the heavens. Truly his war is just, for he is being given great success. I smile a little over Zaynab, who has turned a shameful conquering into a triumph for herself and bound Abu Bakr to her with promises. She is indeed a clever woman, as rumour has it. One day, I think, I would like to meet this woman. No doubt I will for one day, God willing, I will rejoin Yusuf, and we two women will be companions while our husbands fight side by side.

The winter snows come and we huddle in our tiny houses, cramped and impatient, although we know we could not travel in this weather even if word came to join the army.

Spring flowers bloom and the snows retreat. Almost a year has passed and still I am not summoned. I grow resentful, as do the men of the camp, who mutter amongst themselves, disconsolate at being left out of the glory. I think of traveling to Yusuf before I am called for. I know a larger army is amassing and that the new garrison city is beginning to take shape, albeit with tents rather than fine buildings as yet, for the men's strength must be used for fighting, not building. Each time a rare messenger comes to me I grow excited and then am told, once again, that the time is not yet.

"But soon," each messenger assures me. "Soon."

The heat of the summer beats down on us and we grow

sullen. Occasionally the men will fight one another, when quarrels break out brought on by too little to do. I pray that we will be sent for before the late autumn rains come, bringing perilous landslides from the mountains above us and forcing us back indoors after a summer spent in tents. Surely the summons must come soon.

Then news comes that there are rebel tribes in the south. They must be fully conquered and made to swear allegiance, or they will prove a grave danger when the army moves north. Abu Bakr himself decides to head up the men sent to fight in the south. He is leaving command of the whole army to Yusuf. Overnight, Yusuf becomes Commander in all but name. The new garrison city is entirely in his hands. I am proud, but fearful. Abu Bakr could be away for a long time, and other tribes might see Yusuf as only the second-in-command and seize the opportunity to attack. But my fears are laid to rest.

"Your husband's reputation is fearsome," a messenger assures me. "No-one sees him as a lowly second-in-command, to be attacked when the Commander is away – he is seen as Abu Bakr's equal and indeed as his successor."

Winter comes again and this time I do not hope for spring and new messengers, only resign myself. I wonder whether I should return to my home camp but I am afraid of looking like an abandoned wife, left behind not because of safety but because her husband no longer cares for her, barely recalls her name. I walk in the foothills of the mountains sometimes, a thick robe clutched about me, the silence all around me only echoing the emptiness of my life here.

I dream of Yusuf at night sometimes, but as time goes by my dreams grow hazy. I see his hands, his robes, feel his warm body beside me and look for him when I wake, but his face has grown less and less clear in my mind. I have not seen my husband for almost two years, after knowing him for only a few months. I think of Amalu and wonder whether I was nothing but a fool to turn him down. The life I rejected now seems like a more pleasant one than the life I am living. If I had married him I would have children by now, I would live and work alongside my aunt. Amalu and my father and brothers would trade, but visit often and tell me tales of their journeys. Here there is nothing, only an empty waiting. The only pleasure spring brings is that we move back into our tents, which smell sweeter than the tiny stone shelters we must call home. The babies born after Yusuf left take their first steps and I shake my head when Adeola assures me that surely he will send for me this summer. I think sadly that he would not have waited so long if my child had lived. If I had birthed a son, he would old enough to run into his father's arms by now.

It is barely dawn and the ground beneath me is shaking. I wake confused and stumble from my tent, looking about me in the half-light, before shrinking back.

Bearing down on me at great speed are six camels, their riders' robes swirling. They stop only a few steps away in a cloud of dust. A tall figure leaps down from the lead camel and strides forwards. I put a hand to the dagger I keep in my robes before suddenly recognising the man.

"Amalu? Amalu!"

He stands in front of me, his eyes bright with pleasure. I can just see the top of a new scar, which must curve across his cheek before coming close to his left eye.

"Kella," he says and the warmth in his voice makes me so happy that I embrace him. He returns the embrace gently before stepping back from me.

"You are safe," I say happily. "And – and all is well?" I add, suddenly fearful.

"All is well," he reassures me.

"Tell me everything," I beg. "But first – oh you have ridden so hard. Let me prepare refreshments." I call for Adeola and she, all smiles, begins to make tea. The other men go to meet old comrades, while Amalu squats down by the fire.

"We have ridden for so long," he says. "The mountain passes slowed us down or we would have reached you sooner. I have been commanded to pack up the base camp."

I stare at him. "Pack it up?"

He laughs at my face. "Did you want to stay here forever?"

"Then am I – has Yusuf?"

"Yusuf has sent for you," he says, his voice flat.

I give him tea, bread and roasted goat meat. "Tell me more," I say.

He sips the tea. "Abu Bakr's new city is called Murakush. It is still more of a camp than a city, a garrison camp at that, full of soldiers and weapons, but some of the soldiers' families are beginning to join them now. The army will not set out again for a while; we have need of more men. They will need to be trained and we must be fortified. The living conditions are rough."

"I do not care," I say quickly.

He looks at me for a moment and then speaks softly, so that no-one may hear him. "Are you certain that you wish to be with Yusuf, Kella? If it is freedom you want I will travel with you wherever you wish to go."

"He is my husband," I say.

"You barely know him," says Amalu. "I have spent more time with him than you have."

"He is my husband," I say stubbornly. "My place is with him. Besides, now that the war is over we will begin to build the vision he has of the future. Together."

"The war is not yet over," says Amalu.

"It will be soon," I say. "When can we leave?"

"I must pack up the camp," he says.

"Do it quickly!" I say smiling but he lowers his gaze and stares into the fire for a long time.

I have never prepared for travel so fast. I throw my possessions together, in my excitement paying little care to proper packing until Adeola and Ekon come to me gently, take everything out of my hands and set to packing themselves, smiling and speaking softly to one another. Their care and skill mean that everything is packed as it should be in very little time. Within three days I am ready to leave, adding my six camels to the escorts – three which carry my possessions, two for the slaves and of course Thiyya.

Meanwhile, Amalu marshalls the men. They are eager to leave, to join their comrades and partake in their success. Everyone hurries about their work, excited and smiling. The camp is dismantled, the camels and horses are loaded.

There will be an advance party of myself and Amalu with an escort as well as Adeola and Ekon. Then will come the main group, who will travel a little slower than us, for there is livestock to herd as we travel. The little stone shelters we built stand empty, no doubt the villagers will use them once they are certain we have gone.

Amalu comes to me as I approach Thiyya, sitting sedately chewing the cud and waiting for me to mount her. I smile at him and then impulsively turn and hug him fiercely. "I am so glad you are safe, Amalu. I am sorry that my marriage hurt you. But I am so happy! Be happy for me."

His smile is full of a strange sadness. "I will never forget how happy you are now," he says. "I hope you will find happiness in Murakush."

"Of course I will, Amalu," I say. "Yusuf is waiting for me!"

He holds out his hand. On it is a silver shape, an elaborately shaped *assaru ouanafer,* a veil 'key' or fastener. I look closer and see that it is etched with the Tinfinagh's alphabet letter *ezza*, the symbol of our people. My eyes fill with tears. To have this with me is of great comfort as I ride to my new life. I embrace Amalu again and he holds me for a moment longer than he should. When he releases me I see tears in his eyes.

"Come now, Amalu," I say, teasing him a little. "You are not bidding me farewell. We ride together!"

He nods and gives the order to mount. I look behind me at the deserted camp. The only signs of our time here are the dusty outlines where the tents were pitched and the circles where our fires used to burn.

My escort of six men treat me with great deference as we journey towards the garrison camp and I enjoy the feeling of importance. I am the wife of the second in command of a great and victorious army. I think happily that soon I may even be with child again and that the men will be happy for their leader. It will take us almost a month to reach the garrison camp, for the men have strict instructions that we are not to hurry but to travel with the greatest of care for me. We are a small group and often a merry one.

We must cross the Atlas Mountains, and this takes up much of our journey. There are a few trade routes, of course, but they are tiny tracks amongst the towering and precarious rocky slopes. One wrong step and lives could be lost. The only way is to travel slowly and carefully. We meet few people.

Once across that great barrier we begin to see the landscape change before us. We see more plants, even sometimes a crooked little tree. More rain falls in this part of the world, so the closer we come to the camp, the better the grazing for our camels is and the easier it becomes to find good water sources, cold and fresh, sourced as it is from the very heights of the mountains. There are more trees, these unbent, fruit trees and olives. The travelling becomes a little faster, although we do not push ourselves too hard. We enjoy the bright green of the land before the heat of the full summer burns it yellow. The almond trees have already blossomed, now they are full of tender green leaves and the first soft fuzzy buds, which will become the good sweet nuts. The camels are happy with all the new food that they find. I enjoy travelling again, seeing new faces and landscapes, reveling in the luxury of buying our food from villages that we pass rather than cooking and doing other women's tasks. I will reach Yusuf well rested and ready to work alongside him to achieve our shared vision.

"Wait till you see the camp!" says one of the younger men, too full of excitement to contain himself as we draw closer to our final destination. We are but a few days away from Murakush now, and although we have eaten and slept well during our travels, we are looking forward to our arrival.

"You have never seen such an army gathered in one place! Hundreds upon hundreds of men. Camels, horses. More weapons than you can imagine. So many people! Not just the men, but many of their families, slaves, even children. The General Yusuf has great plans. He wants to gather an even greater army. He says we will look back and laugh when we think of how we are now. He says we will have a mighty army of slaves, fighting men from the Dark Kingdom. Already he has secured the trade routes so he can gather taxes from the merchants to allow him to pay for a larger army. We will go north, he says, but for now we must strengthen ourselves. The men are building trenches and walls to fortify the new garrison city. Yusuf wants a great mosque to be built in the very centre, to honour Allah. But for now we all pray together in the space that he has allocated to the building. Yusuf prays among us and we praise His greatness in all we have accomplished so far and all there is yet to accomplish."

I smile to myself at his enthusiasm. "Murakush," I say,

turning the new name over in my mouth. "It is near the old trading city of Aghmat, is it not?"

He nods. "It is. The army took Aghmat and sacked the city. The king was killed in battle and Abu Bakr took the queen of Aghmat to be his wife." He falls silent without adding further details.

I know all of this, of course, but here is a man who will know more details. "Her name is Zaynab, is it not?"

He nods again but does not elaborate, despite his earlier eagerness to talk. I decide to coax more information from him.

"Is she as beautiful as they say?"

He looks uncomfortable but does not disagree.

I smile mischievously, thinking that perhaps he has some feelings himself for the legendary queen of Aghmat, now wife to his Commander. A great beauty will be much admired by soldiers, men far from their own wives, or not even married yet.

"Is the marriage a happy one? Are the lady Zaynab and the Commander well suited?"

He mumbles something. I catch Amalu frowning at him.

I lean forward on Thiyya to catch his words. "What did you say?"

He repeats what he had said and this time I hear him. "They are divorced."

I frown. "Divorced? Already? They have been married less than two years. What happened? Were they so ill-suited?"

The young man looks at the others for help but they are all staring straight ahead as though seeking something on the horizon. He lowers his head and seems to take his courage in both hands.

"The Commander Abu Bakr went into the desert to fight with the rebel tribes. Before he went he decided the lady Zaynab was unaccustomed to a rough life in the desert and that he should set her free as he might be away a long time. He divorced her."

"And now she is alone?"

He takes a deep breath and squares his shoulders. "The Commander gave her in marriage to his second in command, along with the command of the army and the new city of Murakush. When her waiting period is over she may marry him." He takes another deep breath and emphasises his final words with a stubborn nod of his head. "It has been agreed."

I cannot believe I have heard him correctly. Thiyya slows as I let her reins loose and then stops, looking around with interest at the closest trees to see what leaves might be good to eat. The men stop their own beasts and gather around me as I sit slackly on Thiyya's back. I feel the heat sap my strength. After some moments of silence I turn to Amalu. I speak and my voice is hoarse.

"Zaynab is to marry *my husband* Yusuf?"

His silence confirms it.

I grasp at the only part of what has been said that still gives me hope. "He said that she must finish her period of waiting before she can marry again. When was the divorce?"

Amalu clears his throat. "The first month."

I count and recount, but there is only one answer. "She can marry him this month?"

Again silence. Although Thiyya is standing still, I feel that I may fall. "When this month?"

At our present speed we will not get there before the ceremony.

"What were you thinking?" I shout at Amalu. The camels startle.

He says nothing. The men wait.

"Why didn't you tell me? Why did you let us travel so slowly?"

Amalu meets my gaze. His eyes are as angry as mine. "What did it matter whether I told you or not? Yusuf had already decided. Perhaps you should be angry with him for taking a new wife without even consulting you, without even summoning you to his side until now. It was safe enough many months ago for you to join us. He has all but forgotten you in his lust for another woman!"

The men look away as we stare at each other, locked in rage.

"We need to get to Murakush before the wedding," I say without looking at him. "We will ride hard."

"Kella – " begins Amalu.

"Ride," I say.

We ride day and night from then on, stopping only to fill the waterbags. I eat nothing and the men eat as we ride. There is no more banter, no more stories of Yusuf, of the army, of the future. The men are almost asleep on their mounts, Adeola and Ekon's faces are grey with worry but my eyes are kept open with pain and fear. I cannot think properly. I can only ride and pray that I will reach the camp and speak with Yusuf before the marriage takes place.

We see the camp in the far off distance at dawn on the day

of Yusuf and Zaynab's wedding. We ride as fast as we can through the burning heat of that day, but the camels are tired after the last few days and cannot be persuaded to run, ignoring my desperate urgings.

"We will not get there in time," says Amalu. His voice is pleading. "Kella, rest. You are exhausted. It is too late to stop the wedding. Sleep and we will arrive tomorrow when you are strong."

I turn my face away so he cannot see my tears falling and urge Thiyya forwards.

We reach the camp as the sun sets.

Tenfuk – Pendant to Celebrate a Birth

BLAZING TORCHES LIGHT UP THE camp. Songs are being sung and as we approach I can smell a feast – rich roasting meats, good stews, perfumed drinks and the small sweet cakes that Aunt Tizemt so loves.

My aunt seems very far away to me now.

I have never seen so large a camp in one place. The army has expanded beyond my imagining. No doubt all the slaves of the cities they have taken have been pressed into service as soldiers. And perhaps many free-born men have seen that Abu Bakr's army is a force to be reckoned with and have decided to pledge their allegiance to the winning side. Not to mention the many mercenaries who will have seen that there might be spoils of war to be had with this new army, which has such grand plans for the future.

Now many of the men have been joined by their families, or have taken women from the conquered cities as their brides, just as their leader has. There are women cooking. Some are wives, cooking and caring for children, speaking with their men, handsome women, sure of their status and sturdy with years of hard work, women from many tribes but all from the same country.

Other women are there for a different purpose. They are beautiful, of every colouring. One I see even has hair like saffron, her skin very fair and her cheeks as pink as fresh figs. They wear bright clothes and tease the men. They have no need to cook and care for children, leaving them free to wander amongst the tents and chatter amongst themselves. Abu Bakr's men may have been trained as holy warriors, but few would turn away from a beautiful woman. Besides, now there are new men among the army, men who may swear their allegiance to Abu Bakr and profess to worship Allah as required but who are loath to turn away from the pleasures to be had in this world, no matter what the holy book may say on the subject.

There are slave women also of course, their faces visible here and there as they scurry about amongst the tents bringing water, wood, heavy bundles, basins, bags. The slave men herd animals about, cursing in their own tongues, their muscles shiny with sweat, carrying even larger burdens than their womenfolk.

There are tents as far as I can see, of all shapes, sizes and colours, some small and misshapen, faded and greying, kept together more through prayer than good cloth and poles. Some are lavish, elaborate, small palaces amongst the chaos. Animals are everywhere, camels of every colour and size, fine warhorses, old nags, sturdy mules and little donkeys. We pass goats and their kids, sheep and even cattle, for this part of the country has more green fodder to feed them.

Weapons are everywhere. This is no ordinary camp, it is a garrison, and there are signs of warfare wherever I look. Some wounded men groan from their tents as healers seek to remedy their wounds, some of which will not heal or will take a long time to do so. I see missing limbs and terrible wounds to the face and stomach. Fine warhorses are being cared for, brushed and fed and watered, saddles being mended and armour being diligently repaired.

There is food in vast quantities. Great baskets of bread and cooking pots of mouth-watering stews are being carried towards a brightly lit space at the centre of the camp. One day no doubt it will be the great square of the city, but for now it is only a big space with no tents, the ground firmly packed down with the passing of many feet. Huge fires have been lit and whole animals are being roasted over the hot coals, the fat spitting and hissing and throwing up little sparks in the flames. Around the edges are laid out rugs where people can sit and a crowd is already beginning to gather, drawn by the good smells and the chance to sit and gossip before the feast begins.

There are storytellers. Wherever there are a few people gathered and a tale to tell there will be storytellers, and here they are already weaving the army's past two years into legend. The ingredients are all there for the taking – a holy army on a mission from God Himself, a respected leader and his fearsome second-in-command who now leads the army while its founder tames the rebel tribes who dare to challenge their holy cause. A pillaged city. A beautiful queen taken as a bride by first one man and then another. A growing army of fearsome warriors and their glorious future. The crowd listens entranced and people whoop and cheer when their own names are mentioned in the legends being woven by firelight.

Amalu and I have reached this main square, if it can be called that, without anyone taking notice of us amongst the crowd. We have left the loaded camels, the other men of the escort and Ekon and Adeola on the outskirts of the camp, the better to proceed through it unencumbered.

I walk through the crowded spaces as though in a dream, while Amalu brusquely moves people aside, clearing a path for me as he walks ahead. I see everything and yet nothing stays with me. My mind holds but one thought: that if I can speak with Yusuf he can tell me that there has been some mistake, that he has not married Zaynab at all, nor had ever intended to. And yet all around me there are celebrations. A feast is being prepared for everyone to share and I know that the great weight in my belly is there because the marriage ceremony has already been held and now it is about to be celebrated by all the camp. This is why there is so much food, why the storytellers are gathered to tell this latest part of the legend, and why the children shriek and giggle with anticipation of sweetmeats to come. The women of pleasure ply their perfumed trade through the cluttered tents in anticipation of a busy night to come, for a feast will stir a man's senses. A man who sees his leader marry a beautiful woman will turn his own mind to the pleasures that may be his for a few coins or even trinkets, depending on the woman he chooses.

We circumnavigate the edge of the square and as we head towards a large black tent I tug at Amalu's robes.

"Is that Yusuf's tent?"

He nods and I feel my heart race. Now I will see my

husband again and he will embrace me. He will brush away my fears. I put my hand to my heart as though to still its wild rhythm.

We reach the tent, which is more than the height of a man and entirely made of thick black cloth and leather. Amalu stops.

The tent is not decorated in any way; unusual for such a large tent belonging to a person of importance, but then Yusuf has always liked things to be plain, he has little interest in material possessions. The flaps are all closed, which is strange when the night is still warm.

Amalu steps a little closer to the tent and calls out. "My lady?"

Even as he speaks I grab his arm. "I do not want to see the lady Zaynab,'" I hiss under my breath. "Take me to Yusuf!"

Amalu flinches as my nails dig into his bare flesh. He turns to look at me and his eyes are full of pity. "Zaynab receives all visitors when they first enter the camp," he says simply. "Those are my orders. They are the orders given to everyone. No-one may see Yusuf or anyone else until she has seen them."

I see from his face that he is telling the truth and that there is no way to escape this meeting. How has Zaynab taken so much power to herself so quickly? I let go of his arm and take a deep breath as I hear the tent folds being opened. I look down at the bare earth, seeking strength.

Perfume scents the air and envelopes me, a heady mix that I cannot identify, but which tells of great riches, sweet beauty and something else, something dark and dangerous.

Slowly I raise my eyes and see Zaynab for the first time, and something in me grows cold.

She stands in the opening of the tent, ignoring Amalu, looking directly at me. She is tall, and dressed all in black flowing robes, which cover every part of her but her hands and head. She wears no jewellery, not even a belt to encircle her waist and draw attention to her form, making her look almost like a man, were she not so beautiful.

Her eyes are large, and so dark they seem black. The fires of the square dance in them as she gazes at me without blinking. Her hair is very long, falling past her waist, entirely straight and again, unadorned. No head wrap covers it.

Her mouth is wide and her lips are full. Her nose is long and straight, and her cheekbones rise high on her face. Her skin is a honeyed bronze, and although she uses no colourings nor has any tattoos to decorate her face I see the smoothness of her skin. By the way it glows I know that somewhere in the tent behind her is a casket, and that in that casket are the finest oils and powders to make her skin beautiful without any further adornment.

Her clothes seem entirely plain, something a slave might be forced to wear, but I have travelled and traded. I know fine silk when I see it. I also know how hard it is to make any cloth truly black, for the dyes are difficult to come by and it takes a lot of dye to make so much silk so black, like the darkness between the stars when the moon is gone. Her robes, appearing so austere to the ignorant gaze, are in fact the finest silk that money can buy. Only a great noblewoman with many riches has the gold coins necessary to have such a silk used for her everyday robes. Her shoes are likewise slippers of black leather, again without adornment but the stitching of them and the quality of leather tells me in one glance everything I need to know. When I traded I would have paid the very highest price for such leather, and counted myself lucky to have found it at all. I would have struggled to find a good enough craftsman to work it so finely and yet so simply, their only ornament being his skill.

We stand still for a moment, and then slowly, she smiles and I know at once that the beauty I have seen until now is nothing. Zaynab could have had any man she desires, for when she smiles she is the most beautiful woman I have ever seen.

"Sister."

It is all she says, but in the dripping honey of her lips, I hear the scorpion's sting quiver a warning.

I take a breath and extend my hands in greeting. I know a great deal about Zaynab just from looking at her, and I know already that she holds more power in this camp than my husband. How she has come by that power I am not sure, but I know she has it and that from this moment on my life is in her hands.

"Sister," I say and the word is like poison to me.

Zaynab's smile widens, and she takes my hands in hers. They are smooth but strong, slender and well-made.

"I am so glad you have come," she says, and I know she is lying. "It is hard being the only noblewoman here. But now I have you by my side, we will be sisters to one another." She pauses. "Now that I, too, am Yusuf's wife."

I want to strike my husband's name from her wide smiling lips. Instead I force myself to ask what I so desperately need to know.

"Where is…" I stumble over the word, "*our* husband?"

She waves Amalu away without so much as glancing at him. "Ensure my sister's belongings are brought safely to her," she says, "and place her tent close to mine, that we may easily visit one another. Clear those tents away," she adds, lifting her chin to indicate a group of tents on the other side of the square. "She shall have that space, so that we may see each other as soon as we rise each day."

She smiles at me again, a smile of great sweetness which takes no account of the families she has just displaced with that tiny gesture, who had a good position in the camp and will now be relegated to the outskirts, where people go to relieve themselves and the animals are kept.

Amalu hesitates but when he sees that I am silent he does as he is told. I stand before Zaynab in my travel-stained robes and wish that I could sleep and forget all of this, that I could wake to find that all this has been only a djinn tormenting me with evil dreams.

But Zaynab has other plans for me. "Yusuf is in a meeting with his officers. He will join us soon for the feast. We were married earlier but of course his mission must come before his new wife." Her smile grows broader. "I am so sorry you did not arrive this morning," she adds, "for I would have wanted you by my side when I married Yusuf, and to have had your blessing. But I am glad you are here for the feast we will be holding tonight to celebrate the wedding. I will tell my handmaiden Hela to prepare you, for of course you are weary with your long travels."

I try to object, but within moments she has swept me inside her tent and is calling for her slaves, leaving me alone for a moment.

The inside of her tent is like none I have ever seen. It is very plain, with very few colours. Almost everything is dark or sand-coloured. No bright dyes enliven the rugs that cover the floor. Prayer mats are ostentatiously visible in one part of the tent. There are two great chests in the other part, more suited, I guess, to her apartments in Aghmat than to a tent in the middle of a plain. They are made of pale plain wood, with simple geometric carvings, and probably contain her clothes and personal possessions. There are no instruments, no embroidery, no jewels on display. Like her clothes, everything is of the finest quality, but very plain.

The only exception is her bed.

It is huge and stands in the centre of the tent, drawing the eye to it immediately, for in that cool, dark, plain interior it sparkles and glows like a jewel.

It is bigger than any bed I have ever seen and is made of a dark wood, almost black. Every part of it that can be seen, even the legs, is carved. There are fruits and flowers but also the figures of men and women. I step a little closer and gasp. The figures are entwined with one another, showing acts of love in intricate detail, such that they would bring blushes to the cheeks of any woman and make the heart of any man beat faster. Covering the bed are soft blankets, some woven so finely that they seem almost transparent. These are of every colour from darkest red to palest yellow, decorated with silver discs in the manner of our people and with silken cushions to lean on. It is a bed for sweet pleasures, for whispers and moans, a bed that promises a beautiful and fertile woman's touch and nights of wild passion. Any man looking at it would want nothing more than to lie on it and to hold Zaynab in his arms.

I stand alone for a moment in the darkness before the great bed. Then the entranceway is pulled back and Zaynab enters with an older woman, who directs two slave girls to place steaming copper basins of water on the floor to one side. Zaynab turns her smile on me again.

"I know you are tired, sister, and your tent will not be ready for some time. Allow Hela to prepare you for the feast tonight. I have sent a slave to fetch your clothes. I must go and oversee the preparations for the feast, but I will return very soon." She sweeps from the tent leaving me no time to protest.

The slave girls leave. I hear Adeola's voice outside and turn towards the entrance but it seems she has been kept from me. One of Zaynab's slave girls comes back in with fresh clothes for me and a casket containing my jewellery, then disappears again.

I feel a touch on my shoulder and turn to the older woman.

She has large dark eyes, somewhat hooded. Her hair is hidden beneath a grey wrap, her clothes are also plain and dark. She has a stocky frame and her hands are square, nothing like the long elegant fingers of Zaynab. I wait for her to address me, expecting her to use some term of respect, but instead she stands very close to me and stretches out one hand, which she lays on my bare forearm. She does not move her hand, only keeps her eyes fixed on mine.

I shrug my arm away. "You are Zaynab's handmaiden?" I say, not because I care but to remind her of her place.

"My name is Hela," she says. Her voice is deeper than

most women's, her speech almost too slow, as though she is speaking from somewhere far away.

"I can look after myself," I say, unwilling to be stripped naked by this woman who I do not know. "Or my slave Adeola can be sent for."

She shakes her head. She is already unbuckling my fasteners. My clothes slip to the floor. Too tired to stop her, I simply stand and allow Hela to undress me and wash me, comb my hair and then begin to dress me again. When she has finished my jewellery feels so heavy around my arms and neck that I feel I cannot move.

I sit on the great bed, alone and silent, as though stunned by a blow.

I am too late to stop the marriage. My husband, as is his right, has taken another wife. I am no longer his only jewel, for now his time must be split between Zaynab and I equally, according to the Holy Qur'an. Tonight, on our first night together after two years, he will not come to my tent, for tonight is Zaynab's wedding night, and he must favour her. No man would do otherwise. Tonight, in a strange camp far from my home and family, I am about to attend a marriage feast for my husband and his new wife. I will sleep alone in my tent while she welcomes him to this bed. I feel drained, unable to move.

Hela offers me tea. I sip it slowly, my shoulders slumped. I feel only a great sadness, a hopelessness I do not know how to rid myself of. Hela squats low in a corner of the tent, her dark eyes fixed on me in a way I find unsettling. I look away from her but am still conscious of being observed.

I am interrupted by Zaynab, who rejoins me in the tent. I am conscious of how different we look, standing side by side. I am smaller than her, perhaps ten years younger, dressed in colourful clothes and loaded down with beautiful jewellery. By rights, I should draw the more favourable glances. But Zaynab's beauty, her imposing height and the extreme simplicity of her clothes draws the eye immediately, making me look almost foolish beside her, like a love-struck girl dressing to impress young men rather than the acknowledged wife of a great commander. I feel uncomfortable in my clothes and make a gesture as though to remove some of my jewellery, but Zaynab puts out her long slim hand to stop me.

"I have a gift for you, sister, a gift of welcome. I had it made for you when I knew that you would soon join us here."

She turns away and lifts the lid of one of her great carved chests. I catch a glimpse of many bottles, jars, measuring spoons and pestles, pouches, small decorated boxes.

She closes the lid and comes back to me. In her hands she holds a glorious *tenfuk*, a woman's pendant. It is large, hung from a string of onyx beads. The sharp triangle of metal holds within it an arrow-shaped carnelian. The pendant is a suitable gift for the birth of a daughter, or could even be given to a pregnant woman as a wish for a daughter, with its connotations of sunrise, of life and birth.

I have lost my first child and am not yet carrying another life. Tonight my husband will take another woman as his wife. It is a breathtakingly malicious gift, loaded with calculated hatred. My hands tremble as I take it from her and put it round my neck. There is no other choice available to me. I cannot refuse her gift.

Zaynab is all smiles as we leave the tent. "I rejoice that

you can share in my happiness tonight, sister," she says, as we walk towards the centre of the square and people fall back to let us past. "Yusuf will rejoice also, for I know he wanted you here with us."

I let her words wash over me. I feel helpless, swept along in the crowd towards a husband I no longer know.

My meeting with Yusuf might as well be a meeting with a stranger. He comes into the square and is greeted with cheers, many blessings and congratulations as a new husband. He is also the recipient of ribald jokes and teasing by some of his men, which he waves away good-naturedly. When he sees me he smiles and embraces me.

"My dear wife," he says. "You are welcome here."

I swallow. "Husband," I say, the word sticking in my throat. "I am glad to be by your side again."

"It must feel strange to you to join me here on my wedding day to a second wife," he says. "I am sorry I could not speak with you of it before. I hope you understand that this marriage is important for our mission's success."

I want to argue with him but I do not even know where to begin. "Yes, husband," I reply, cursing myself for my meekness. What else can I say? The marriage is already complete, all I will do is cause enmity with Zaynab.

His expression lightens. "The wedding feast is being served," he says. "You will sit by me."

He treats me with nothing but honour and kindness throughout the feast that follows. He inquires after my health, the journey I have made to reach him, my time in the garrison without him. He feeds me choice morsels from the dishes brought to him.

But his eyes stay on Zaynab.

She does nothing to draw his attention. She sits modestly by his side, accepts food from the servers and from Yusuf when he chooses to offer her food from his own dish. She keeps her eyes downcast, a soft smile on her lips and her back straight. Her calm and graceful demeanour make her the very model of a good wife. She praises Allah every time she opens her mouth, which is not often, and smiles at me as much as she smiles at her new husband. She pours his drinks before I can and sends the best dishes to me first. Yusuf speaks to me as a beloved sister, while he looks at Zaynab with a hunger in his eyes I have not seen before. I cannot escape the sinking feeling that he is already lost to me.

The feast over, there is dancing, singing, storytelling. At last it is time for the bride and groom to retire. I stand trembling and watch them go to Zaynab's tent, surrounded by people singing, offering blessings and lewd advice. I feel a soft touch on my arm and turn to see Adeola, the combination of her dark skin and clothes making her barely visible.

"I bring drink," she says in her halting way.

I wave her away. "I do not want to drink."

She shakes her head and tries again. "To sleep."

I frown. "Sleep?"

She nods earnestly and summons all of her vocabulary

to make her meaning plain. "Drink. To sleep deeply. Not to hear." She makes a small gesture towards Zaynab's tent, looming within the darkness of the emptying square.

I feel the tears fall hot and fast on my face and nod. I would give anything, drink anything, if it will make me sleep so deeply that I will not hear one single murmur from Zaynab's tent as she spends her first night with my husband, barely a stone's throw from my own tent, foolishly decorated with colourful embroidery promising good luck and happiness and children to its miserable owner. I follow Adeola slowly back into my tent, which she and Ekon have arranged as though I had never left my aunt's camp. I sit on the bed and Adeola undresses me with the care of a mother for her child. When she has finished and has pulled the blankets around me, Ekon brings in a small bowl cupped in his hands. It steams and has a pleasing scent. I do not know what is in it. I drink it without questioning, seeking oblivion.

Oblivion comes, but not before I hear the first moans from Zaynab's tent, leaving my body rigid with despair before I sink into darkness.

When I wake my jaw is so tightly clenched that I fear my teeth will shatter when I open my mouth, but it is daylight and that first terrible night is over. This camp is now my home.

The camp is like a city of tents. Aghmat may still have a few people who live there, but it lost its soul along with its riches. Those who wish to be rich and powerful in the future have seen that this new army is a force to be reckoned with and their best chance is to align themselves to it. The once bustling souks of Aghmat have grown small. More and more people come to the first souks held outside the camp, which are growing rapidly. Craftsmen begin to set up their own little tents and do their work close by the camp, for the camp holds more customers for their wares. The herds of goats and sheep kept nearby grow larger and the first few stone and mud buildings begin to be constructed, small and humble for now, but more will soon be built and they will grow larger in due course. Ramparts will be needed soon, for no important city can afford to be without them and the garrison-camp of Murakush will soon be an important city. It will form the base for the army when they move further north to such cities as Fes, part of Yusuf's plans for the future.

I see little of him. He is busy with his plans for the army. Men must be trained, horses purchased as their steeds. New weapons must be forged, plans drawn up. Negotiations must be made with important men, tribal leaders sought out to create the alliances that will support the army when the time comes to move north. He is a figure that I see only at a distance. At first I wait eagerly for Yusuf to come to me. I have resigned myself to my situation. Our religion allows Yusuf to have more than one wife, however much that pains me. That same religion states that he must treat Zaynab and myself as equals, giving us the same privileges and care. I think that at least I am here at last, in what will one day become a bustling city. If I can speak with Yusuf, spend time with him, remind him of our plans together

I may be given a role to play. Perhaps I can manage the traders who wish to set up permanent stalls here. Once I try to speak with him.

"The army must need many provisions," I say. "I could manage the traders who supply you with the traveling food, the weapons…"

Yusuf pats my arm. "Zaynab manages all such things," he says, still walking towards his destination.

I follow him. "I want to be useful to you," I persist.

He pauses for a moment and gives me a quick embrace, such as one might give to a beloved but nagging child. "I must go to the council," he tells me. "You have everything you need?"

"Yes," I say, "But I…"

"Good," he says and is gone.

I stand still, watching him stride away, angry with myself for not telling him that I am unhappy, that I am bored, for not reminding him of our plans, the way we used to talk together. But what is there to say? Zaynab all but rules Murakech, she is its queen. Everything that is done here is done under her command and her voice is respected in council.

Days pass when I do not see Yusuf at all, then I will see his dark robes pass in the distance, always surrounded by other men, always earnestly discussing something. Sometimes I see him at prayers, but he is too far away to speak with before or afterwards. Often he prays alone or only with his men. I am a married woman without a husband. I am treated with courtesy but mostly left alone. Aside from

Adeola and Ekon I know no-one except Zaynab, and I avoid her as much as I can. She is too busy overseeing the camp, for nothing escapes her hawk-like eyes. She chooses where the craftsmen may ply their trade, what food will be prepared, where the herdsmen may take their animals. There is nothing she does not know.

I wonder how Amalu fares but I can hardly go visiting him alone, it would not be right for a married woman to do so.

At first I believe that Yusuf is so busy that he has time for neither of his wives. When night after night he does not come to me, I believe that he does not go to Zaynab either. Every night Adeola cooks good food. I sleep deeply and dreamlessly and hope that he may come the next day, or the day after.

One night, though, I have no appetite, for I have idly eaten too many dates while I sit at my loom. When Adeola serves my food, I only pick at it. She looks worried but I reassure her that I am well, although this does not seem to give her much comfort.

Later on I understand why. It takes me a long time to sleep that night, far longer than it usually does. As I lie in my tent I hear the sound I least wish to hear, soft moans coming from Zaynab's tent. Disbelieving, I creep out.

The camp is quiet and dark, for it is very late. I come closer to the large dark tent and hear, unmistakably, the sounds of lovemaking and Yusuf's own voice as he groans with pleasure. My legs shake and my breath seems to be stopped in my throat as I hear him cry out and then speak Zaynab's name softly and her golden laughter answer him. I return to my tent in a daze and find within it Adeola, her head bowed, a cup of the steaming drink from my first night in the camp in her hand. I looked at her and then comprehend her earlier concern.

"The food you make for me each night…" I begin, feeling my way towards the truth, which I do not want to touch.

Adeola shrinks back a little. "To sleep," she says, looking at me in fear. "Not to hear."

I nod wearily. "Every night?"

She lowers her eyes, as though even to look at me is to add to my suffering. "Yes," she says softly.

I take the drink from her and drink it in large greedy gulps. It burns my tongue and throat but I do not stop until it is all gone. I let it fall to the floor with a clang and wave her away. She bends to pick it up and then leaves me alone to the coming gentle darkness.

After that I know the truth. I do not torment myself with it. I eat all the food that Adeola brings me each night, taking large portions so that whatever herbs she is using to make me sleep will be sure to take effect. I eat well and sleep well. My eyes grow bright, my skin grows polished, my curves grow more rounded and the men of the camp watch me pass with more interest. Adeola watches me and says nothing, but one day she comes to me when the sun is high and without speaking begins to undress me, then bathes me and perfumes my skin. She pulls out my finest clothes and dresses me, adorning me with all my jewellery, taking especial care to leave aside Zaynab's *tenfuk* pendant and to ensure all of the jewellery Yusuf has given me can be seen.

"What are you doing, Adeola?" I ask her.

She smiles and shakes her head.

I let her have her way, for the days are long and often dull and my mind needs distraction from its old paths worn bare with my pacing.

By the time she has brushed my hair and hennaed my hands and feet it is growing dusk. She leaves me sitting there in all my splendour, laughing at myself for allowing a slave to treat me as though I am her plaything. Outside I can hear her putting the final touches to the cooking she started this morning. I smell the good smells and lie back on the cushions of my bed, trying to enjoy the simple joys of being cared for by such a devoted slave. Briefly I think of the old garrison camp and regret leaving it. There I was a married woman, respected in my own right and cared for. Here I feel like a child's forgotten toy, discarded for sweetmeats.

"I hope I do not disturb you, wife?"

I sit up, shocked. In the doorway is Yusuf. I have not seen him close to for so long that I stare at him as though he is a stranger.

He smiles. "May I enter?"

I spring to my feet and throw my arms around him, pulling him into the tent. He chuckles, a deep rumble in his chest, making me weak with relief that at last I have him to myself.

Adeola comes and pours water over our hands before bringing in heaping platters of good food; well made but not too elegantly prepared, for everyone knows that Yusuf prefers his food to be simple.

Yusuf smiles at her. "Your slaves are very devoted to you," he says as he takes his first mouthfuls of food. "Your other slave... Aykron?"

"Ekon," I say.

"Ekon, yes. He came to me today and said you had asked that I join you tonight to eat. I told him I was busy, but he was very insistent. He said that you would be very unhappy if I did not come to you." He laughs, taking more food. "So here I am."

I doubt it was so easy. I know that Ekon must have planned his moment and his words carefully, perhaps for many days, for he is a mere slave and cannot insist that Yusuf bin Tashfin, general of a great army, should come to me simply because he, Ekon, has asked him to. I keep my eyes lowered for a moment so that Yusuf will not see the tears welling up as I think of Ekon and Adeola's faithful attempts to make me happy again.

I say nothing. I have a night alone with Yusuf, and I hope that in spending time together he may remember our previous happiness and plans for the future and that over time I may take back at least my own share of my husband. I try to tell myself that he spent much time alone, and that he then spent time with Zaynab for many months, longer than he had even known me, in fact. Perhaps it is to be expected that she comes foremost to his mind rather than a wife whom he has not seen for so long, who has not shared these important past months with him. Tonight I will try to be a loving wife, and we will rediscover the tenderness and partnership between us and then the future will not be so hard for me, for I will do my best to accept Zaynab, even as she must accept me as Yusuf's first wife.

As we eat I speak at first of daily things, the grazing of the many herds of goats and sheep that keep the camp supplied, the training of the horses that takes place every day on the plain, the storytellers, the craftsmen, the souks. I seek to make him feel at ease, to enjoy the meal and our time together, to make him laugh.

I succeed, and after the meal, when Adeola has brought water to wash our hands, we lie propped on cushions on my bed, our faces closer together and talk a little of our time apart and of the time we had spent together when we had been first married, which makes him smile.

"Your face when your father told you I wished to marry you," he chuckles. "I thought you would fall off your camel."

"What kind of man proposes marriage after one camel ride together?" I retort.

"Ah, but you had already joined my men and ridden a great distance with us, you had proven yourself," he says.

I am happy to talk of the time when we first met. I do not press him to talk of the time since then, of the battles, the fear, the killing. Nor do we talk of the future, of the battles yet to come, the difficulties of leading such a large army. Abu Bakr's absence weighs heavily on him, for they have worked well together and been of comfort and support to one another. He talks of these things every day, carries them in his heart and in his prayers. I want him to leave all of that outside my tent and to have only kindness and good memories with me. A place to rest his body, but also his heart and mind.

We have lain together for a while when at last Yusuf takes me into his arms and begins to stroke and undress me.

His movements are unhurried and gentle, as I remember from the past, and I close my eyes, my own hands reaching out to him.

We are interrupted. A sweet voice calls from outside. In a moment Zaynab stands in the doorway of my tent, Adeola visible behind, attempting to stop her from entering. Zaynab ignores her. In her hands she has a red wooden cup, which she holds out towards us. I shrink back, pulling my clothes around me.

Yusuf frowns. "What are you doing here, Zaynab?"

Zaynab's smile falters. "I brought this for you both to share. It is a recipe taught me by my mother," she lowers her long lashes almost coyly, "for loving nights. I wanted to offer my sister a gesture of my love for her." She looks up again towards me, her face gentle, hopeful. "I know it is not easy to welcome a new sister as a wife to your own husband, but you have been so gracious, so kind to me." She gestures uncomfortably. "But I am interrupting, I am so sorry. It was not my intention." She holds the cup out awkwardly, almost pleadingly.

I glance at Yusuf. He has lost his frown and is smiling, pleased, no doubt, that his wives are getting on so well, without much of the trouble that can often happen for a man caught between jealous wives.

I have no choice. I hold out my hands for the cup, my clothes slipping as I do so. Zaynab modestly lowers her eyes so as not to see my nakedness, places the cup in my hands and bows her head to both of us as she backs out of the tent. "May Allah bless your bed," she says softly as she goes.

I sit back on the bed trying not to spill the cup, which is full to the very brim with a perfumed drink. It smells of rose petals and honey, with other spices and herbs, which I cannot readily identify. I look at it doubtfully, unsure that I want to drink any peace offering from Zaynab. I do not fully trust her. I take a very small sip, barely wetting my lips, and look at Yusuf.

He smiles and takes the cup from me, then drains it in a few easy gulps. "It is a good drink," he says. "Zaynab often makes it for me. She will not tell me what it contains, for she says it is her handmaid's secret."

I make an effort to smile and draw Yusuf back onto the cushions, for I am not about to spoil our night together turning over Zaynab's strange actions in my mind. She has done nothing but bring a drink to her husband and speak peaceably to me. I lay my hand upon Yusuf and feel him stir in response.

In the morning he is gone, and I lie alone in the cold air of early dawn. The call to prayer goes out but I lie still, unmoving or heeding. My God has shown me no mercy, I cannot shape my mouth to praise His name.

I am bruised inside and out. There are shadows on every part of me, growing darker as the day grows lighter. My thighs ache and my innermost parts are torn and bleeding. Strands of my hair lie on the bed and my scalp hurts where they have been pulled out in a frenzy. My bed is in disarray and I lie half uncovered, too shaken to warm myself, too hurt to move, too ashamed to call for Adeola.

She comes without my calling, her small dark hands reaching out to my body before drawing back in fear. She stands still for a moment and when she sees me look away and slow tears begin to trickle down my face she calls out to Ekon in her own tongue, commanding him to do many things. I can hear him outside, bringing water, lighting the fire and making it blaze to heat the water, a pause and then his return from milking, the milk being heated with honey and herbs all to her instructions. Occasionally he calls out a question and she answers, supplying him with further instructions or his large hand will appear through the flaps holding something she has asked for and she will take it swiftly and ask him for other things and the flaps close again, his hand disappearing at her behest.

I lie still while she strips the bed and brings warm water, washes me and bandages me where she can. I wince as she rubs soothing salves on my bruises and scratches. I groan when she makes me get up and stand for a moment so that she can make up my bed with clean sheets and soft blankets. She moves quickly, and I sink back onto my bed and feel her strong arms lift my head and shoulders and place me back down gently onto the cushions, which cradle me. All the while, when she is not calling to Ekon, she sings to me, little snatches of half-finished songs made for children. Her gentle soothing kindness makes my tears fall faster. She wipes them away and then brings the warm milk, sweetened with honey and spices, soft breads and little pieces of tender meat. I do not want to eat, but she treats me like a child and like a child I obey and eat some mouthfuls until she is satisfied. After that she brings the drink that makes me sleep, and I grasp the cup with both hands and drink eagerly, for I want to fall into darkness and escape those hours of the night that I have just endured.

After that night I no longer pray for Yusuf to join me. My bruises slowly fade and I am still afraid. The gentleness I had known from our early days of marriage was there at first, but something in the drink Zaynab brought changed him. His desire was insatiable, a raging fire within him that sought ever more extreme ways of being quenched. My body was sorely tested by that one night, I do not think I can bear such treatment again. Now I know why he visits Zaynab's tent and never comes to mine. Every night he is given that drink and spends the hours of darkness with her. He is a strong man, or his body could not bear the strain and so Zaynab binds him to her, for she seems to have the strength to hold his fire in her hands and quench it. Whether she is burnt by it herself I do not know or care. She has stolen my husband, taken his tenderness and kindness and turned a gentle beast into a roaring lion that can be tamed only by those foolish enough to risk their lives. I am too cowardly to risk mine, or my child's. That one night has brought life in my belly but another night like it might well take it away again. So I turn inwards, stay out of sight, and Yusuf goes to Zaynab while life grows inside me. I know that when I tell him he will be gentle with me, but I also know that if he is offered that drink again within my own tent I must find some way to avoid him drinking it.

Time passes and yet I do not share my secret, for I want my baby to be strong within me before Zaynab knows of it, for I know she will be angry. If I give Yusuf a child when she has not yet done so I will be favoured and I can see that Zaynab is not a woman who will accept such a state of affairs.

But Zaynab's eyes are everywhere. She sees everything, she hears everything. She sees the day when I emerge from my tent in the morning and sway before Adeola grasps my elbow and takes me back inside. She hears when I retch. It takes only those two signs and Zaynab comes to see me.

"Sister!" she cries, entering my tent unasked and unwelcomed. "I have barely seen you these past weeks. You are not unwell? The camp life here is very harsh for a woman of refinement."

I want to laugh. I, refined? I lived as a boy for sixteen years, traded all over the country, have always lived in a tent. It is she who has lived her life before here as a queen of a rich merchant city, being pampered and perfumed, with many slaves and servants to do her bidding. I say nothing, but Zaynab knows what she is about.

"I have decided to give you my own handmaiden Hela and take away those two you have, for evidently they are not taking good enough care of you," she goes on happily. "My own servants are well trained and will make your life here so much more comfortable."

I sit up. "I would prefer to keep my own," I say, barely remembering to be polite in how I address her. "They are very loyal and they have taken the greatest care of me."

Zaynab waves her hand dismissively. "They are quite young," she says. "Slaves improve with good training and I have trained many slaves. I have already brought you Hela and two slaves whom she will command. I have sent yours to my tent. I do this for your benefit, sister," she adds kindly, taking my hands in hers.

I am trapped. Zaynab has completed the change without even allowing me to say goodbye to Adeola and Ekon, whose loyalty and kindness to me will now be rewarded with Zaynab's no doubt harsh training. I begin to weep, for I cannot see how my situation will ever improve. It seems to me that I am at this woman's mercy, alone and friendless.

Zaynab is not at all distressed by my tears. She sits and holds my hands gently and then calls for Hela.

She enters bringing a hot broth with small pieces of good lamb in it. She hands this to Zaynab, who holds it to my lips in a kindly manner. I taste it and it is good, if a little strong with parsley. I can taste nothing in it that might do me harm, so I drink it and eat the pieces of lamb under Zaynab's watchful gaze, then sit alone as she departs, all my fighting spirit gone.

She leaves me with Hela and two additional slaves. One is a scrawny girl whom I soon discover is mute. The other is a male slave, who has a permanent cough. He is strong enough but lazy and insolent. All three of them watch me whenever they are near, and I have no doubt that they are spying on me for Zaynab.

Hela cooks all my meals. Her food is good but always heavy with parsley. Despite my reprimands, she continues to add that herb to everything I eat in copious quantities.

I dislike Hela. Her face seems to have no expression to it, she watches me with her large dark eyes in a way I find disconcerting.

"What are you thinking?" I ask her one day, when she has stared at me too long, even for her.

"Whether you are happy," she says.

"I would have thought everyone knows I am not," I say, not bothering to lie.

"You could divorce Yusuf," she says, as though suggesting I might take a stroll around the camp.

"Divorce him?" I repeat in horror.

"You will never be happy here," she says.

"How dare you speak to me like that?" I ask her. "You are only a handmaiden."

She says nothing but she does not drop her gaze, nor apologise.

I try to go about my work and ignore her but at last I turn back to her. If this is a time for honesty then I will have honesty. "Why would you suggest I divorce my husband?" I ask.

"Some women can live with another wife," she says. "Zaynab cannot."

"Why?" I ask.

She shakes her head. "Too long a story," she says.

"Tell me it," I challenge her, but she only shakes her head again.

"It would not help you," she says. "You would be better off divorced."

"I have no intention of divorcing Yusuf," I tell her, but I am shaking.

I wake in pain. At first, half asleep, I think I have a belly-ache, but then a horrible fear steals through me. I put a hand on my belly and feel a cramp run through it, just as wetness trickles over my thighs and I know without doubt that if there had been a child in my womb, there is a child no longer.

I lie still, not through any vain hope that I might save my baby by so doing, but out of a great numbness.

This is the second child I have lost. Perhaps I am barren. Perhaps I have not been granted my mother's fertile womb. Without a child I can never again hope for Yusuf's tenderness, for Zaynab will always be on hand to make him take that drink to unleash his drugged lust on me. No doubt, no matter how rough he is, eventually Zaynab will have a child in her womb. Then I will be a barren and unloved wife, useless and fit only to be set aside.

I lie still until dawn, as the cramps eat at my belly and the blood flows down my thighs. When I do not come out, Hela comes in and when she sees what is wrong she brings washing water and clean blankets and clothes. I let her wash and dress me, give me rags to staunch the flow, remake the bed. Then I lie down and ask for food, for I feel weak.

She brings me a good stew of lamb with apricots. For once there is no parsley in it. I say as much.

She frowns and turns away. "No need for that now," she says.

I turn her words over in my mind as I doze through much of that day, feeling the blood that should have been a child trickling out of me. When the cool of evening comes I leave my tent and walk through the camp, my plain robes and covered head shielding me from passers-by. I head to the outskirts of the camp, where there is a stall, which I have seen before, selling fresh herbs. It belongs to a Christian slave woman who grows many herbs in a small field near the camp, working the soil alone and carrying water to the plants each day. Everyone in the camp uses her mint for tea and her other fresh herbs for cooking. They say she knows all the properties of plants and that many can be used for healing as well as food.

She is of normal height, but stands a little twisted and limps when she walks. She is older than Zaynab, I suppose, although it is hard to tell. Her face is scarred. Her skin is fair compared to mine, but her thick dark hair and deep brown eyes make her seem one of us, although I have heard that she comes from Al-Andalus, the land north of our own across the sea. Her hair is tucked back oddly in a white cloth, not wrapped high up like our own, but perhaps that is how it is worn in her country. She speaks our tongue well enough, but with an accent.

I ask her for parsley. She takes up a large bunch.

I shake my head. "More."

She adds another bunch and then another before I nod.

A shadow falls over her face and she indicates the huge bunch I am now holding, ignoring my hand outstretched with payment. Her voice is clear although her accent is heavy. "Do not eat too much."

I raise my eyebrows as my heart begins to thud. "Why not?" I ask, waiting for her to say what I know already, what I knew as soon as Hela spoke and yet what I cannot bear to believe until I am told it to my face.

"Parsley can take away life from within the womb," she says simply.

I leave her standing at her stall, watching me as I walk away, the vivid green leaves fallen from my hand to be trampled into the dust by passers-by.

Tiraout — festive pectoral necklace

*N*ow I know that I cannot trust Zaynab. I was wary of her before and jealous too, but now I understand that she will stop at nothing to ensure that my status with Yusuf will be lower than hers. I have heard it whispered that she was a concubine to a minor vassal before she became queen of Aghmat. She showed no remorse when her husband the king died, only sought to become Abu Bakr's wife as quickly as possible. When her status might have been in question as Abu Bakr left the camp to go south, she somehow obtained a divorce and married Yusuf, perhaps thinking that his life was in less danger than Abu Bakr's, who would be in direct combat while Yusuf trained the troops and made plans for the future. This is a woman who is more ambitious than most men. And she is fulfilling her ambitions in the only way open to her: through marriage.

I do not care about Zaynab's ambitions. I am not interested in marrying higher and higher.

But I want a child. I want the child that was taken from me by a quick blow of a camel's leg. I want the child that I lost through eating what I thought was an innocent flavoursome herb but which was turned into an evil brew by a crone who works for an ambitious sorceress. Just as Zaynab will stop at nothing to hold her status as the wife of more and more important men, so I grow stubborn. I will do whatever it takes to feel life stir within me again. When I have a child I will live quietly. Zaynab can have Yusuf every night. She can sit by his side in council. She can follow her own dreams and leave me alone with my baby. My child will be a symbol of the vision we shared: of what the Maghreb could be one day, when the blood has been shed and the battles are over. A son for Yusuf will be the beginning of a peaceful era. When he sees his son he will be reminded of how we were together and our plans for the future.

I brace myself. I buy healing salves and drink herbal teas to encourage life within me. I buy them from the herb seller and when she sees what I ask for she adds other herbs.

"For a child," she says and I nod without replying. The kindness in her eyes threatens to undo me and I must be strong.

I order fine foods to be made and eat heartily. I buy new clothes and polish my jewellery. I obtain a sweet perfume and use it on the intimate parts of my body. I wash with fine rose-scented soaps and sit and brush my hair until it gleams. Then I send for Yusuf.

He comes to me and I am kind. When Zaynab inevitably sends her drink for him, I let him drink it with a smile and then lie back and let him have his way with my body, although it hurts me and I long for his old gentleness. The next day I use the salves. I make sure to eat well, drink and eat my fertile herbs. I pray.

Again and again, whenever my body is strong enough, I send for Yusuf. Sometimes I manage to avoid him taking the drink, or manage to spill a part of it. Then he is gentler and I know some pleasure. But drink or no drink, bruises or no bruises, I call him back to me. I want one thing from Yusuf, and then I will be satisfied and trouble Zaynab no more.

He still spends more nights with her, but I do not care about that. I need time for my bruises to fade between our nights, to eat and regain my strength.

I summon up my courage and dismiss Hela. "You may leave me," I tell her. "I will not have a witch like you serve me."

She looks at me for a long moment. "You should keep me by your side," she says. "I know that you hate me but I did not use magic on you, I took life when it was still early. There are worse ways to lose a child."

"Are you threatening me?" I ask her, feeling my legs tremble although I try to sound strong.

She shakes her head. "I stood between the two of you," she says. "You should be grateful Zaynab did not have her way."

"I don't believe you," I say. "I believe you are a witch who works for a serpent."

She does not answer, only gathers together a small bag of her possessions and commands the two slaves to leave.

"Why do you work for her, Hela?" I ask. "What possible hold does she have over you that you would take a child's life to make her happy?"

She pauses in the doorway, without looking back. "You would not understand," she says, her face hidden.

I send word to Zaynab that I demand the return of Adeola and Ekon and they come back to me that very day. I embrace Adeola tightly and Ekon kisses my hand, holding my fingers in his large palm, all of us relieved at being back together.

I stand a little taller now, dress with care and wear my fine jewellery when I leave my tent. I go about my days with light feet and a smile on my lips. I sing when I weave or when I embroider cloth, laying out the symbols and shapes my Aunt Tizemt taught me, although my time with her seems so very long ago.

Sometimes I walk through the camp and sit where I can see the herb seller. I see her answer the anxious questions of those who are unwell and her calm responses, her instructions of how to prepare a herbal tea or tincture, how many days they must eat or drink a herb to cure their ills. She is precise, her voice quiet but firm. Sometimes her eyes will flicker towards me and she will meet my gaze for a moment. I do not know what she thinks when she sees me watching her. She cannot know that I find comfort in her presence even if I do not speak with her. I think of Hela, using herbs against me rather than to cure those who have need of healing and I vow she will not come near me again. Whatever her reasons, she has chosen to serve a woman who does not baulk at demanding the life of an unborn child and neither of them is to be trusted. The sight of the herb seller reminds me that not all those with power or skills are evil, she makes me feel protected.

Zaynab leaves me alone for a time, perhaps lulled into a feeling of safety by the fact that Yusuf still goes more often to her tent than he comes to mine. Besides this, she is widely acknowledged as his right hand. Her days are spent in council with Yusuf and his leaders, for she is a clever woman and has contacts in many of the important cities to the north, which are important to Yusuf's plans for the future. I wish a little that I could be a part of those meetings, for Yusuf to see me as an important strategist too, but I have to admit that although I traded for years, I do not have the knowledge of the noble families that Zaynab can offer. She has been queen of Aghmat, and can advise on the loyalties, strengths and weaknesses of many high-ranking tribal leaders across the land.

When she emerges from these meetings she is drained. I see it in her beautiful face when I catch a glimpse of her as she passes, but she hides it well, retiring to her tent for a few hours and then emerging fresh and calm, despite the stream of visitors she has received during that time.

She is visited constantly by people wanting orders. Zaynab holds court from inside her great dark tent. It is she who specifies how many and which men should stand guard, where new tents should be erected, what foods are to be prepared when there are big feasts. She directs all the daily life of the camp. There are those who do grumble, although quietly, that lady Zaynab has too much power in the camp. But Yusuf does not deny her power nor does he ever countermand her orders. In truth, he has no interest in such day-to-day arrangements, and is probably glad that Zaynab has taken such work off his shoulders. He is too busy training his men and planning for the future. Sometimes important leaders of tribes visit him, and then his council will sit long into the night.

Meanwhile I carry out my plan, and one morning when I open the tent flaps I take a deep breath of the good stew Adeola is making and nearly vomit up all of the milk porridge I have just eaten. Hastily I retreat into my tent and drink water, then lie on my bed and loudly berate Adeola for having made bad food the night before, which has made me feel ill, all the while making a face at her which she understands. I get up as soon as I can and walk about the camp until I feel better.

From then on I cherish my secret and am careful to protect it from the camp. I feel better this time, for after a few days I do not feel so sick when I smell food, only deeply desire fresh milk, which I drink in large quantities, refusing much other food under the pretext that it is too hot to eat much. I see Hela watching me from Zaynab's tent, but there is little she can report, for I keep my distance from her and so I escape her notice for a long time. But not long enough for my liking.

Zaynab sends a message to ask me to dine with herself and Yusuf in her tent. This is an unusual request and one that makes me suspicious. However, I dress well, order Adeola to prepare fine cakes as a gift for Zaynab, and arrive as the sky grows dusky. Flaming torches light up her tent, with smoking lamps inside. A space has been made for a sumptuous meal, where Zaynab is waiting. Yusuf joins us and Hela pours water for us to wash our hands. As we eat we exchange meaningless pleasantries. The food is good and plentiful. There is a silence after we have washed our hands again. It is broken by Zaynab, who reaches out and touched Yusuf's hand. He looks up at her and she smiles. It is the smile of a virtuous and beloved wife. I brace myself for whatever is to come.

"Dearest husband," begins Zaynab. "I have been blessed." I feel a lead weight sink in my belly. Zaynab turns her eyes slightly towards me and a smile curves her beautiful lips. Yusuf only raises his eyebrows and smiles, waiting for her to finish.

"I am with child," she says. "Allah has answered my prayers. Blessed is His kindness to this unworthy woman."

I shake my head as Yusuf embraces Zaynab, and then smile widely for his benefit and embrace Zaynab myself. I can contain my secret no longer, so desperate am I to strike back at her.

"You are twice blessed, husband," I say brightly, and feel Zaynab's hate flow towards me as she hears my next words. "I am also with child, blessed is Allah."

Yusuf, of course, is delighted, and once again we all embrace. As Zaynab leans towards me, her glorious smile struggling to stay on her face, I whisper in her small perfect ear.

"My son will be born before yours."

Then I lean back and smile warmly at her. Shortly after this I make my excuses and leave them alone.

I wait for Zaynab's retaliation. I keep a dagger by my side, for the threat I now pose to her is so great that I think she may well abandon all her subtlety and simply attack me herself, or worse, send an assassin to do away with me. The nights seem very dark and cold to me; any small noises make me wake with a start and then lie awake for many hours until my eyes close without my knowledge or consent.

I wait. And wait. Then I hear the rumours flying around the camp. Abu Bakr is on his way back from the south. He will arrive in a few days. I can sleep again. Zaynab has a far greater threat coming towards her than I, and I know she will have to work harder than she has ever done before to preserve her own status. Although Abu Bakr has been away a long time, and although he gave Zaynab in marriage to Yusuf and left him in charge of the army and the new garrison city of Murakush, he is still Commander of the Almoravids. It is his name that appears on the gold dirham coins that are cast, not Yusuf's. Yusuf might seem to have greater power at his command, but he is Abu Bakr's subordinate. He is also tied to Abu Bakr by blood, being his younger cousin.

If Abu Bakr is truly returning, there are only two options. Yusuf can either accept him back as commander and obey his orders, thus reducing his own status, or he can challenge Abu Bakr for leadership.

The camp is in turmoil. All the men have sworn loyalty to Abu Bakr. But they love Yusuf. He is their general. He is their true leader, the man who prays, fasts, eats and trains beside them. He is the man they look to in battle. The men mutter in corners, for and against. They do not want to see Yusuf lose leadership, but to challenge Abu Bakr could well be disastrous, perhaps leading to splitting into factions, the unnecessary loss of much-needed men, the possibility of their mission failing when it has only just begun. For Zaynab, there is danger too. If Yusuf is demoted, she will lose her status, something I cannot imagine her accepting. But if Yusuf makes a bid for leadership of the Almoravids and fails, Abu Bakr might have Yusuf killed for daring to challenge him, making Zaynab a widow once more and vulnerable. She is Yusuf's right hand, she may well be considered to have been behind this challenge and might even face death herself.

I risk making myself visible to Zaynab, knowing she has more pressing concerns than her jealousy for me. I wander the camp, listening to all sides. There are rumours of ambushes, of formal challenges. There are those who shrug their shoulders and say that Yusuf will have to swallow his pride and accept that he will no longer be the leader of the troops, that he will be a general again, not a commander.

But although I listen to the people of the camp, be they high or low, I watch only Zaynab. I have learnt by now through my own experience and rumours that she is the mistress of such situations, that she can and will bend any situation to her own advantage. If Zaynab looks happy, things are going well for her, no matter how the wind blows or who may fall to make way for her.

She looks terrible.

Her skin is pale and her immaculately plain dark robes grow dusty and stained by sweat under the arms, despite the weather beginning to cool as summer ends. Her thick glossy hair has grown dull and wispy. She grows thinner than before, so that her hands are bony and her face is gaunt. Her eyes are as bright as ever, but they are disturbing to look at, shining like the last embers in a dying fire, a fevered patient about to leave this world. If she had a mother alive, that mother would make her rest, would feed her good foods and soothing drinks, and would bath and care for her, protecting the tiny life within her. I myself rest and eat well and am careful not to over-exert myself, but I see that Zaynab does none of this. The whole camp hears her retching in the mornings, sees her paleness and weakness when she walks, but no-one can stop her.

She sits in council every day, can be seen in Yusuf's company at all hours of the day and night, their dark heads close together, their voices low. Slaves bring food and take it away again barely touched. Yusuf eats as simply as ever and Zaynab cannot stomach anything but a little unleavened bread. The smell of yeast has her on her feet and running to vomit again and again. Perhaps I should feel sorry for her, but like the rest of the camp I mostly feel curiosity. How can she keep going like this? And what will happen when our Commander, Abu Bakr bin 'Umar returns?

We wait.

Despite all the guards it is of course the children, with their keen eyesight and their games on the plain outside the camp, who spot them first. They come running with news that a sizeable number of men are making their way towards the camp. That they are Abu Bakr's men is quickly ascertained, but as they draw ever closer it becomes clearer that Abu Bakr is not among them.

Many of us, especially the women and children, have spent the morning on the outskirts of the camp, leaning on the low mud walls that are slowly growing in and around the camp or sitting on the dusty ground watching their steady progress towards us. We have not been watching Yusuf and Zaynab, nor seen their preparations. As the men draw closer all of us begin to look amongst the crowds to see where they are. Yusuf will surely have to come forward to greet the men and inquire after the Commander, his cousin? And Zaynab should be at his side. But they are nowhere to be seen. A good smell of roasting meats begins to fill the air and I, along with most of the crowd, follow our noses back to the main square, then catch our breath as we see the scene before us.

The square has been cleared, fires have been built and slaves are bustling back and forth, cooking great quantities of food. On a hastily-built raised platform covered with fine rugs sits Yusuf, with Zaynab by his side. Although plainly dressed as ever, both wear clean fresh clothes, and Zaynab suddenly looks as though she has drunk some magic elixir of youth. Her cheeks are tinged with pink, her lips are full and red, her hair glistens as though it is made of precious metals. They sit in comfort, surrounded by coloured cushions, the very picture of a king and queen even though the camp is not a fine city. They look powerful, healthy, at ease. They look like rulers.

Behind the platform stand many of Yusuf's warriors.

They are fully dressed for battle, and make an imposing spectacle, like a king's royal guard. Many are the black warriors from the south, whom Yusuf favours for his own protection. Very tall and dark, their faces gleam in the sun. All the men chosen have fearsome battle scars and their bodies are hardened. No-one entering this square could think that reclaiming leadership would be easy, nor think lightly about challenging Yusuf for the command of these men who stand by his side.

We stand, amazed, then scatter amongst the crowd as Abu Bakr's men enter the square behind us.

These men have fought side by side with Yusuf before following Abu Bakr to the south, and it is clear from their faces that they are taken aback by what has happened since they left. When they left Murakush it was a glorified version of their own garrison in the desert – tents of all shapes and sizes, none very fine, scattered here and there. Food was scarce and simple. It was a training camp, not a fledgling city.

It has changed. The tents are larger, better made, laid out in a more pleasing formation, with more space between them to pass by. There are the beginnings of real buildings; small mud-brick walls being worked on here and there, a few small edifices already completed. The square is larger. There are regular markets, craftsmen ply their trade. There are more women and children, older and younger men. It is no longer a training camp. It is a new city and it is growing rapidly.

It is clear that Yusuf has recruited many new men and that they obey him as their commander. The powerbase has shifted. There are many more fighting men in evidence; not only the new black warriors, but also other men of our own lands, from important tribes beginning to align themselves to this new rule.

This larger army and new city has rulers. Yusuf is clearly the commander here, no matter where Abu Bakr might be at this moment. Sat in a position of influence by his side, Zaynab is an imposing consort; a powerful and beautiful woman. The men will remember the prophecy that Zaynab would marry the man who would rule all of the land, and as they look at Yusuf sitting above them they cannot help but wonder if he is indeed that man. The reins of power are held in different hands from those they had thought, the wind changing the shape of the dunes before their very eyes.

There is a long pause, a silence while everyone waits for the first move to be made. Yusuf waits long enough to make everyone uncomfortable, then rises to his feet. At his side, Zaynab rises also, her dark silken robes fluttering in the breeze. Together they come to the front of the platform, where Yusuf holds out his hands to the men.

"In the name of Allah, I welcome you back to Murakush, my brave and noble warriors." His voice is calm and hospitable, his use of a possessive word to refer to the men smoothly uttered. "Come eat with us, my brothers, for you must be tired and hungry." He claps his hands and the slaves spring into action, fetching jugs of scented water to wash the hands of the guests.

The officers ascend the platform where they are warmly embraced by Yusuf while Zaynab turns her dazzling smile on them. The common soldiers gather near to the platform. Water is poured, then generous amounts of food are served to all. I am helped up to the platform, to take my place near Yusuf. The food is richer than the men have been used to, fighting rebel tribes in the desert and scrubland of the hot south, and they fall upon it, enjoying the rest and comfort so long denied them. The rest of us eat less hungrily, still amazed at the spectacle Yusuf and Zaynab have created and wondering at what will happen next.

The feast over, Yusuf entertains the officers in Zaynab's tent, which I avoid. I am uneasy about what exactly Zaynab's plans are, for I detect her hand in all of this, her smiling face hiding some secret plan. I see the men emerge later on, each one carrying noble gifts that Yusuf has showered on them. Even the common men are given golden coins. I wonder whether these gifts can so easily sway the men's loyalty, but they are a small part of the greater impact that the homecoming is having on them. These men have been away from loved ones, fighting and living hard. Now they return to a place of nobility and riches, of bountifulness and kind words. They are dazed, impressed, keen to be part of all that they had seen.

It becomes clear that Abu Bakr has sent these men on as a reconnaissance so that he may know how the land lies. He himself, with a smaller number of men, is now based in Aghmat, which when he left had still been of some importance. Anyone can now see that it is as nothing compared to the authority of Murakush. He will have seen for himself how things have changed since he has been away.

Not all of his men ride back to him. Only a handful of those who were sent out return to him and these are messengers. They are charged with telling him to meet with

Yusuf on an appointed date, at a place between Aghmat and Murakush.

They ride out at dawn. Yusuf rides ahead, Zaynab at his side. Behind them follow a party of people of importance. I have been granted a place in this group, not by Yusuf's side. The black warriors come immediately behind the officers and tribal leaders, now Yusuf's vassals and partners. Then come all of his men, in their full battle dress.

The place chosen for the meeting is an open plain, a good place to spot any troops approaching, but with nowhere to hide. A small shelter has been set up to shield the negotiators from the heat of the day, and as we approach we see that Abu Bakr has already arrived and set up a very small camp with his remaining men. He sits under a shelter, a little older and grayer but still the stocky kindly-looking man that I remember. His eyes take in the sight before him as we slowly come to a halt.

There are not just hundreds, but several thousand men gathered behind Yusuf, in tight fighting formations. A personal guard has formed around Yusuf and Zaynab, made up entirely of the black warriors, their height adding to their imposing battlewear.

On either side of Yusuf and slightly forward are guards who carry great chests. These guards stop as we all draw to a halt, then gently put down their precious burden and step back, lifting the lids as they do so, displaying a fantastic array of gifts. There are jewels, rolls of fine cloths, skins, gold, weapons, rich robes, fruits and much more, heaped up in glittering mounds.

There is a long silence. Yusuf should of course dismount and greet Abu Bakr, as Commander, his own cousin, his brother in arms. It is offensive not to do so, but still he waits. Yusuf on a magnificent stallion with his queen by his side, Abu Bakr sitting on the ground on a plain rug beneath a simple shelter. It is a great show of strength and power, riches and importance, a challenge without a challenge needing to be spoken out loud.

Abu Bakr is not a stupid man. He knows Yusuf well, but he also knows Zaynab and what a formidable opponent she can be, perhaps of greater value than any army. No doubt he sees her hand in this. Besides, he is getting older. Perhaps he does not relish the idea of commanding a greater and still greater army, of taking them across all of our land and beyond, fighting, always fighting. He does not have the ambitions of Yusuf, nor certainly those of Zaynab.

I see his broad gruff face sag slightly, a weariness stealing over him. Then he straightens his back and his head comes up. He smiles at Yusuf and his words come smoothly, for he has surely rehearsed them since he has learned of Yusuf's change in status. His eyes are kind and his tone carries with it a sense of inevitability, as though he has waited all of his life for this very moment.

"Will you join me, cousin?"

Yusuf waits a moment, while the men tighten their grips on their weapons. Then he dismounts and slowly makes his way to the shelter, where he sits down. They look at each other for a long moment before Abu Bakr speaks again, finishing what he has no choice but to say. "My cousin Yusuf. My true brother before God. There can be no man more worthy than you to command this army of holy warriors and to undertake a holy war in the name of Allah."

There is a palpable release of tension as he speaks. The men's hands relax on their weapons and I see Yusuf's shoulders loosen. I see Zaynab nod, a small confidant gesture.

Abu Bakr continues. "I am a simple man, one who loves the desert, home of our families and seat of our power. I wish to return there with a small force of my own men. There we will continue our work, fighting back the rebel tribes and securing the trade routes for our own needs. Brother, I ask you to assume command in my name, and I will return to the desert quickly, for this is no longer my place."

After that all goes as smoothly as Zaynab no doubt planned it. A document is drawn up to transfer power. Abu Bakr will retain his nominal power as Commander; but Yusuf is now officially the head of the army, the cities conquered so far and their mission in the future. Witnesses and the tribal leaders watch while all is agreed and at the end of it all the two men embrace and set off back to their respective futures. I look back over my shoulder and see Abu Bakr's small group slowly making their way across the vast plain, never to see Murakush again.

The army comes back to the camp victorious. Abu Bakr's name will be inscribed on gold coins until the day he dies, but the true Commander is now Yusuf. The army is his to command, Zaynab is his undisputed wife. Murakush will remain under his rule, and Abu Bakr, his own leader and once-loved cousin, will retreat into obscurity.

I feel a grudging respect for Zaynab. She is no pampered

queen consort, she is Yusuf's right hand. It is her skill that has brought this negotiation to a peaceful conclusion and heaped greatness on Yusuf. My own plans for the trading routes seem simple in comparison with a woman who can think so vastly, so strategically. The never-ending battles and negotiations for power tire me even to think of. I wonder if the wars will ever end, but feel my baby stir within me and promise him that one day there will be peace.

As we reach the square I shake my head. She has done it again. On the raised platform, food being prepared below her, lies Zaynab. How she has managed to dismount, rid herself of her outer robes so fast and appear to have been here all along I do not know. Perhaps she is truly a sorceress, able to fly like a bird, appear in one place and then another in the blink of an eye.

I am helped up onto the platform and Yusuf gives both Zaynab and I *tiraout* necklaces, heavy pectoral pendants, one large triangle with two smaller ones dangling beneath it, appropriate to this festive occasion. Certainly she has earned hers a hundred times over.

Zaynab lies back on silken cushions, a beautiful woman, her smile warm towards all, but dazzling for Yusuf. While I quietly take up a place towards the back of the platform, he takes her in his arms before the whole camp. She lowers her eyes and waves him to a place beside her, then orders the food to be served. As she does so, she makes a tiny gesture, smoothing her silk robes across her belly, where there is now a small but unmistakable curve. The camp roars its approval. Danger has been averted. They have a clear line of command. There has been no violence, no ugly scenes. Yusuf is now their ruler, with the beautiful Zaynab by his side, and now all the camp knows she is expecting his child. There is food, drink and the promise of a great future to come. People eat, dance, laugh, tell stories and sing.

I watch all of this for a little while, then slip away to my own tent. I sit on my bed and gently rub my own belly, sing an old lullaby to my tiny child. I pray that he will be born safely into this dangerous life, where victory and defeat walk on the blade of a dagger, one twist of the handle turning the fate of many in one direction or another with no notice. Into a world where the new commander of a great army is forever in debt to the woman who has made him so.

Issaran — Celebration Necklace

*T*HE ALMOND TREES COME INTO blossom as our two bellies swell. Zaynab's seems larger, for her voluminous and loosely worn robes add to its size. My own robes, shaped to my body with brooches and a belt, make my belly seem a little smaller, although I am sure that I am due a full month before her, a secret only she and I share. While I begin to feel better, Zaynab seems to continue with her sickness, day after day. I do not know how she can stand it.

The camp is happy and busy. Now that Yusuf has official command of the army, he is ready to swell its ranks beyond all imagining. A strong army will allow him to move swiftly as he goes north, making battles both brief and victorious.

Two thousand black slaves are added to the troops, fighting men, who quickly learn the fighting style required by Yusuf. The men train day and night on the plains near Murakush. From Al-Andalusia he brings two hundred and fifty men to whom he gives horses. These form his own personal guard, reflecting his new importance.

All of this costs money, of course. He levies a tax on the

Jews living within his own jurisdiction. Besides this he also has taxes from the traders who journey the trading routes, as his men take more and more control of such stretches of land and can offer protection.

The size of the main army now allows him to send out small parts of it to the surrounding areas, under the command of men close to him. These go to different tribal areas and either negotiate alliances or conquer them. The choice is theirs. Many choose to recognise Yusuf's authority without engaging in debilitating battles.

In this way Yusuf gains the region of Salé where the tribes submit quickly, not wishing to take on the might of the new army, of which by now all have heard. Yusuf's position is very strong. If a tribe wishes to fight the smaller army sent out to them, they know that a victory for them will only result in a far larger army being dispatched to finish them off. Those tribes who submit, however, will come under Yusuf's protection, which is worth their allegiance.

The first real assault on the north comes when an army is sent to the city of Meknes. It is close to Fes, which has always been an important target in Yusuf's plan. The amir of Meknes, Al-Khayr bin Khazar az-Zanati, is offered mercy if he will surrender without fighting. Although his people react with anger and suggest he fight back and dispel not just the army but Yusuf and all his men and their mission from the land, the amir is a clever man who can see that this is a growing impossibility. Yusuf is simply becoming too strong and winning over too many allies. Instead he settles for negotiation, offering to take his own key people and decamp to a new settlement, leaving the city free for occupation by the army, who enter it peacefully. The fallen amir visits us in Murakush, where Yusuf greets him with great honour and kindness and gives him permission to remain in the region of Meknes for the rest of his life.

Meknes is an important victory for Yusuf. It is hardly any distance from Fes, and now he turns his attention to fortifying the army in Meknes so that in due course he can order them to take Fes. His territory is growing almost daily.

Yusuf does not head up these armies himself, for he prefers to remain in Murakush and develop not only the city but control his conquests, setting up administrative centres in each of his conquered areas. They will report back to him, collect taxes and recruit more men. He still oversees the training of new recruits, of primary importance in developing a coherent army.

Now Murakush begins to develop like a real city. An outer wall is built with high ramparts patrolled by soldiers. More and more buildings spring up, their apricot-coloured mud walls glowing in the first and last rays of the spring sun, shining in the full heat of the day. No longer is it a chaotic sprawl of tents, a garrison for soldiers. Now come the first houses for the generals and their families, for the officers. There are the first buildings for administration.

Huge water tanks are dug so that the city can have water brought to it more easily, for baths and irrigation. Gardens are built to supply food to the ever-growing population. Already many palms are beginning to grow in a great grove outside the city walls and it is jokingly said that they come from all the dates that the soldiers ate when they first came here after sacking Aghmat, that where the soldiers spat the stones, palms sprung up.

The first quarters begin to develop; a few buildings, little streets between them, the first communal ovens built, one for each quarter. They begin to have everything that a real city would have – the steamy hammams where all can become clean, small shops selling basic necessities for when the souk is not open. Qur'anic schools begin to teach, informal at first, but growing larger. Many of the men recently recruited into the army have no understanding of Islam, and Yusuf insists that they should be taught as well as the many children who now make the city noisy with laughter. The souk grows ever larger as the city's population grows and becomes more demanding. Now there is need for jewellery, for perfumes, for baskets, pots, carved wood, cloth, rugs, good leather and shoes. There is demand for more and better food; some luxury after the early days of camp life when the food was simple. Now the people have a taste for sweet treats, for fruits, fish and seafood from the coast, more herbs and spices. The herb seller seems to have stopped plying her trade, leaving it to the local farmers and traders who have set up permanent stalls. I no longer see her in her usual place.

Metalworkers join the weapon-makers, beating out not just swords and daggers, but great brass and copper dishes, trays and jugs to satisfy the families now expanding their kitchens and the amount of food they must provide. Their part of the city is hurtful to the ears; the great hammers rising and falling, children accidentally scattering brass dishes as they run past and the shouts of the craftsmen at the small disappearing legs.

Now other craftsmen come, their skills suddenly in demand as the builders complete their work. Expert carvers begin their work on the plasterwork inside the houses of the more important people. Tiny intricate designs are worked ceaselessly into wall after wall, elaborate twirls and curls, stylised calligraphy. Never-ending geometric repetitions are shaped, the white dust from the work covering the men until they look like beings from the other world.

The painters sit over wooden panels for doors and ceilings, chests and balconies, painting in vivid colours what the plasterworkers carve in pure white. More flowers, leaves, great arches and circles, squares, triangles. Greens and oranges, gold and blue; the panels slowly transform into works of art and are then lifted into place with much effort and curses. The metalworkers bring their crafts to the woodworkers, their hinges, heavy door-knockers and locks sliding neatly into place.

In the streets clothes grow more elaborate. Brighter colours adorn the women, finer fabrics float around their new owners, shoes are made of softer and brighter leather. Even the weapons carried become more elaborate; no longer strictly utilitarian, they grow elegant scabbards and fine scrollwork on their handles.

There is a prayer hall. It is not nearly large enough, but it is a real building, and that satisfies Yusuf for now. He wants a great mosque, but that will have to come later. For now there is at least a space where people can come together in prayer.

The tileworkers labour over tiny pieces of colour, fitting

one after another, each only a tiny part of no importance, but as we pass by them each day their patterns unfold, stretch out, each tiny piece now a part of something larger and more beautiful.

There are still tents on the outer parts of the city where the more lowly live, where the foot soldiers and the cavalry sleep. There are tents of traders for the souks, and there are tents here and there between the buildings, but the city is changing fast. Slaves work daily under builders and surveyors, their bodies and clothes marked with splattered mud indicating the nature of their work even after they have finished, exhausted, for the day.

The petals fall from the almonds and the sun grows hotter. As Yusuf's wives, of course, we now have our own separate dwellings, for although Zaynab and I never waver in our public politeness towards one another, even Yusuf seems to sense that all is not as it seems and when the time came to build him a house, he ordered two. One is larger, for Yusuf spends most of his time there and Zaynab has her own rooms within the building. It has bigger rooms for entertaining, for this is where important guests will come. For all his love of simplicity, even Yusuf knows that an amir such as he now is must offer his guests a certain elegance in hospitality, and so there is a great room in which guests can be received. It is simpler than it would have been had it belonged to a man who loved luxury, but still it is decorated and his courtyard is full of flowers. There are rooms where guests can sleep, as well as kitchens large enough for his growing retinue of slaves and servants.

My own house is nearby, but I am grateful that it is mine alone, despite it being smaller and less grand. Strictly speaking I could complain, could demand all that Zaynab has, for the Holy book would give me justice. But I crave my own space, my own little kingdom rather than to be always under Zaynab's watchful eye. Yusuf offers me more servants, more slaves, but I refuse and keep only Adeola and Ekon with me, for they are all I need and the only people I trust. I do not trust Zaynab not to pay off someone to spy on me in my own home. It is small with a pretty roof terrace, which I fill with flowers in tubs and a great basin of water, which ripples in the breeze. An elegant city house should have fountains but we are not so elegant yet. Inside, the rooms are cool; dark in the heat and brightness of the day, and there I rest, surrounded by my own possessions. I see little of Yusuf, although he visits me occasionally, bringing me fruits and asking after my health. I do not try to make him stay longer than he wishes and he has much to do. We are kind and courteous, but there is little intimacy left between us now. He is wrapped up in his new-found power to take his mission forward, I am wrapped up in my pregnancy and Zaynab stands between us.

My own rooms are simple. I keep the decorations plain, the carved white plasterwork and vibrant rugs enough for my liking without filling the rooms with fine objects. I am used to tents, not living in buildings, and it seems strange to me at first. I feel shut away from the elements. Inside my rooms the breeze cannot come at night for heavy drapes are hung over the windows, and the heat of the sun is kept away by the thick mud walls and wooden shutters. I wonder how

Yusuf fares. He was raised as I was. I laugh to myself when I hear that he often sleeps in the courtyard of his fine house.

I eat, sleep and watch the world go by. I marvel at the city and how it grows daily, keeping pace with my own belly. It is a quiet time for me; alone but not lonely in my own little world, while all around me great plans take shape around the growing army, city and Yusuf's power.

My child kicks within me and sometimes a little foot presses against the tight skin of my belly. I rub my fingers against the bump and smile when it is quickly retracted. Soon I will have my babe in my arms and will be able to play with it. I think of stroking its silken hair, of a tiny hand clutching mine.

Yusuf visits me, offering me a box. I take out a beautiful necklace of silver and amber, an *issaran* pendant traditionally worn for a great celebration, perhaps held at the full moon, when the great circle of amber held within the silver will reflect the beauty of that celestial orb.

"For you," smiles Yusuf. "And this is for our child, when he comes."

He pulls out a string of silver beads, each one a thick tubular shape. I smile. These are *ismana,* 'long bones' beads, given to a child to promise good health and that their bones should grow long, leading to a tall child. He shows me how each one has been marked by the jeweler with my own name and Yusuf's.

"When you first see your son he will be wearing them," I promise.

Yusuf pats my heavy belly. "It cannot be long now," he says.

I awake to a strange sensation, which fades as I stir. I think I have been dreaming and lie half asleep as the pale dawn lights my room, thinking to sleep again, for I was restless and slept badly in the night, my body uncomfortable whichever way I lay. Then a slow return of that feeling takes hold of me; a squeezing and tightening in my belly and suddenly I am wide awake, for I know my baby is on its way.

I tell Adeola what is happening and warn her that no-one must know. She has Ekon close the heavy shutters of the house and hang blankets in front of each window, the better to muffle any sounds.

My pains come slowly, building all through the day. I walk up and down in my rooms, restless and in growing pain. I am certain that my baby will be born at any moment, but still time goes by and nothing happens. I want to cry out with pain but I must be silent and so I clench my fists and teeth and try to stay silent.

"You need a midwife," says Adeola.

I shake my head. There is no-one I trust.

But as the pain goes on and on I grow afraid. How will I know if something is wrong?

"Fetch the Andalusian woman, the herb seller," I say at last to Adeola. I know that she has healing knowledge and I have need of someone as calm as she has always seemed to me.

Adeola slips out of the house and returns some time later with the woman.

She looks about her as though curious and when she sees me she looks shocked. "Why do you not have a midwife with you?" she asks.

"There is no-one I trust." I tell her, panting between the pains. "Zaynab…" I do not finish the sentence but the woman nods as though I have said more.

"What is your name?" I ask her.

She hesitates. "Isabella," she says, as though the name is both familiar and strange to her. I do not know if she is lying to me but I do not really care, I only need a name by which I can call her.

"Your child comes too soon." she says before she examines me. Everyone believes that Zaynab will be delivered of her child before me, so she must be worried that I am birthing too early.

I shake my head, awash in a wave of pain.

She frowns and comes closer, giving me her hands to hold, which I do gratefully, drawing on her steady calmness, her air of being unworried by anything. I badly needed her reassurance. As the wave dies away she sits down with me.

"Not early?"

I shake my head again.

She thinks for a moment. "Zaynab…" she begins.

I shake my head again.

She looks at me, eyebrows raised, then nods to herself. "So."

After that she questions me no more. She examines me and I look hopefully at her.

"I think it will be born very soon," I say. "I have been in pain for a long time."

She looks at me kindly. "You have not yet felt pain," she

says matter-of-factly. "And your baby will not be born for a long time yet."

I gaze at her with horror and disbelief. She smiles and pats me on the shoulder as I bend over again with pain.

She is right. The hours go by until they are nothing but a blur, the waves by now not even separate, only coming again and again till I cannot distinguish between one and the next.

At last there comes a most terrible moment when I believe I will be ripped in two. All about me goes dark and then at last I feel some relief. The pain brings me back to the light and I hear a small cry.

Isabella busies herself, then comes to my side, where I have fallen back on my bed in exhaustion. In her arms she holds a tiny form, which she hands to me.

"A son," she says.

I hold the strange tiny creature in my arms. He is wet and slippery, and I fear I will drop him. He is still partly blue as well as an angry red. I think of how the indigo robes stains the men of our tribe blue and leads to all who meet them calling them the Blue Men and I laugh so hard that I think I will never stop. I am drunk with happiness for at last I hold my own child, a son for Yusuf. I remember his choice of a name for a son, and now I whisper to the tiny creature who nuzzles my breast impatiently, uninterested in my fits of laughter which make him bounce up and down on my belly. He makes grumbling sounds and I try to help him, although it takes Isabella's help to show us both how he should drink.

"You shall be called Ali," I say to him. "As your

father wished. You are his first son, and you will be much loved."

I am interrupted by Isabella who has brought me a strong golden broth made by Adeola under her direction, as well as two raw eggs, the traditional food given to a new mother. She sweeps aside my refusal of her horrible concoction, insisting that I must have something to help me regain my strength. She holds Ali while I reluctantly swallow the raw eggs, which I do not like at all. Under her stern gaze I finish them and then hold my arms out for my son. She shakes her head and hands me the bowl containing the broth, in which I can taste garlic, saffron, thyme and mint, along with pepper in such large quantities that I cough and splutter.

I wipe my streaming eyes as I finish and then set the bowl aside and look up. Isabella and Adeola have disappeared with Ali and before me stands Zaynab. I feel myself cringe at the sight of her.

"You have a son?" she asks, looking this way and that.

I thank Allah that Isabella has already taken Ali somewhere else, away from Zaynab's cold eyes, for I do not trust her not to dash him on the floor if she could lay her hands on him. I stay silent.

"It is my own children who will follow Yusuf," she says and there is a note of desperation in her voice that almost makes me pity her.

"Why do you hate me so much, Zaynab?" I ask. "I am nothing compared to you, yet you hate me and pursue me. You seek to do me harm at every possible opportunity. I have done nothing to you."

She looks away, around the room, still searching for a

glimpse of my son. "I am always second," she says, almost to herself.

"What do you mean?" I ask. "You are Yusuf's right hand, you are a queen."

She shakes her head impatiently, as though I cannot see something obvious. "You may have a son," she tells me. "But I will have many more. And if I can do your son harm, I will do it and I will not hold back. Every time I see that life grows in your womb I will find a way to take it from you. Before or after it is born, while I still live each one of your children will die."

Her words are not only horrifying, they sound as though she has repeated them over and over to herself, they sound like a charm, a spell.

"Get out," I say, trying to sound strong, although inside I feel as though I am about to faint. I feel like a tiny bird, watching in horror as a snake eats its young, unable to protect them.

Zaynab leaves, still twisting her head this way and that. When she has gone I call out and Adeola comes in, clutching a newly-wrapped Ali to her chest.

"Where is Isabella?" I ask.

"Gone," says Adeola. "She slipped away but it is well, I have your son here."

I reach out and take back Ali, then hold him to my breast. I look down at him and my tears begin to fall on his head.

"What is wrong?" asks Adeola. "Do not think of Zaynab's words."

"She will find a way to bring harm to him," I say, sobbing now. "You heard her. She will do it."

224

Adeola's face is worried. "Tell Yusuf?" she says.

"He will not believe me, Adeola," I say. "Yusuf loves Zaynab, she is his right hand. He barely remembers why he once married me."

Adeola doesn't answer. There is not much she can say.

"Go and sleep," I tell her.

"You who should sleep," she says.

"I will, I will," I reassure her.

Reluctantly, she leaves the room, making me promise that I will call for her if I need anything.

I have lost track of time but the streets are very dark. I walk quickly, my shoulders hunched around my tiny son, the hooded robe Adeola uses when she goes shopping in the marketplaces covering every part of me and shielding my face.

I know where Isabella lives; a part of town where the foot soldiers and their families live, not a wealthy area. I find the house I had pointed out to me once when I enquired: plain red mud walls with no decorative moulding, a heavy wooden door. I knock softly, not wanting to draw attention.

She is surprised to see me. "Is the baby ill?" she asks. "Do you bleed?"

I shake my head. "May I enter?" I ask.

She steps back, allowing me to pass by her into the courtyard of the house. It is tiny, only a couple of dim lanterns illuminate the space and I can see a doorway into the house.

The room she ushers me into is extraordinarily plain. There is no carved plasterwork, no paint. The walls are white, the floor is plain gray tiles. There is a table and a chair. Nothing else. The only decoration in the room is a large wooden cross, hung on the wall. I stare at it for a moment, already half-regretting my plan.

"Kella?"

My attention is caught by the table. On it is a stack of good paper marked with fine calligraphy, although it is not our own script. It must be Isabella's work, for writing implements and inks lie to hand. Few people can read and write, especially such fine script. This is the work of a scribe or a religious clerk. I am confused by this room, it feels as though there are clues as to who Isabella is and I yet do not understand them. All I know of her is her calmness, her abilities with herbs, that she is a very educated woman and yet also a slave. I turn to face her, frowning.

"Why are you here?" she asks.

I swallow. "I want you to take my son."

She gazes at me for a long time. "Why?"

"Zaynab... threatened him."

"You could go to your husband."

I shake my head.

She does not argue the point and I wonder what she knows of Zaynab.

"Will you take him?" I ask and I can already feel my tears welling at the thought of her agreeing.

I see her make a tiny movement towards me, as though about to take Ali. "For how long?"

"Forever," I say.

She steps back. "Forever? Where will you be?"

I shake my head. "I do not know," I say. "I may have to leave this place to ensure Ali is safe. But I cannot visit him, cannot see him again or Zaynab will know I am his mother."

"She came to your house."

"She did not see him," I say. "I will say he is dead." Even the thought of him dying brings a wave of nausea. I hold him more tightly and he stirs in my arms, lets out a tiny cry but then settles again.

"And his father?"

I swallow again. "He will know him when he is old enough."

"How?"

I fumble in my robes and pull out the *ismana*, the string of silver beads marked with my name and Yusuf's. "His father gave me this for our child. He will recognise it when he sees it. You must keep it safe and give it to Ali when he is old enough to make himself known, when he is a man."

She stands silently.

"Will you take him?" I ask again.

"I must pray," she says abruptly. She turns away from me and kneels below her cross.

I watch her. I have never seen a Christian at prayer before. Her hands are clasped together, her head is bowed. She stays silent and still for a long time before she opens her eyes and looks up at the cross. She makes a movement with one hand echoing its shape across her face and shoulders, then rises and turns back to me. Her face is very calm, but her voice shakes a little when she speaks, at the enormity of what she is about to do.

"I will take him," she says. "I will keep him safe until he is grown to be a man and I will bear witness to your husband that he is your child and his."

She holds out her arms, her hands open to receive Ali.

I try to move, try to hold him out to her but my whole body convulses in sobs. I rock him in my arms, my face buried against his skin, trying to smell him, feel him, kiss him for the last time. Isabella watches me with a vast pity in her eyes. When she sees that I cannot let him go she reaches out and takes him from me very gently, her hands cradling him. My fingertips stay in contact with him until the last moment and when my arms fall back empty by my sides I let out a low moan of pain, tears falling so fast down my face that I cannot even see. Ali begins to cry and at once my hands reach out for him but Isabella shakes her head.

"You must go now," she says. "Or you will be found out."

I look at the back of Ali's head, at the tiny tuft of black hair, which is all I can see of him. I back away from Isabella and then turn. I walk through the darkness of her tiny courtyard and pull the door behind me, its heavy thud echoing inside me over and over again as I run through the dark streets back to my own home.

When I arrive Adeola is waiting. "Where is Ali?" she asks, seeing my empty arms.

I shake my head. "He is dead, Adeola."

She gasps, stares at me in horror.

I lay one hand on her and look into her face, tears streaming down my own. "You must say he is dead," I tell her. "You must take a wrapped body and have it buried."

She nods quickly, hurries away from me while I walk unseeing to my own bed. When I lie down I weep as though I will weep forever.

It is light when Yusuf comes. Behind him is Zaynab. The two of them look down on me where I lie weeping on my bed.

Zaynab's face takes on a mask of sorrow and she kneels, embraces me, her black robes stifling me, their silk slipping across my mouth and nose like sliding snakes, making my skin tense with disgust and fear. "My poor sister. Your newborn son was weak and now he has been taken from you. It is the will of Allah. We must not question His decisions." She looks up at Yusuf. "Our son will be born soon," she says, as though to comfort him. "You will have an heir, to mend your heart."

Yusuf nods. "You may leave us now," he says and Zaynab, unwilling but unable to refuse, goes out of the room.

Yusuf kneels by my side. His own eyes fill with tears and gently he strokes my disheveled hair.

For a moment I think of telling him the truth. He is a good man, a kind man. I will explain how things are between me and Zaynab, beg him to keep Ali and me away from her, to let us live in peace. But I do not trust Zaynab. I do not trust that there will be no mysterious accidents, no illnesses. Ali is more precious to me than Yusuf's feelings.

"I named him Ali," I say, and then stop, for my sobs are choking me. I close my eyes against the new swelling of pain at speaking his name and when I open them again I see that Yusuf, too, is weeping.

We sit together, embracing, weeping, for a long time.

It is almost nightfall when Yusuf rises and I am left alone again.

In the days that follow, Adeola and Ekon treat me as though I am their own child. They wash me and comb my hair, they dress me in fresh robes each day. They hold sweet orange juice to my lips, make me eat rich meat stews and drink broth to give me strength. They bring fresh fruits and the little honey cakes Aunt Tizemt loves. One of them sits by my side day and night, they hear my sobs in silence.

Zaynab is safely delivered of a son. They name him Abu Tahir al-Mu'izz, and the city rejoices that Yusuf has an heir at last. Yusuf holds a great feast. Zaynab is showered with gifts and praise. Her son is said to be strong and healthy; a fine boy who will one day be a great warrior like his father. Those around me lower their voices when they see me coming and tiptoe about. I do not attend the feasts for the boy, only weep at my loss, sleep and weep again.

Amalu comes to me. He kneels before me and his eyes are serious.

"Come away from here, Kella," he says. "There is nothing good left here for you. Come with me. We will trade together, as you once asked me to. I was a fool to refuse you. I have cursed myself every day since, for we would have been happy together and I would have saved you all of this pain."

I look into his dark eyes and I almost speak the truth, for I trust Amalu, but I am too deep in my loss to imagine the life he offers. Instead I shake my head in silence and he kisses my hand and leaves. Later I look down at my hand and imagine what it would be to live a life filled with love and tenderness rather than this unending pain.

Tiseguin — Ring with Container

FES. THE WORD SWEEPS THROUGH the city. At long last, Yusuf is ready to attack Fes.

Fes is a twin city. Long ago, one city was built on one side of the river, then another on the opposite bank. One city is inhabited by the descendants of refugees from Cordoba in Al-Andalus; the other by Kairouanis, from Tunisia. The walls of the two cities are so close to one another that, to an outside observer, they appear as one city, but they are still in fact two cities, each with their own customs. It is known that the neither of the two amirs who govern the two parts of the city will peaceably surrender as did the rulers of Meknes. There will have to be a siege.

Yusuf places the command of much of the army under a relative of his, Yahya bin Wasinu, and preparations for the siege begin. There are troops already at Meknes who are well placed to go to Fes and begin the siege. But more troops will be needed before they can begin. Every day new men are recruited and more soldiers set out on the journey to reach Meknes, where they will be welcomed and provisioned to then make their way on towards Fes.

Yusuf wants both parts of Fes to fall to his men, for he has in mind to destroy the wall which separates the two parts of the city, thus making it into one single, larger, city.

Fes has been his dream for a long time, for with Fes as his base in the north and Murakush in the south, he can plan future campaigns to the north and the east of our land, as well as further into the south, with Abu Bakr's help.

The stately dinners with leaders of tribes and cities are all but stopped, for Yusuf, always the warrior, only ever undertook them because he knows that negotiation and good relations with his new subjects is important. Now that there is a battle to be fought he sweeps all such events to one side. The servants of his household are idle without the great feasts to prepare or the guests to care for. Their master spends much time in training or poring over plans with his generals. They calculate the number of people in Fes, how much food they may have within the walls, how best to attack when the time comes and the greatest threats to their own men. Having two amirs each with their own soldiers will complicate matters. They sit up talking all night and train men most of the day. When I see Yusuf he is always in a hurry, always surrounded by generals and of course his own personal guard who now go everywhere with him.

As for Zaynab, she has a child to care for but she leaves him with nursemaids and is always by Yusuf's side. While the men train she returns briefly to her own quarters where she will beat anyone who has allowed any harm, real or imagined, to come to her son. She inspects him as though he were a prized object rather than her own flesh and blood, then goes to the outskirts of the city to watch the training, taking up a place in the shade and keeping her eyes narrowed against the sun. Her dark eyes miss nothing. Later she will speak with Yusuf about men who held back, who have not shown courage, strength or stamina. Those men will find themselves withdrawn from the troops riding towards Fes and made to train even harder until Zaynab's lips stop speaking their name. Sometimes I see her in the distance and wonder at her. She does not hold her child and cover him with kisses as I yearn to do with my son. Her eyes light up when she sees him, but the light in them is cold and hard, the eyes of a good trader when they spot a precious gem that they may use to make their fortune.

She uses a gem to attack me.

I come to my rooms one night as the siege of Fes begins and find on my bed a small casket. Inside is a *tiseguin*, a large ring of silver topped off with a very small box, the lid to which is fastened by a tiny chain. The lid of this box is made of carnelian, a stone known for its protective powers. It is customary to fill such a box with kohl for the eyes or with perfume, so that a woman may have her favourite beautifiers carried with her wherever she goes. I am puzzled by the gift and a little suspicious.

"Where did this come from?" I ask Adeola.

"A guard delivered it. He said it was from Yusuf for you."

I open the tiny box and find it to contain a sweet perfume, very light and fresh. It smells of flowers and fresh air and salt, such as one might smell close to the sea. I smile to myself and rub the perfume where my pulse beats. I wear the ring proudly, hoping to see Yusuf soon and have him smile at my delight in his gift.

The first day of the siege must be terrifying for the people of Fes. They have heard of the great army, of course, but few have seen its full might, for until now Yusuf has never had the need to use all of it at one time. Many cities and tribal leaders have simply surrendered when he has so demanded, seeking to avoid his wrath. Those now looking out from the ramparts of Fes can see thousands upon thousands approaching them, their ranks tight and steady, the men approaching without hesitation, their great shields held high, their weapons glinting in the sun.

My head feels light and my feet seem to float. I feel free. All my fears of Zaynab suddenly seem foolish. What harm can she do me, after all? I am alive and healthy. My son is also alive, even if I cannot hold him. Zaynab is fallible, she will not always win our battles.

I dress in my best, wear my jewellery and apply more of Yusuf's perfume. When evening comes I sit by his side during the meal, laughing and joking, telling old stories from my days as a trader, when I was dressed as a boy. I tell of all the scrapes I got into, the lies I told my father about my camel racing, the tricks I played on my oldest and most serious brother. Yusuf looks surprised but pleased at my lightness of spirit and I make sure that he can see the ring he has given me. When the drums are played I clap my hands and tap my feet. I smile at Zaynab and she smiles back at me, her hands keeping my rhythm.

The drums are never silent; day or night their pulse beats, the inhabitants of Fes unable to sleep so that even their soldiers begin to feel fatigue without even fighting. Babies cry, children whimper, the men and women begin to feel a real fear.

I awake feeling strange. The colours of my rooms seem very bright and I think perhaps that I have slept late, for the rays of sunlight at the window hurt my eyes and make my rugs seem too bright. I wear plainer clothes that day for none of my usual reds and oranges seem right. I take some comfort and pleasure in my new perfume, which smells so fresh.

Yusuf's army never comes forward when the enemy retreats, to avoid a false retreat, allowing the enemy to suddenly turn on them when they follow. But neither do they fall back, staying always together, always facing the enemy. The soldiers of Fes must come forward to be killed or escape back to the safety of the city walls to remain under siege while their water supplies and food dwindle and the people grow ever more fearful.

I cannot stop thinking of Fes. I see our soldiers, blood running outside the walls of a great city, limbs and heads rolling helplessly away from their owners. The weapons gleam so brightly that I shield my eyes even when they are tightly closed. I rub the perfume into my skin and breath it deeply, hoping to wash away the smell of blood in my nostrils, the sound of drums and steel on steel, hurting my ears in my silent room.

There are camels, allowing our men to fight the foot soldiers from a great height, cutting off their heads with one quick stroke of a sword. There are horses, who change direction at great speed, avoiding the enemy's weapons and allowing the riders to chase after those who seek to escape their fate. The great shields, tanned with ostrich eggs and camels' milk, are like iron, protecting the men from any weapon wielded by the soldiers of Fes, such that their attempts to protect their city seem foolish.

I lie on my bed and moan, thinking I hear the men scream as they plunge to their death from the ramparts, the terrified howls of women and children as they see their fathers, brothers, husbands die. I smell the perfume but it does not seem to take away the sound, no matter how much of it I put on. The little box is almost empty and I want to ask Yusuf to bring me more of it, so that its sweet fresh smell might bring me comfort.

Still the siege continues. More lives are lost while the two amirs hide from the conquering army, coming closer every day as their own armies shrink.

I rub on the last of the perfume, feel the room seem to float about me. I think of my life, which seems full of bright colours and sensations.

My childhood, the thick dark indigo of the robes that my father, brothers and I had worn and the pure soft white of Thiyya. The gold of oranges and the orange of gold, the pink rose buds of rich perfumes, the yellow of lion skins, their once-fearsome manes soft to the touch. The choking dust and the blinding sand. The heat and the endless journeys, the flickering warmth of fires and the good smell of roasting kid.

My Aunt Tizemt. Her warm hard hugs, the sweetness of her cakes dripping with honey, her roars when she was angry and her grumbles when she was happy. The waterfall of gaspingly cold water as Tanemghurt prepared me for my wedding night.

Yusuf's warm hands slipping over my body, his hardness melding with my softness, his sudden unexpected laughter and his smell, of horses and leather. His smile, his face at prayer.

My two lost children, the red red blood creeping down my thighs and the sinking pain of helplessness.

My third child gone from me when I had only held him, smelt him, fed him once.

Zaynab. The blackness of her eyes clothes tent deeds.

Darkness.

It is dawn when I stagger to Zaynab's rooms. My heart seems to beat loudly in my chest and I falter, hesitating at each step or uneven surface in the tight streets, for every time I put my foot down it does not seem to touch the floor. I sway as I walk. People draw away from me, whispering. *The amir's wife, swaying as though drunk, her eyes rolling back or even closing as she walks, clutching at anything close to her hand as she tries to take a few more steps to her husband's house.* Some of Yusuf's servants see me. The guards hurry forward and take me inside, away from prying eyes, calling for Yusuf. But I stop them, asking instead to be taken to Zaynab's rooms.

Two of the guards almost have to carry me up the tight stairs to Zaynab's own bedroom. Once there, they sit me down on a thick rug piled high with cushions, facing her great bed. They bring water and food, which they offer me, perhaps thinking my faintness is through fasting. I refuse and ask instead that they bring Zaynab to me at once. They look doubtful but obey me.

I wait and look around me. Zaynab has recreated her great tent here. The walls are white now, the plasterwork intricately carved with the names of Allah, with passages from the Holy Book. The floor is a thousand thousand tiny chips of tiles, making up a simple geometric pattern. There are great wooden chests against the walls but they are unpainted, or painted only with the simplest of flowers. Their wood, however, is precious. Cedar, ebony and citrus wood are used as inlays. The room is austere at first glance, dazzlingly complex and costly when looked at again. Her great bed is the same. It still smells of power and sex, of ambition and lust. It is glorious and frightening. I cannot keep my eyes away from it.

I smell her before I see her or hear her, that strange perfume she wears wafting towards me as she comes up the stairs. I hear the soft rustling of her silk robes, the gentle tread of her fine leather slippers on the steps. I close my eyes and wait, a wave of fear washing over me. When I open my eyes again my fingers are crushing a silken pillow and Zaynab is seated on her bed opposite me, looking down on me with interest, as though I am a rare specimen of some strange beast from foreign lands, brought here for her amusement.

She sits on the edge of the bed, her feet tucked neatly under her long lean thighs, her black robes draped becomingly all around her. Her slippers lie to one side, discarded. Her hands lie loosely in her lap and she leans forward, her elbows resting on her knees. We gaze at each other until I moisten my dry mouth and speak.

"What have you given me, Zaynab?" I ask.

She looks at me in silence.

I go on. "I thought the perfume was from Yusuf, but now I know it was from you. It does strange things to me, I see visions of terrible things and I hear things I do not wish to hear. My feet stumble and I feel that I might fly like a great bird if I were only to leap from my window. I talk and talk, telling all that is in my heart, no matter who is listening. I feel light, and then the colours grow so bright they hurt my eyes until I grow afraid."

She gazes at me silently as though I speak a foreign tongue. Then she frowns, straightening up as though she has much to do. She speaks briskly.

"You are stronger than I thought," she says. "I thought if you rubbed it in day after day, thinking to please your husband – " she allows herself a quick smile " – that you would surely die. But you seem to be stronger than that. The man who sold it to me showed me what only a few drops would do to an animal." She smiles. "It was unpleasant, but quick."

I shake my head. "Why do you hate me so much, Zaynab?" I ask in despair. "I have not tried to fight you. I want only to help my husband succeed in his mission, to bear him children, to build a great country. Yet you treat me as your greatest enemy. What more can I give you? You have taken my husband. You have taken my children – one from my womb, one from my arms – "

Her eyes narrow to slits and she closes the space between us with a single leap. I see a cloud of black silk flying through the air and draw back with a shriek. Her hand comes quickly across my mouth to silence me. When she is sure I will be quiet she withdraws it and brings her face close to mine.

"*Taken* your second child?"

I gasp. "He is dead."

She shakes her head. "You said I took him. He is *alive*?"

I shake my head slowly, terrified. Zaynab stands, looking down on me, then reseats herself on her bed as though she has all the time in the world. She smiles, a loving, kind smile.

"He *is* alive. That is why you stopped your grieving so soon. Where is he? Your *son*. Ali. Where is he? He is alive somewhere in this city. Not with you, I know that."

I tighten my lips.

"No matter," she says, still smiling. "I will find him. I know what a son of Yusuf looks like, for I have my own. Soon he will be Yusuf's only child."

I whimper, unable to stop the sound.

Zaynab relaxes. "So. I need to find your son. Then I will simply… watch you. I have spies everywhere. I will know when your womb is filled, and I will kill all your children, one by one, whether in your womb or in your arms. I will not trust my servants again, not even Hela; I will do it myself. In time everyone will know that you are barren and that your children do not live long. Who would want such a wife? What ill-luck. Yusuf will set you aside, or perhaps being such a pious man he will simply send you away, to live alone in one of his many cities. Who knows?"

"Why?" I ask.

She shrugs. "You are a threat to me," she says. "You diminish my own status. I will be Yusuf's only wife."

I hold out my hands to her. "Why did you even let

me come here?" I ask. "Yusuf sent for me. You could have arranged it so that I never received the message, so that I was killed by bandits. Why let me come?"

"I thought you were old and barren," she says as though it was obvious.

I frown. "What made you think that?"

"Yusuf said you had lost a child in the first months of your marriage. I thought you had lost it naturally. It was only later that he told me about the camel. I thought you were much older than you are. I thought you would come here, a poor simple desert woman, withered and barren. That you would be no kind of competition to me." She gestures at me. "Then you arrived. Ten years younger than me. Beautiful. Innocent to the point of foolishness. Dressed in your bright robes, your shining silver. His first wife. He spoke of you with tenderness, your trading skills, your vision matching his for the future of this land. Your womb filled with life so quickly, so easily."

I rise, unsteady on my feet and look down on her. "I am leaving, Zaynab. You have tried to poison me. No doubt you will try again. What do you want – my life in exchange for my son's?"

She smiles. "I might consider such a bargain," she says.

My son is alive. Zaynab knows this now and I know that she will not stop until she has found and killed him, this time with her own bare hands.

If I were dead, Zaynab might let my son live. She might believe that with my death his identity will be lost. If I am gone, who can name him as Yusuf's heir? And who can prove it if his mother cannot vouch for his paternity?

I shake my head as the darkness comes closer. I have to think.

I could take Zaynab's poison in a larger dose and surely die. Then she might spare my son.

That evening Yusuf calls me to him. Zaynab sits by his side and I try to avoid her gaze, keeping my eyes fixed on him alone.

"When Fes falls, as it will shortly," he begins, "there will be a time of rebuilding, of making it into a great city. But we have many men, and it will not take long. One of the buildings that I will order to be constructed will be a great palace where I will take up residence in due course, for there will be many campaigns in the north. I must be able to be closer to my generals when they set out to conquer new lands."

I steal a quick glace at Zaynab. She rules Murakush with an iron grasp. Will she take kindly to moving to a new city?

Yusuf continues. "It is my wish that when I move to Fes my two wives will accompany me. You will both live within the palace, for I wish all of my family to be together under one roof. In this way we can share meals together and welcome guests together. You will of course have your own rooms within the palace," he adds. "Zaynab has requested that you and she have your rooms close to one another, for she believes that as sisters you will draw on one another's strength and love to become used to a new city."

I feel my heart sink. I am certain that I have escaped many of Zaynab's plots and schemes on a day-to-day basis by living in a different building, and even so she has managed to do me more damage than I would have thought possible. What could she do to me if we were under the same roof, her servants preparing my food? How much easier it will be for her to poison me, to blame an unlucky slave perhaps, who might be killed for having dared to harm me, while Zaynab looks on and weeps false tears for her 'sister'. I shudder inside but keep a smile on my face as I answer Yusuf.

"I will be glad to be closer to you, husband," I say gently and it would be the truth if Zaynab were not part of the bargain. As it is I know now that my days are numbered. Living in Murakush or living in Fes will make no difference. Zaynab will not be satisfied until I die.

Or disappear.

The next day I send gifts to my family. I spend many hours in the souk, wandering from stall to stall, even in the heat of the day when many retire to their homes for food and prayer. I wander on, making good use of my trader's eye. I hold my family in my heart as I walk from one trader to the next. For my brothers I buy fine saddles, each with different colours woven into them, as well as tiny trinkets and toys for their children who will no doubt be numerous by now, although I know I will never see them.

For my father I buy a fine sword, the best that can be found in a city supporting a great army. It is the finest I have ever seen and indeed the maker does not even want to sell it to me, for he hopes an officer or even Yusuf himself will desire it. He has no interest in selling it to an unknown woman, even one as wealthy as I obviously am, with gold coins already held in the palm of my hand while I bargain. But I disclose my identity to him, leading him to believe the sword might find its way to my husband's hand. Then he grows eager and even gives me a fine scabbard for it.

My aunt I heap with gifts. Everything I see that I think may please her I buy. Brass bowls, copper jugs, wooden spoons make their way into the hands of slaves who walk wearily behind me, wondering at my sudden desire for purchases, for I am known for my simple house and belongings. I choose pots made from clay, a rarity for Aunt Tizemt for our earth is not suitable for the potters' wheel. I buy cloth and jewellery, powdered henna and tiny silver discs for her weaving. I laugh to think of her grumblings as she unpacks my gifts, her mutterings that I must have more money than I know what to do with and all the while her good strong hands admiring what her mouth cannot bring itself to say, that I have good taste and that the things I have sent her are useful and beautiful. They will colour her life a little brighter.

I even send a gift for Tanemghurt, though I do not know whether she is still alive. In a tiny pot I place precious rose perfume such as might adorn a bride, paying many coins for it, for it has come from far away and is the finest of its kind. I buy it hoping she still lives and may use it one day on another innocent young bride such as I was before I learnt some cruel lessons regarding marriage. I think of the cold waterfall for her astonished brides and her secret pride in such rituals, the creations of her own imagination.

I hold the tiny pot in my hands, think of her wrinkled old face and struggle to stem my tears.

While I wander through the souk with my slaves running back and forth behind me, some taking my new purchases back to the house, others coming to take their place and carry my new items as I walk on, I hear a baby gurgle. I look up at once, for I always hope that I might catch a glimpse, however brief, of Ali in the streets, held by Isabella. My breasts dripped milk for days after losing him and even now, so much later on, they still seemed to ache when I hear a child cry.

It takes me a moment to locate the child, but when I do I feel my heart, so eager to reach out, suddenly pull up short. The baby is Zaynab's boy Abu, only a little younger than Ali. I steer clear of him whenever I can, for his sweet smiling face hurts my heart and his chubby little hands hurt my very soul. Now he is just ahead of me, held as ever by his nursemaid. He smiles over her shoulder at me. She is oblivious of me, striding along as best she can carrying a heavy baby, jostled by the many people who walk along the tight streets.

I gaze at his tiny jolly face and sigh. Certainly I could plot against Zaynab's child as she has done against mine, but I cannot bring myself to harm a baby, nor to wish any bad fate upon him. He is only a baby and knows nothing of his father and mother, nor of me and my secret child who is, after all, his brother. He smiles broadly and reaches out his tiny fingers. I hold out my own hand, unable to resist his enthusiasm and happiness. His fingers grab mine for a brief moment before he is pulled away as his nursemaid finds a gap in the crowd.

I watch him disappear, his bright eyes still fixed on mine, then turn back to the craftsman with a heavy heart. He has been bargaining all this time and appears to have haggled me into a ridiculous price, so I clear my mind. I think of my father and brothers, trading their way across the dunes and begin to barter in earnest.

That night I supervise the packing of all the gifts I have bought and wave goodbye to the men and the camels as they set out on the long journey to my old camp. I wish I might lead them there, but know that for now my fate holds me captive in Murakush, for the news we have been awaiting has finally come.

Fes has fallen.

Taneghelt – The Key of Love

T HE SIEGE IS SUCCESSFUL ON the eighth day, when
the army breaks through the defences of Fes and
crushes the twin cities beneath its might. Buildings
are sacked for riches and some even destroyed with brute
strength or fire. The inhabitants pay a high price for their
stubborn defence. Bodies lie slaughtered in the streets,
while the two kings, who were proud enough to refuse to
surrender, are now forced to beg for mercy at the feet of
Yusuf's general Yahya bin Wasinu. He in turn makes them
wait, grovelling, spending each day in fear of their lives,
while he sends word back to Yusuf to ask for his clemency.
Yusuf gives it, allowing the two toppled kings to live
where they may choose. They slink out of their conquered
fortresses like beaten dogs, taking those few who are still
loyal to them to a new life of lowly status.

Those people who have not lost their lives have a choice
– to leave the city with or without their kings, or to stay
and swear allegiance to their new ruler. Some leave, unable
to bear a new ruler, some to seek their now-demolished
fortunes again. Those who remain must accept the changes
now ordered by their new unseen amir, Yusuf, far away in
Murakush. The wall between the two parts of the city comes
tumbling down, men of the city itself conscripted to do the

back-breaking work alongside the army's muscular soldiers. Rich merchants cut their hands to ribbons handling heavy tools and curse in whispers over their blisters at night.

Once the wall is down the people have to live day by day, side by side with those who have been strangers to them, now suddenly become neighbours in the rubble.

The city begins to change shape. Now it is truly one great city rather than two placed side-by-side. New people come to it from all over the land, and every day more men join the army, which numbers many different nations within its ranks.

Yusuf has ordered that building must begin as soon as the rubble is cleared away. Mosques are to be built, baths, water canals, mills. The city will be transformed, ready to take its place as one of Yusuf's most important cities in his plans for future conquests.

He has also ordered the creation of the palace he promised. It will be a fortified castle, its ramparts high above the city offering a lookout post where his guards can spot any attackers stupid enough to try and take Fes from Yusuf's army. The rooms will be bigger and more beautiful than those in Murakush. Craftsmen will be called from far and wide to design complex tiled floors, to carve the plaster into swirling gardens of leaves and flowers, and to fill every room with fine rugs and cushions, low tables of scented wood, brass and copper dishes engraved with every possible shining design. It will be a very different life from the one Yusuf and I once knew in the desert, where our only homes were our tents and our meals were plain. Now foods will be brought to us from far away, great banquets will be held, growing ever more formal. Our clothes will become more

and more costly, our servants and slaves multiplying day
by day. Zaynab's great bed will take up residence in her
rooms and we will all live in the palace together, her eyes
everywhere, my life in danger.

Murakush is in ecstasy. The army has triumphed yet again,
and now Yusuf rules over cities both north and south. His
army is huge and each city taken is another part of the
greater plan.

There is feasting the night that word reaches us about
the success of the army. Torches burn brightly, lighting up
the city's growing fineness. Good food and drink are made
and eaten, the storytellers fill the squares and people gather
to listen to the latest tales spun around Yusuf and his holy
mission, his handsome baby son, a new city conquered, two
new kings subjugated to Yusuf's mercy. Fes is described to
those who have never seen it, its great riches now part of
the wealth that Yusuf can command, the wall of division
between its people felled at his orders. My husband is
becoming the stuff of legend, his conquests something
from a fairytale, peopled with extraordinary heroes and
princesses. Zaynab, of course, has her own legends, and
they grow greater by the day. I have even heard the story of
my own younger days when I entered the camel race and
my veil fell from my face, showing that a young girl had
beaten the men at a camel race. I shake my head when I
hear these stories, for I am described as more beautiful and
daring than I truly was. No longer a silly headstrong girl
who risked her father's wrath in order to please herself and
make fun of proud young traders and their sons. Now I am

a stunning beauty who defied her father, beat off princes and warriors to claim a great prize and who amazed all when her fine robes unveiled her true loveliness, drawing the eye of Yusuf bin Tashfin himself.

I sit at a window where I can overlook the streets and watch the feasting, listen to the stories being told, the dances and songs that accompany them as the night draws on. Children gradually fall asleep and are carried back to their homes, while the men and women continue celebrating. I see a few men and women who should not be in one another's company, for the night hides much. I hear rumours passed from mouth to ear. One of these makes my heart beat faster.

Two women stand in the street below me. One I recognise, a slave woman in Zaynab's household, who washes her clothes and makes her bed. The other I do not know, a slave from another household no doubt, the two perhaps friends.

"She has not bled this month," says Zaynab's woman.

"By many days?" asks the other.

I lean further out of my window, wondering whether they can truly be speaking of Zaynab or whether they speak only of a slave girl or servant who has been a little too friendly with the soldiers.

"Enough," says Zaynab's woman, nodding knowledgably. "She looked faint today, pale. Like she was with the last one. She will give the Commander another child for sure."

I sit back and breath deeply. Zaynab, who somehow managed not to give her three previous husbands any children, seems fertile after all; her first son not a stroke of luck but perhaps the first of many.

"Praise be to Allah," says the other, although there is not much praise in her voice. Zaynab is not a favourite in her household, for she is harsh with her punishments and entirely lacking in praise. She works her servants and slaves hard, thinking nothing of having them whipped or starved if they displease her in even a small way. Her fertility is not a source of pride to them as it might have been with a more beloved mistress.

They continue talking as they walk slowly back to their own beds, while I allow the night air to cool my hot cheeks and slow my heart.

The next morning I go to the stables where all the camels of Yusuf's own household are kept. I find Thiyya. I have not seen her since I first came to Murakush, but she is healthy and well-cared for. I thank Allah Zaynab has never known she is precious to me or no doubt she would have found a way to harm her. Thiyya recognises me but makes a great show of ignoring me until I offer her the dried figs I have brought. She immediately fights off the other camels and flutters her long white lashes at me, daintily picking each fruit from my hand, then greedily nuzzling me for more when she has eaten them all. I pat her gently and smooth her fur. I look around the stables but cannot see any racing saddles that would fit her. There are large men's saddles or dainty women's saddles, neither of which are what I like to use with her. I stroke Thiyya's small ears while she tosses her head. She has never liked to have her ears touched. I pat her forehead and leave her.

I am walking back through the streets when a little slave boy runs up to me.

"Lady, I have a message for you from a man."

"What man?" I ask.

He shrugs. "I do not know, lady. He asked me to find you." He pulls out a little pouch. "He said to tell you that a veil sometimes allows you to see more clearly."

He looks at me as though to see if this makes sense to me. I shrug and give him a coin for his trouble. I let him go with my thanks and go up to my bedroom, calling for cool water to be brought to me. When Ekon has left the room I open the pouch.

Amalu has sent me another veil key, one that matches the first one he gave me when Yusuf summoned me.

I sit and look at the little silver fastener for a long time, thinking about the time he had given its twin to me. I was so full of innocent excitement and pleasure, a free and happy woman on her way to see her husband after too long apart. Before I had met Zaynab, before I had lost two more children by her hand. Now I feel like a prisoner, my innocence crumpled and dirtied by all I have experienced.

Amalu knew me before, when my man's blue veil covered my face, allowing my shaded eyes to see clearly in the blinding desert sun.

I see clearly now the path I wish to travel and I begin to take the steps to lead me there.

I leave my room and spend the afternoon in the souk, at the saddle-maker's stall. I make him show me all of his stock, rejecting all the heavy men's battle saddles and all the ornate women's saddles, forcing him to find me the light racing saddles that young men favour. He is mystified by my demands, muttering to himself as he fails to make me take an interest in the more appropriate women's saddles, extolling their softness and comfort. I laugh and wave them away, examining the racing saddles for their quality and workmanship. I find one that reminds me of my days as a trader, one that I think will fit Thiyya well. I pay him more than the saddle is worth, throwing gold coins at him with no attempt to bargain him down, leaving him blessing Allah while looking somewhat bewildered. I give the saddle to a passing slave boy and pay him to take it back to my house, which he does, walking slowly, dwarfed under its weight.

More than once I take up my outer robe with its heavy hood and take a pace towards the door, before turning back. At last I take a coarse cloth and use it to cover my head so that no-one will know me. I slip out of my home and take the smallest streets I can find until I reach Isabella's house, looking behind me more than once in case I am being followed. I hesitate again, my hand held up to knock. At last my knuckles strike against the wood, but there is no answer. I swallow, then open the door myself and step inside her courtyard. I have not been here in daylight. It is very small but pretty, full of herbs and flowering plants. I think to call her name but the silence around me tells me she is not here. I push at the door to her house and enter the room I remember from the night when I gave up my son.

It is still sparse, as I recalled it. The large cross still looms over the small room, but now there are signs of its new inhabitant. I see a bowl of water in which are soaking cloths to keep a baby clean.

The other item lies on the floor, discarded by its tiny owner, perhaps in a fit of temper. It is a little rattle, such as are given to small babies to please them when they cry. They delight in the sound that the beads make when they are shaken. This rattle is made of ivory, a rare and precious substance to be used for a careless baby's toy. I kneel and take it in my hand. I touch its fine smooth surface and then bring it to my lips and kiss every part of it, hoping that when my son next holds it to his rosebud mouth he may feel his mother's kiss touch his lips.

I wipe away my tears, which have begun to fall, and then leave that house. I could walk up the stairs and see every room, could even wait for their return from wherever they have gone, but it is enough for me to have stood in my son's home, to see where he lives each day and to leave a kiss for him. I am not certain that I could see my son, perhaps even hold him again, then walk away for a second time.

I close the door softly behind me and when I have walked three streets away I take off the coarse cloth and give it to a beggar girl, who blesses my name as I walk home.

Now that I have made my farewell to my son I seek out Amalu's home. Yusuf's men no longer live in the barracks formed from tents. I make enquiries on a morning when the army has left early for the plain outside Murakush, where they will practice manoeuvers all day. I find his house tucked down a side street, its plain orange-painted door unlocked. I push at it and enter a small courtyard, modest in size and bereft of comforts: no fountains or flowering plants here. His few rooms are also plain: a simple bed and blankets, a worn prayer mat along with some weapons, perhaps not needed for today's practice. No decoration, no cooking utensils save a water jar and dipper, a cup. I think sadly of all he has given up to be close to me. He, who was always at the centre of a group – playing with the camp's children, playing the drums in the oasis, talking with friends, eating with his family – now lives in this silent house, fights faceless in Yusuf's army and eats alone, perhaps something bought from a stallholder and eaten quickly without the pleasure of company.

I return to my own rooms and call for Adeola and Ekon.

"I have a task for you," I say and tell them what I want of them, leaving them with a generous purse of money.

I visit the hammam where I allow myself to be soaked and scrubbed until I feel newborn. When I return to Amalu's rooms I wear a very simple pale robe and none of my jewellery, but my hair is soft and shining, falling down my back like a great waterfall. My hands and feet and face are marked with henna, in beautiful patterns and the symbols of my people. My body is clean, my skin is soft and hairless. I smell of fine perfumes and the roses from the soap that cleaned my hair. My eyes are outlined with kohl.

I push open the orange door and look about me in awe. The courtyard has been filled with flowering plants and hung all about with lanterns in many colours. A great basin of water ripples in the breeze and sends tiny flower petals scudding across its surface.

"Food will be brought at the appointed hour," says Adeola.

She shows me to a room where a tub of water, cloths and a clean robe await Amalu's return. She gestures to the stairs, scattered with yet more flower petals and I follow her to his bedroom, now lined with wall hangings and fine carpets, his bed draped in soft sheets and colourful blankets. Bright strips of cloth hang at the windows, billowing as though we were back in a tent. More lanterns are hung here, while platters of fresh fruits and little cakes have been placed on two small tables.

We return to the courtyard, where Ekon waits for us. I take a deep breath and feel my eyes fill at what I am about to do.

"I did not know why I bought you, Adeola. I thought it was the heat, that I was foolish to be sentimental. Now I know better. The two of you have been far more than slaves, bound to obey my orders. You have proven yourselves friends to me when I needed you most. There is no way in which I could thank you for what you have done but to give you your freedom, and I do it now."

They stare at me.

I half-laugh, although I can feel tears falling. "You are free," I say. "I have already had documents drawn up, your freedom will be made known and I have left money for you. But I tell you now that you are free. You are no longer my slaves."

Adeola meets my gaze and her own eyes fill with tears.

She embraces me and I clasp her tightly to me, our muffled sobs and laughter joining together. When I release her I look to Ekon, who has been watching us, his face solemn. Now he steps forwards until he is almost touching me. I hold out both hands to him but instead he kneels before me.

"You do not have to kneel," I say. "You are no longer a slave."

But Adeola shakes her head. "It is the way of our people," she half-whispers, her eyes still shining with tears as she watches him.

Slowly Ekon bows forward until his head almost touches the ground at my feet. He presses first one cheek and then the other against the cool tiles of the courtyard and I think of the golden sand that clung to his lips when he thanked me in this same way for the purchase of Adeola. When he rises I bow my head to him before I am suddenly embraced, enveloped in his crushing arms, my face buried in his chest which shakes with the violence of his sobs; the years of enslavement he has endured in silence now being released from this most reserved of men.

It takes a while before we are all composed, little bursts of laughter and more tears coming from us as we speak together.

"You must go," I say at last. "Amalu will return soon."

We embrace again and they leave me alone in the courtyard, where I wipe my eyes and try to see myself in the basin of water. Certainly I am not as elegant as I was, the kohl lining my eyes has been somewhat marred by all the tears I have shed but then what I have to say to Amalu is greater than such petty matters.

I find myself a little nervous. I have prepared what I will say to Amalu but what if it is his turn to reject me? I have not been kind to him, I think, yet he has shown me nothing but devotion and care. What if he laughs at my proposition or sends me away? I pace through the tiny courtyard, arrange and then rearrange the flowers to my liking although none of them look right. What looked beautiful when I first saw it now seems too much, a foolish show of affection come too late.

"Kella?"

I spin round, my hands dirty with earth, my face flushed with the effort of lifting a heavy flowerpot. Amalu stands in the doorway of the courtyard, staring at me. For a moment I say nothing, flustered. I had meant to be calm, elegant, clear in what I have to say to him. Instead I am aware that I am sweating from my efforts, my hair is disheveled and my kohl is smeared from the tears I wept earlier.

"Kella?" says Amalu again, coming closer. "What are you doing here? Is something wrong?"

I can't help it. I laugh. "I'm sorry," I gasp. "I meant everything to be perfect and instead..." I gesture helplessly at myself.

Amalu frowns. "What was to be perfect?"

I brush the dirt off my hands and step close to him. "I made a mistake a long time ago," I say. "I mistook freedom for love." Fumbling in my robe I pull out a tiny necklace, black and silver beads intertwined, tiny dangling strips of engraved silver.

Amalu's eyes narrow. "That is a *chachat*," he says.

"It is the engagement necklace you gave me," I say.

"You kept it?"

I nod. "Now I return it to you, Amalu."

His face falls. "No need," he says gruffly, pushing my hand away.

"I have not finished," I say. "You always were impatient."

He waits.

"I return it to you and ask whether you would offer it to me again," I say. My voice wavers.

"I am not sure of your meaning," says Amalu but I see his eyes and the hope that is within them.

"I would marry you," I say. "If you will go away with me from this place."

"Where to?"

"To trade together," I say. "I would like to travel far to the north and east, beyond Al-Andalus, perhaps across the great trade routes to where silk comes from."

"And what is stopping you?"

"You are," I say. "I do not want to go alone. I want to go with you by my side."

"Is it the trading or me you want?" he asks.

"Both," I say honestly.

He laughs a little.

I hold up the tiny necklace again. "It is for you to say," I tell him. "I made the wrong decision. Now I wish to set it right."

"You are married," he says.

I shake my head. "I did not marry for love," I say. "I married for freedom."

"And you have not found it?"

"I am imprisoned," I say. "I would have been better off staying with Aunt Tizemt forever."

He laughs and for a moment his eyes shine with unshed tears.

I wait while he looks down at the *chachat* in his hands. Then slowly he raises his arms and puts it about my neck. I step forward into the circle of his arms as he fastens it and when he is done I lift my face to his and gently unwind the dusty wrap from his face. Veiled, he looks a fierce warrior, unveiled I see a young man, most of his face pale except for the dark brown strip of the sun's heat across his eyes and the scar that crosses his cheek. He looks at me, his whole face serious.

"You could kiss me," I say. "I am your betrothed."

He puts his hands on either side of my face and kisses me so gently I lean forward, wanting more of him, more.

He washes and puts on a clean robe. Food is brought to us by a stallholder as arranged. We sit and feed one another as though we have not eaten for days, lips brushing against fingertips and slowly we begin to speak, not of anything of importance, only the goodness of the food and the colours of the petals all about us, the heat of the day and the cool water we drink. When we have eaten we wash and Amalu takes my hand in his.

"You are my betrothed?" he asks me.

"I am," I say and he leads me to his room.

I am unsure of how we will be together, but my robes fall to the floor and I am not shy, it is as though Amalu and I have been in one another's arms many times before. He is tender to me but our desire grows until our kisses and caresses are fierce and yet still full of love. There is none of the fear I felt when Yusuf drank Zaynab's brew. Instead, we laugh even between passionate kisses, we hold each other tightly even while murmuring endearments, we collapse exhausted even while reaching out for one another again. Afterwards we lie together, the room growing dark as we share the moments we had thought lost.

"I have a secret," I say.

He waits.

"I have a child," I begin. "A son. Yusuf's son."

Amalu props himself up on one elbow, frowning. "But they said… Where?"

"I gave out that he was dead," I say. "But he is not. I gave him to the herb seller."

"From Al-Andalus? The Christian slave woman?"

I nod.

"Why?"

"She was kind," I say. "There was a calm about her. I saw her house, she is no common slave. And I had no-one else to turn to."

"You should have told me. I would have taken him away. I would have taken both of you. He will come with us now."

I shake my head. "He must stay here."

Amalu stares at me. "You wish to leave your son behind?"

I feel tears well up. "No," I say. "It breaks my heart."

"Then bring him."

"I cannot take him away from the only mother he has ever known," I say and the tears begin to fall. "I cannot do that. And besides, he is Yusuf's son."

"Yusuf does not even know he exists."

"He will one day," I say. "I left a sign for him. One day he will know that Ali is his son and he will claim him as his own, as his heir. And then there will be peace."

"Peace?"

"All this endless warfare," I say. "It is not what we had planned."

"We?"

I stroke his face. "Yusuf and I were united by a vision of what the Maghreb might one day be," I say. "Not by love. There was some tenderness between us, but what we saw together was a time when all of the Maghreb would be united and peaceful. When trade could flourish, when great cities could spring up."

He shakes his head. "You expect all this from a babe?"

"When he is grown to be a man and Yusuf makes him his heir," I say, "he will bring peace and prosperity. There will be no more need for war."

Amalu sighs. "There always seems to be a need for war," he says. "I am tired of it."

"We will go away," I say. "You and I. We will travel the trade routes, we will go far to the north and the east, beyond the sea. It will be a great adventure. And we will be together."

"And you will never see your son again?"

I press my head against his chest and let my tears fall. "I will trust in Allah to protect him," I say and feel Amalu's arms embrace me.

We doze for a little while and then Amalu stirs. We light the lanterns, then drink cool water and eat some of the fruit I brought, feeding one another fresh orange dates and tiny red pomegranate seeds, their colours like gems scattered across our bed as we drop them and laugh at one another for our clumsiness. I marvel at the lightness between us, the simplicity of happiness.

"Tell me a story," he says idly.

"A story?"

"Yes. It is dusk and dusk is when the storytellers come to the squares and the people gather to hear a magical tale," he says, biting into a late fig, its delicate pink insides and green-purple skins splitting under his hands.

I shake my head. Then I rise from the bed and stand before him entirely naked. I begin to clap my hands loudly.

He laughs. "What are you doing?"

I point to him. "I will dance for you if you will play for me."

Amalu chuckles and makes himself more comfortable on the cushions. He takes up a little drum from the corner of the room, and begins to beat out a slow rhythm. "Here is your music. Begin, oh most wondrous dancer."

I stand still for a moment, the soft breeze caressing my body. I let my feet begin to move, following the slow beat. My hips undulate and I let my head fall back, my hair whispering from side to side across my back. My hands come up my body, the fingers forming shapes as I dance, a smile growing on my face and on his.

I dance for a long time, the beat growing faster until I can no longer keep pace with it. I fall onto the bed, exhausted, sweat running down my body. Amalu laughs and pats away the drops with a blanket, then pulls me close to him and holds me in his arms again.

"Your turn," I command.

He looks at me in feigned horror. "You want me to dance?"

I nod firmly. "Oh, yes."

He mimicks my movements until I am almost choking with laughter. When he returns to me we laugh together until we subside into weak giggles.

"Sing to me," I suggest.

"I sing like the vultures," he says, making a raucous sound.

"You can tell me a story, then. You must find a way to amuse me after I have danced for you."

"I thought you were amused a moment ago," he says, poking at my belly until I wriggle away. "You could barely breathe for laughing."

"Tell me a story," I insist.

"As you command."

I lie soft in his arms and lose myself in his warm voice.

"There was once a noble young man who loved a princess. She loved him in return and they wished to marry, but her father, the leader of the tribe, was stubborn and thought no suitor was good enough for his daughter. Many men sought the princess's hand, but her father turned them all away. When the suitors attempted to visit the princess by night, her father, a fierce old warrior, devised an extraordinary system of twenty-one locks throughout his palace. Each lock was made by a different locksmith so that there should be no one key that would open all the doors. No one could now reach the princess in her rooms without opening the twenty-one doors and locks that led there."

I open my eyes and look up at Amalu. He smiles and

gently closes my eyes again with one fingertip before continuing his story.

"The princess and her young lover were determined that they should be together, and the noble young man was also very clever, and so he went to a silver smith who was his friend and begged him to help them. The smith thought for a long time, and at last he took the two syllables of the word for love: 'ta' and 'ra' and made a shape in poured silver which combined the male and female shapes and the two syllables of the word 'love', making a cross with a circle, a perfect symbol of love. This he gave to the young man, who asked what it should be called. The smith replied '*taneghelt*', meaning melted liquid, for it was in this way that he had made the jewel. The young man paid him well and thanked him profusely, then took the silver piece to the palace wherein his beloved lived.

That night, the young man approached the first door. He touched the lock with the silver jewel and the lock at once melted and the door opened before him. In this way, each of the twenty-one locks opened and when the king came to rouse his daughter the next morning, he found her in the arms of the young man. Astonished at the daring and tenacity of the couple, the father at last gave his blessing to their union."

I smile without opening my eyes. "Was there only one of these magical keys?" I ask, knowing the answer but wanting him to tell me it anyway. His voice is low and tender and I bask in hearing him talk like this, as though we have all the time in the world to spend together, with nothing to worry or threaten us.

"Today there are twenty-one forms of the key, just as

there were once twenty-one locks, for different jewellers designed *taneghelt* pendants to their own pleasing. Lovers give these jewels to show that they have the key to one another's hearts."

"And do I have the key to your heart?" I ask him, for I can see that he is hiding something in his hand.

He smiles at my guess. "You know me too well," he says, and gives me a *taneghelt,* slipping it into my hand from his, still warm from his body. I hold it gently in my palm.

"How did you come to have it?"

He shakes his head. "I have had it ever since you came to Murakush. I thought one day to give it to you, to let you know that you still had the key to my heart, though I did not have yours."

I touch the *chachat.* "You had my heart all along," I say. "It was I who did not know you had it."

"I must go now," he tells me. "I must prepare for our departure."

"I will come with you," I say.

He shakes his head. "Sleep," he says. "You will have need of all your strength, for we will have to travel fast to get as far away from here as possible before your absence is noted. Yusuf will not take kindly to his wife running away with one of his soldiers."

"He barely remembers who I am," I say.

"He will remember when you run away," says Amalu. "He will send men after us."

I shake my head. "I doubt it," I say. "Zaynab will be glad I am gone. She will find a way to persuade him not to follow me."

"Not to bring back his own wife?"

"Zaynab always gets her way," I say wearily. "She will be delighted if I leave."

"I wish I was as certain as you are," says Amalu. "Either way, I would like to get far away from here before anyone finds out you are gone."

I nod.

"Sleep, then meet with me. Do you need a camel?"

"I have Thiyya," I say. "She is in the stables, I will find her."

He smiles. "An old friend to accompany you on a new adventure."

I nod and he kisses me very gently on the forehead before leaving. When he is gone I lie back down on the bed and allow relief to wash over me. I will be gone from here soon, I think. I will not have to live in fear. I will travel the trading routes as I once did, with Amalu by my side, knowing that my son is safe. I feel sleep coming and I do not struggle against it, only let its soft embrace comfort me.

I wake to a bitter taste, a wetness on my chin and neck. When I open my eyes Hela is hovering over me, holding a carved wooden cup. I throw out one arm, shoving her away from me and she clutches at the cup to stop what is left of the liquid within it from overflowing, then crouches in a corner of the room, her eyes fixed on me.

I spit the taste from my mouth, a dark bitterness that will not leave me.

"What have you given me?" I ask her but she does not answer.

I grab at the water jar and rinse my mouth again and again, spitting the water onto the floor at her feet. She does not move, only watches me.

"How did you find me?" I ask.

"You were watched," she says. "Zaynab found you growing too free. Wandering about the souk buying all manner of things, your face no longer sad. She set a watch on you and when they reported back to me I came to find you."

"Why do you serve Zaynab?" I ask. "What possible reason do you have to carry out such dark deeds on her behalf? What hold does she have over you?"

I do not expect her to answer but she half-closes her eyes as though my question wearies her. "It is too long a story," she says.

"Did she threaten you? Did she do something to you?"

"I did something to her," says Hela, her voice almost sing-song. "I did something that can never be forgiven."

"What was it?"

She shakes her head. "Too long a story," she says. "Too long. So long."

I stride across the room and grab at the cup. Startled by the suddenness of my movement, she lets go of it. I pour the liquid on the floor and she holds out her hand. She does not look at the liquid, only at the now-empty cup, as though it is precious.

"Give it back to me."

I draw my arm back and throw the cup at the wall. There is a cracking sound as it hits and when it falls it is in two pieces. I hear a low moan and turn to look at Hela. She is rocking on her heels, her whole body curled up, only her eyes showing, staring at the cup as though seeing something terrible.

"I have a son," I tell her. "He is Yusuf's firstborn son. One day he will make himself known and all your evildoing will have been for nothing."

Hela is not listening to me. She crawls across the room as though I am not there, her robes brushing against my feet, still moaning, a low painful sound. When she reaches the cup she picks up one half in each hand and looks at them, her body still rocking.

"What is the cup to you?" I ask, unnerved. "I threw away what was in it."

She does not answer. She stays crouched against the wall.

I feel faint. "What was in the cup, Hela?" I ask.

She shakes her head. "It does not matter what was in it," she says, her voice husky. "It never matters what is in it."

"Am I going to die?" I ask her. I can feel my heart thudding and I am not sure whether it is from fear or her potion, whatever it was.

She shakes her head. "You broke the cup."

"You put some of the mixture in my mouth while I slept," I persist. "Was it enough to kill me?"

"You broke the cup," she repeats, as though her mouth cannot form any other words.

Her voice and eyes frighten me more than the bitterness in my mouth. Slowly I edge out of the room, expecting her to leap at me, to attack me somehow but she does nothing and I leave her there, still rocking back and forth, her body hunched around the broken cup.

Back in my own rooms I put on a plain robe. A wave of nausea washes over me and I wonder whether I am poisoned, whether Hela's potion was strong enough to kill me or whether I spat it out fast enough. Or perhaps it is only my own fear. I touch Amalu's *taneghelt* and open my casket of jewellery. Even though I should hurry, I cannot help but linger over the contents. I lift up each piece and adorn myself, one by one. Only one piece is missing, the *ismana* long bones.

I think of my little son. All he has left of me is my love. And a string of silver beads.

Marrakech, Morocco, c.1074

*Y*OU HAVE SEEN EACH OF *my jewels as I have adorned myself. Now you know my journey and how I came to be here.*

The city is quiet. It is dark and only a few torches flicker, making me freeze for a moment when I think I see a person in the shadows, but then all is still and I move again. A drunken guard is snoring. I can smell the orange blossom through the darkness even as I falter beneath the weight of my saddle. One of my jewels slips and falls from my neck but I cannot stop to pick it up. It tinkles as it falls to the ground, but no-one hears me. Zaynab would hear me if she were here, but if she saw me she would say nothing. She would not call for the guards to stop me. Perhaps when I am gone she will be set free from the jealousy that cripples her life.

Outside the camp the camels sigh and make their low groans when they see me. They toss their heads — the day is done, their work is finished, they seem to say — why trouble them now? Can I not sleep like their masters? Only my own camel, my Thiyya, whitest of camels with her strange blue eyes, makes no sound but stares at me coolly as I approach. It is a long time since she was used and she rolls wearily upright, then stands to allow me to fasten the saddle straps. She twitches her head when I put on her head harness but the small silver sounds of the dangling triks seems to soothe her. I finish my preparations and lean against her for a moment, feeling faint. She looks at me scornfully when I do not climb swiftly up her side as I used to and sinks to the ground again with a soft impatient huff.

I turn Thiyya to the north and let her walk at her own pace, unhurried and unbothered by the misfortunes or misdeeds of mere mortals. I curl my bare feet into the soft fur of her neck and feel a great weight lift from me. I leave behind my child and doing so leaves a wound in my heart but I believe that he is in safe hands and that my distance will protect him from Zaynab.

A soft glow appears; the rising dawn. The desert spirits whisper around me even as the birds wake. Did our queen, Tin Hinan, come this way once, long ago, on her white camel? Thiyya continues her long slow strides and I face the rising sun a free Tuareg woman, as I was born. My jewels sway with the rhythm of the riding. I hold my head high and then close my eyes to feel the first warmth of the sun touch my face.

I think of my son, of the power he will inherit and the gentleness with which I hope he will rule a peaceful kingdom. I pray for him. I pray that his father will recognise him and claim him for his own when it is safe to do so and that his life will be a happy one. When I open my eyes I see ahead of me the outlines of Amalu, Ekon and Adeola. Behind them stand many loaded camels and Amalu's slaves, ready for the trading routes that we will travel together.

As I draw closer Amalu comes towards me, as though he cannot bear to wait for me to reach them. Thiyya stops by him without my command and I look down on him. His eyes shine with love.

"Not dressed as a man?" he asks.

I shake my head. "I am a free woman," I say. "I have no need to hide."

He nods. "Ekon and Adeola are with us," he says, gesturing to where they stand.

"I set them free," I say.

"They would not leave you," he says. "They travel with us as friends."

"I come to you with nothing," I tell him.

He shakes his head and holds up his arms. "You are everything," he says.

I slip from Thiyya's back and feel his strong arms about me, claiming me for his own at last.

For Readers

I hope you have enjoyed this book. It forms part of a series of four novels, *The Moorish Empire*, following the rise of the Almoravid dynasty, which ruled over the whole of North Africa and Spain. Each book follows the life of one woman but many characters recur in the other novels, so you can enjoy seeing them from a different perspective.

The first book, *The Cup*, is Hela's story, Zaynab's handmaiden. It is a free novella which you can download from my website, www.MelissaAddey.com.

The second is *A String of Silver Beads*, which is Kella's story, who finds herself pitted against Zaynab as a rival. The third book is Zaynab's story, *None Such as She* and the final book is *Do Not Awaken Love*, which is the story of Isabella, the Andalusian slave woman who raises the child who will one day rule the Almoravid empire.

Author's Note on History

I have tried to be authentic to the period and setting, incorporating as much of the history as possible, however this particular era has some large gaps in the sources available and so I have allowed myself some storytelling freedom. The idea for this story came from a trip to Morocco, where I loved the traditional jewellery and had the idea for a woman's story told through the individual pieces she gathers over a lifetime. I then began my research into Moroccan history and was fascinated by the Almoravid dynasty.

In 11th century Morocco Abu Bakr bin 'Umar and Yusuf bin Tashfin headed up a holy army, the *al-Mourabitoun*, starting a dynasty of rulers known later as the Almoravids (I have used this later name for simplicity), intent on bringing the country under Islamic rule. Up to this time Morocco, along with Tunisia and Algeria (collectively known as the Maghreb) was primarily a set of tribal Berber states with more or less strict adherence to Islam.

They were successful, taking the important city of Aghmat early on. Abu Bakr married the queen of the city, Zaynab, said to have been a very beautiful and clever woman known as 'the Magician'. When southern tribes rebelled Abu Bakr left both the foundling garrison city of

Murakush (modern Marrakesh) and Zaynab to Yusuf (who married her) and went to deal with the tribes. When he returned Zaynab advised Yusuf on how to negotiate keeping his power. They came to an amicable agreement and Abu Bakr went back to the south, leaving Yusuf as commander of the whole army in all but name and Zaynab as his queen consort. My version of Zaynab's story is told in *None Such as She*, while her handmaid Hela's story is told in *The Cup*: a free novella which you can download from my website www.MelissaAddey.com.

Yusuf went on to conquer the whole of Morocco, plus parts of Tunisia and Algeria. When Muslim rulers in Spain asked for his aid he went to Spain and conquered almost all of Spain (this included fighting against El Cid). He died when he was very old. He had been a very religious man who disdained the riches of the world such as fine clothes or elaborate food, and was said to be quite a kindly person.

Although Zaynab is said to have borne Yusuf a lot of children and was most certainly his right hand in ruling the empire, he chose as his heir Ali, the son of a Christian slave woman, who was apparently a favoured wife, called Fadl-al-Husn, or 'Perfection of Beauty'. She could well have been Spanish (Andalusian) and thus would have originally had a Spanish name. I found this odd and I have invented Kella's story to account for this choice. In this series the Christian slave woman is named Isabella and her story is told in *Do Not Awaken Love*, the last of my Moroccan novels.

Ali became ruler when Yusuf died. A very religious man, not given to warfare, Ali held the empire for only part of his life before the Almoravid dynasty was toppled by the Almohads.

Your Free Book

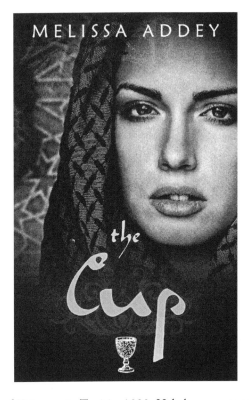

The city of Kairouan in Tunisia, 1020. Hela has powers too strong for a child – both to feel the pain of those around her and to heal them. But when she is given a mysterious cup by a slave woman, its powers overtake her life, forcing her into a vow she cannot hope to keep. So begins a quartet of historical novels set in Morocco as the Almoravid Dynasty sweeps across Northern Africa and Spain, creating a Muslim Empire that endured for generations.

Download your free copy at
www.melissaaddey.com

Biography

I mainly write historical fiction, and am currently writing two series set in very different eras: China in the 1700s and Morocco/Spain in the 1000s. My first novel, *The Fragrant Concubine*, was picked for Editor's Choice by the Historical Novel Society and longlisted for the Mslexia Novel Competition.

In 2016 I was made the Leverhulme Trust Writer in Residence at the British Library, which included writing two books, *Merchandise for Authors* and *The Storytelling Entrepreneur*. You can read more about my non-fiction books on my website.

I am currently studying for a PhD in Creative Writing at the University of Surrey.

I love using my writing to interact with people and run regular workshops at the British Library as well as coaching other writers on a one-to-one basis.

I live in London with my husband and two children.

For more information, visit my website
www.melissaaddey.com

Current and forthcoming books include:

Historical Fiction
China
The Consorts
The Fragrant Concubine
The Garden of Perfect Brightness
The Cold Palace

Morocco
The Cup
A String of Silver Beads
None Such as She
Do Not Awaken Love

Picture Books for Children
Kameko and the Monkey-King

Non-Fiction
The Storytelling Entrepreneur
Merchandise for Authors
The Happy Commuter
100 Things to Do while Breastfeeding

Thanks

My thanks go to many people. Ryan, for all our adventures shared together, especially in Morocco and his steadfast love and encouragement. The members of www.YouWriteOn.com, for their feedback and encouragement in the early days of this manuscript. Helen, for reading with care and editor Sam Bulos who made me read my own work with new eyes. Dr Michael Brett of the School of Oriental and African Studies, for discussing my timeline right at the start and Professor Harry Norris of the School of Oriental and African Studies, for taking the time to read the first draft and for sending me a lovely letter of encouragement which I still treasure. All errors are of course mine.

A big thank you to editor-authors Debi Alper and Emma Darwin and the June 2018 Jericho Writers editing group – so much learnt! Thank you for all the encouragement and useful insights received. Thank you to Kathryn from www.refresheditorial.co.uk for her eagle eyes and thoughtful feedback. And to the University of Surrey for three years of funding, allowing me to do so much more than my PhD. Such a precious gift.

Thank you to Streetlight Graphics who always make something beautiful with no fuss at all. Thanks as always to my family and friends who encourage me to keep going.

Thank you to Bernie for missing your stop. My usual suspects Etain, Camilla, Elisa, for being great beta readers. And to Seth and Isabelle, who were not even born when I first started this story but still give Mamma time to write... thank you, my honey-bunnies.

Printed in Great Britain
by Amazon